Yesterday's Eyes

JAN 13

CH

Yesterday's Eyes

Catherine Flowers

www.urbanchristianonline.com

Urban Books, LLC
78 East Industry Court
Deer Park, NY 11729

ISBN 13: 978-1-60162-741-4
ISBN 10: 1-60162-741-6

First Printing December 2012
Printed in the United States of America

10 9 8 7 6 5 4 3 2 1

*This is a work of fiction. Any references or similarities to
actual events, real people, living or dead, or to real locales
are intended to give the novel a sense of reality. Any simi-
larity in other names, characters, places, and incidents is
entirely coincidental.*

Distributed by Kensington Corp.
Submit Wholesale Orders to:
Kensington Publishing Corp.
C/O Penguin Group (USA) Inc.
Attention: Order Processing
405 Murray Hill Parkway
East Rutherford, NJ 07073-2316
Phone: 1-800-526-0275
Fax: 1-800-227-9604

Yesterday's Eyes

Catherine Flowers

Dedication

This book is dedicated to all those who remain imprisoned by the memories of a painful past. You *can* be set free.

Jesus said, "Come to me, all you who are weary and burdened, and I will give you rest. Take my yoke upon you and learn from me, for I am gentle and humble in heart, and you will find rest for your souls. For my yoke is easy and my burden is light" (Matthew 11:28–30).

All scripture is taken from the NIV.

Acknowledgments

First, I would like to thank God, my Heavenly Father, who has guided me throughout this writing process. He is *always* in control, and His blessings are endless!

Thank you to my editor at Urban Books, Joylynn Jossel-Ross. You saw something in my writing and took time out of your busy schedule to send me an e-mail full of encouragement and advice (Blessing #1).

Many thanks to my agent/editor, Dr. Maxine Thompson. I have grown so much under your guidance. Your knowledge, support, and encouragement have been invaluable. Thank you for accepting me as your client (Blessing #2).

I would also like to thank my children, Walter, Fatima, Nick, and Kiana. You all believed in me from start to finish, and understood when I could not spend as much time with you as I wanted to because I had to write. I am grateful for your unwavering encouragement and support as I embarked upon this journey (Blessing #3).

Finally, to everyone at Urban Books who played a role in the publication of this book—from Carl Weber to graphics design—thank you!

Preface

May this book be the seed that is planted in the souls of many, watered by more, and made to grow by one. And if the seed has already been planted and watered . . . let the germination begin. Amen.

Part One
Chapter One

Ida needed to escape. Not for the moment, but forever. Her six-year-old daughter, Tia, sat at the kitchen table looking at her silently as Ida brought the bottle of vodka up to her lips. She took a long swallow and felt the hot sting of the fiery liquid as it rushed down her throat. Her shoulders slumped over.

"I can't take it no more!" she cried out. "I can't take none of this no more!"

She stiffened her back suddenly. "You," she said, pointing a rigid finger at Tia, "ain't nothing."

She turned and pointed the same finger toward an old bassinet sitting in front of the kitchen window. "Your brother, *Him*, ain't nothing either. You know that, don't you? Y'all just like me. You ain't got nothing, ain't never gone have nothing . . ."

She stopped abruptly and stood up, steadying herself with the back of the kitchen chair. "I gotta get out of here. All of this," she spread her arms wide to embrace the sparsely furnished four-room upper flat, "all of this," the anger in her voice gaining momentum, "is about to drive me crazy!"

Tia followed her mother as she staggered to the bedroom. She tried to ignore the familiar growling pang in her stomach as she watched her mother stand in front of the bedroom mirror and apply a thick layer of blue powder to her tiny slanted eyes. Next, she drew a straight red line with what looked like a crayon down each of her cheeks, and then gently rubbed it into her skin until only a lighter version of the redness remained. It made Tia think of caramel with a cherry on top, and her stomach growled again as she swallowed her own spit. Using the same crayon, her mother began to color in her lips until Tia could no longer see the natural tan color of them.

Finally, she squeezed her small frame into an even smaller black dress with sequins that sparkled and glittered every time she moved. Tia picked up her mother's wig and began twirling it, thinking how it reminded her of a Halloween mask with its long brown strands of hair that, no matter how vigorously her mother brushed, would never stay in place.

"Here," Tia said, handing it to her mother.

Ida snatched it from her, and without turning away from the mirror said, "Now go to bed."

Tia walked into the living room, which was adjacent to her mother's bedroom. A tan chair with brown and gold flowers on it sat in the center of the floor, and there was a matching sofa pushed against the wall that served as her bed.

"I'm hungry," Tia said, plopping down onto the chair. "I didn't eat dinner." No sooner had the words left her mouth did she realize her mistake. She had only meant to think those words; to actually *say* them, she knew, would make her mother mad.

"Then go in the kitchen and fix a hot dog. You see I'm busy."

"Ain't no hot dogs."

"What you mean ain't no hot dogs? It was two in there this morning. What happened to them?"

Tia was silent.

"What happened to them?" her mother repeated as she walked unsteadily from the bedroom to the kitchen. She swung open the refrigerator door and found a half-liter bottle of cola and a handful of grapes inside. Turning her head swiftly to the left, she looked down into the wastebasket and saw the empty package that had once contained the last two hot dogs. "Tia, get in here!"

Tia slowly pushed herself up from the chair and went into the kitchen. Her arms and legs felt like a stretched rubber band that, after being plucked, continued to wiggle for a while.

"You ate the hot dogs, didn't you?" Ida grabbed her arm and stared at her with eyes that were like an inferno. "Didn't I tell you not to go eating up all the food? Didn't I?" Her grip was tightening around Tia's thin, right arm, and saliva was beginning to form at the corners of her mouth.

Tia inhaled the smell of alcohol on her mother's breath, and it made her nauseated as she nodded her head up and down.

"Get in the living room and sit down."

Slowly, with small steps, she followed her mother's orders. Every muscle in her six-year-old body twitched in response to the increased danger signals being sent from one nerve ending to another.

Four steps and she was out of the kitchen. She counted with dismay the next four steps that would place her directly in front of her mother who stood watching her with both hands on her hips. Now, just five more steps and there sat the sofa, waiting for her, beckoning her to safety. She squeezed her hands into tiny fists. She could do this. She could make it to the sofa. But halfway into that first step she felt the sting of her mother's hand on the back of her head. The blow sent her stumbling two or three steps along her course, but she maintained her balance and quickly scurried to the sofa.

"You get on my nerves!" her mother yelled.

Now, shaking uncontrollably, Tia kept her head down and tried hard to focus on the top of her dirty white canvas shoes. If she raised her big toe high enough, she could almost poke it through the hole that had formed on the top of the left shoe. But with each blinking of her eyelids, the hole became secondary to the spreading circle of moisture just below them.

"Didn't I tell you not to eat those hot dogs?" Ida stood bellowing from the kitchen. "Didn't I?"

Still looking down at her shoes, Tia began nodding her head, crying silently.

"Then why," Ida was crying now, "why didn't you listen to me?"

Tia kept her head down and did not answer.

Suddenly Ida was angry again. "Look at me when I'm talking to you!"

Tia raised her eyes just in time to see the half-empty two-liter bottle of cola fly directly toward her. As she dodged the bottle, she heard it smash into the wall behind her and felt its cool liquid dance across her hair and face like rain. Only it wasn't rain. It was soda, soda that she could have been swallowing instead of feeling it running down the side of her face.

"Lie down on the couch and go to sleep, and you better not move. I'll be back," Ida said, slamming the door behind her.

Slowly, Tia bent down to pick up the empty cola bottle from the floor. She could feel the lukewarm liquid trickling down the back of her ear. She ran her hand over the top of her head and felt the moisture intermingling with the coarseness of her hair, the sticky substance clinging to her ebony, bonelike fingers. Warm droplets took turns landing on the back of her neck after the liquid had reached the end of her two ponytails.

A cockroach had already begun making its way toward the puddle on the floor, having sensed sweetness nearby. She watched it for a while as it enjoyed its newfound treat before she finally gave it one good stomp with her foot. It lay almost void of life, semi-paralyzed from the weight of the heavy pressure. Even if it had wanted to crawl away, make its way back to safety, it could not for its insides were crushed, its tiny legs weakened by the unexpected blow.

She looked around the small upper flat. It was dull and colorless with a slightly putrid odor reeking throughout its four rooms. The square kitchen was barely big enough for a stove and refrigerator to fit into, and its walls were gray and dirty. It was in this room that the odor was strongest, and the screen-less window, propped open with an empty soda bottle, did little to diminish the smell. Directly below the window was the bassinet that her brother slept in, had always slept in since her mother had brought him home from the hospital two months ago.

The bedroom had an adjoining bathroom that, like the rest of the apartment, was dull and lifeless. The walls were a dingy off-white color and had cracks in the corners of the ceiling just above the bathtub and toilet where the paint had already begun to peel. Each time Tia went in to the bathroom, she would automatically look up to see if there were any paint chips about to fall onto her head, and the worn-out toilet seat always moved, shifting to the left or right whenever she sat on it, causing her to fear that she would one day fall into it. Baths were always a torturous occasion ever since she'd seen the rat.

"It's not a rat," she remembered her mother saying. "It's a mouse."

Mouse or rat, all she knew was that it had poked its little head out of a hole in the baseboard of the cabinet beneath the sink. She had been playing in the tub when, from the corner of her eye, she'd detected a sudden movement. She'd turned just in time to see the rodent's head rapidly turning from side to side, its tiny, beady eyes moving back and forth frantically.

"Momma!" Tia had cried out.

"What?" Ida responded.

"A rat!"

"Where?" Her mother had stood calmly in the doorway with both hands on her hips.

"There." Tia remembered pointing toward the baseboard that had no longer shown any signs of a rodent having been there.

"Here?" she recalled her mother saying as she handed her a towel. "Just get out. You done, ain't you?"

"Uh-huh," she lied.

The green bar of soap with tiny white streaks running through it had not even made contact with her washcloth, much less her body. But she had to get out of that tub, out of that room, and from that point on, Tia McElroy held the world record for being able to take the fastest bath in the world.

Sitting on the sofa now, Tia tried to figure out why her mother had been crying one minute and was so angry the next. Had it been the rat she'd seen months ago? Was it her and her brother now? And what about that thing called nothing? Was that it? She would have liked to have comforted her mother, to have given her a hug and a kiss, and told her everything would be all right, but she knew her mother did not like hugs and kisses, and anyway, she had her own nothingness to deal with. It kept occupying her stomach, serving as a constant reminder that she was hungry, and their refrigerator, like her stomach, was empty.

Her mind drifted back to earlier in the month when she had accompanied her mother to the grocery store. She had wiggled with anticipation, thinking of all the food she would see, knowing that they would be bringing some of it home with them. Her mother had pushed the shopping cart full of plastic bags—eight to be exact—through the exit doors looking for a driver to take them home. It was always the same toothless, gray-haired, old man who would ask, "Need a ride?" and her mother would nod her head.

They would get into the back of his old station wagon, the torn vinyl seat cover sticking to Tia's small thighs as she would reposition herself to get a better view of the scenery passing before her.

In any given city, there is a street named after Martin Luther King, Jr. In Tia's city, Martin Luther King Drive ran approximately six blocks south before turning into Old World Third Street in downtown Milwaukee, and two miles north before turning into Green Bay Avenue. It was located in the center of southeastern Wisconsin in the heart of a city that was looked upon as "the ghetto" by those who lived on the outskirts.

In the '60s and '70s, it had been booming with business that boasted a variety of shops where one could buy quality clothing or furniture. Reasonably priced haircuts or relaxers were advertised at the local barbershop or beauty salon. And bargains on quality meats were a constant at the Good Deal butcher shop. There had even been a full-scale grocery store where drivers like the one Tia and her mother always rode with sat around waiting to take families and their groceries home. When the economy dropped, most of the booming businesses were systematically replaced by window-less, burnt-out, and dilapidated buildings. However, the one business to remain a constant throughout the years was Oscar's jewelry store. Perhaps, having gained a familiarity to this type of clientele, he knew that no matter how broke some folks got, they would still find a way to satisfy their desire for gold necklaces and rings. And so he stayed, catering to—and exploiting—the poor.

Since the renaming of Third Street to Martin Luther King Drive several years ago, there had been a campaign to bring life and vitality back to the small community. The first effort had been in the form of a brand-new pharmacy that had been erected across the street, diagonally from the jewelry store. Next, was a community health clinic for those who had no health insurance or were underinsured. At the same time, restaurants, low-income apartments, and other businesses began to plant themselves in various areas of the neighborhood. And what had once turned into a ghost town was slowly trying to resurrect itself. But there was still a long way to go.

Turning right or left on Martin Luther King Drive would lead to many run-down single- and two-family homes. Some of the homes hinted of an effort by their occupants to keep the property up, while others blatantly displayed a lack of concern that was evident by dirt in places where grass should have been, and abandoned, underinsured vehicles parked in unkempt backyards. There were also many boarded up houses with "For Sale" signs on the lawn, posing as eyesores to the city. And there were plans in the making to refurbish many of these properties.

Long before they arrived home from the grocery store, Tia would begin the begging ritual, having carefully planned which food items she would ask for first.

"Mama, can I have some cookies when we get home?"

Ida had pressed her lips together and waited a few seconds before answering. "We'll see."

"No, I changed my mind. Umm, can I have some cookies and potato chips?" she asked, then quickly revised her plan. "No, I want some cookies first. Then I want some potato chips and a hot dog, okay?" She had known that she was running the risk of being slapped for talking so much, but the thought of relieving the hunger pains in her stomach outweighed the pain of a slap across her face.

"Hush your mouth, girl," her mother had said. "We ain't even home yet, and you begging already. This food's got to last us all month because when it's gone it's gone, and I don't want to hear nothing about you being hungry."

Another wave of hunger pangs brought Tia back to the present. She went into the kitchen to check on *Him,* who, through it all, had not cried out. A warm breeze drifted in from the window, causing the putrid odor to intensify momentarily. She looked up at the sky and knew that when her mother came home all the mini marshmallows now covering it would be gone, replaced by darkness and maybe a few stars.

She pulled the blanket back from *Him's* face and was again reminded of the odor that permeated the small apartment. She stood still as he stared up at her with eyelids that did not blink. She pulled the blanket all the way down to his feet. He was a small baby with a stomach that seemed to take up most of his body. His tiny feet had patches of purple covering them, and she wondered why he never cried. Even *she* knew that babies were supposed to cry sometimes. Her mother had said it was because he was such a good baby. But even so, didn't good babies cry too? She rubbed his arm, and the texture made her think of a plastic baby doll. But he wasn't a doll. He was her baby brother. She touched his other arm and wondered why he was so cold in the middle of July.

Chapter Two

Ida stepped onto the porch and looked at the house directly across the street. She recognized the shadow staring down at her from the upstairs window. The woman stood still with both hands placed on her wide hips and made no attempt to hide herself from Ida's view.

"Hey, Trip," Ida yelled to the shadow, while waving her hands wildly above her head. "I see you!"

The woman maintained her posture and did not return the greeting. As Ida began walking slowly down the street, she thought about the silhouette in the window. That shadow, her mother Mavis—also known as Trip—had always been the source of her misery. She blamed her for everything that was wrong in her life. Even now, as she left Tia and *Him* alone, she blamed the shadow because if she had been any kind of a mother at all, maybe they'd still be speaking to each other, and she could have asked her to watch them for her. After all, she was their grandmother. She shouldn't even have to ask. But there had always been a distance between them that Ida had never understood.

Growing up with her, she recalled her mother always getting upset over one thing or another. *"Don't sit there. Put that back. Hang that up. Clean that up. Why are you wearing that?"* Always a constant flow of commands or corrections for the things she did wrong.

It had started out in her mind—calling her mother Trip. Ida would silently wonder why her mother was always tripping about things. Eventually, the silent wonder found strength through her increasing rebellious nature, and she began to ask the question out loud. And when she did not receive what she felt was an acceptable answer to her question, she would let her dissatisfaction be known by calling her mother a trip. Even though her mother never showed it, Ida knew being called Trip irritated her, and so she did it that much more with glee.

"Trip, Trip, Trip," Ida repeated as if she was singing a song. Suddenly, her tone changed, and she yelled angrily over her shoulder, "Say hi to your preacher man for me!"

The shadow forcefully pulled the curtains together and disappeared from the window.

Ida continued down the street, an occasional stagger—the effect from the half pint of vodka she'd consumed earlier—interrupting her gait. She had moved to the area when she was sixteen years old—four years after her mother had married Henry. That had been eight years ago when the mention of Forgery Boulevard on the northwest side of the city meant that financially, a family was doing all right in life. Most of the houses she passed were still owner occupied, including her mother's. But there were several rental properties as well, and the one that she rented across the street also belonged to her mother and her mother's husband, Henry. The people in the neighborhood were a mixture of ethnic backgrounds, and everyone kept to themselves most of the time with an occasional quick greeting in passing.

When they had first moved to the neighborhood, Ida had felt a sense of pride. Their house had been categorized as a standard bungalow with an upstairs attic partially remodeled to include two of three bedrooms. The roof was comprised of rustic-orange, brown, and maroon-colored tiles with beige vinyl siding, and there was a tan awning with vertical brown stripes hanging in the front of the house above a single-pane picture window. She was happy to be living in a real house, something nice. But her joy soon turned to resentment when she discovered that it did her no good to have a nice house with furniture that she could not sit on because it was reserved for guests that they seldom had.

Through the years, homes had been sold, and the new owners were not as predisposed to keeping up their property to the same degree as the previous owners had done. Other homes were rented out under a government program known as rent assistance, and slowly the neighborhood began to deteriorate. To this day, Ida was waiting for an answer from her mother about when the peeling paint on her own bathroom walls would be removed and repainted.

As she neared the bus stop, she thought about Henry. How was he able to deal with a woman like her mother? But then, he was just a man, wasn't he? And he was different from her unknown biological father only in that he had stuck around and married her mother. But that's where the difference ended.

She could tell her mother a few things about her preacher man if she wanted to. And maybe she would one day. Now that she was twenty-four years old, maybe she would tell her mother about all the things Henry had been doing to her, and she to him, for the past three years. And how each time, she made him pay before he received those little pleasures that he said he could not, and would never receive at home. So, she reasoned, he really wasn't dealing with Mavis. He was conducting business with Ida. Every Monday night.

She would watch him from her living-room window as he left his house, got in his car, and drove off. Minutes later, he would be knocking on her back door. It was always the same. She would open the door and hold out her hand. He would place fifty dollars into it, and they would walk up the stairs without speaking.

She thought about how badly she could use that money now. She was well aware of the empty refrigerator in her kitchen. And she didn't need Tia reminding her that there was nothing to eat. She still had one-and-a-half weeks to go before her food stamps would come or before she would receive another check from the county. What was she supposed to do until then?

The rent she had to pay took away half the amount of the check she received every month, and her mother refused to lower it. She was eligible for energy assistance every year, and that helped to keep the electricity and heat on in the small apartment, but there still was not enough money to live on. The food stamps were only good for food items; she could not buy things like toothpaste, toilet paper, and soap. That too took money.

She had tried to supplement her income by getting a part-time job at a fast-food restaurant, and her first paycheck had been less than $200. Still, when she went to see her caseworker for her review, she was told she had committed fraud because she had not reported the extra money. The caseworker told her that since the amount in question was under $1,500, she would not refer her to the district attorney's office for prosecution. But she would have to agree to pay it back. She did. And out of frustration, she quit her job.

Child support was out of the question because she did not know where Tia's father was. And the baby's father . . . Well, she didn't want to think about the baby right now, and she would see his father soon enough.

He had persuaded her to keep quiet about him being the father of her baby, saying that his image would be destroyed if she said anything. He'd promised to help her take care of the child financially for the next eighteen years. But it had been two months since his birth, and she was going to tell him that he was going to have to up the ante. She was going to let him know that if he didn't start bringing her more money, he was going to find his precious image completely destroyed.

She finally reached the corner and stepped onto the curb, swaying from side to side as she peered down the street to see if she could see the #57 bus coming. There was no bus in sight. She stumbled back as the streetlight turned green and several cars sped past her. The sound of a honking horn and verbiage meant to be a compliment caused her to return the gesture with a few expletives of her own as she held on to the light pole in order to maintain her balance. Minutes later, the car with the honking horn was back again, driving slowly this time as he pulled up to the pole she was clinging to.

"Need a ride?" he asked. His face a bit pale with skin weathered by too much sun, and eyes that were weary from age.

"A better question," she said looking him straight in the eyes—she was not too drunk to know it was money-making time—"is, do *you* need a ride?"

He nodded his head. "How much?"

"Fifty."

"Fifty?" he raised his eyebrows.

"Five-zero," she spoke slowly. "I'm not stuttering, am I?"

He opened the car door. "No, you're not," he said grimly.

She sat down hard in the front passenger seat and slammed the car door closed. The smell of new leather combined with the scent of sweet cigar smoke filled her nostrils. "Just pull up some and turn down that alley," she said.

She knew the alley would be deserted and dark, and as he steered his vehicle into the blackness, she reached over and began to fumble with the leather belt on the polyester pants worn by the man sitting beside her.

Fifteen minutes later, she had him drop her off at her original destination, the downtown district. If she was lucky, she would return home with enough money to get them through the rest of the month.

Some people choose to drink their pain away, while others choose to fly high above it, cushioned by a drug-induced euphoria. Others search for relief in the arms of a lover, believing that the solution is to be found somewhere in between that first glance and the promise of love ever after. Still, others simply crawl into a shell made impenetrable by the negative thoughts they harbor.

Mavis, Ida's mother, was the latter of these people, solid as steel on the outside, and just as firm and unyielding on the inside. She stood at her bedroom window looking down at her daughter as she yelled and staggered down the street. She thought about her own dysfunctional upbringing, and snatched the curtains closed.

Her mother, an emotionally unavailable woman, had married her father, a physically abusive man. The combination of the two taught her to keep her emotions well under control. The last time she could remember crying had been when she was thirteen years old, and she still had the small scar in the middle of her forehead to remind her.

She had been sitting in front of the window daydreaming and had not heard her father calling her name. Enraged, he'd entered her room, and when she turned around, she saw the can of deodorant flying toward her head.

"Mavis," he'd shouted, "when I call you, you answer!"

Both of her parents were dead now, having died of cancer years ago. Still, she continued to resent them for the terrible childhood she'd had to endure.

She'd made a promise to herself that if she ever had a child, things would be much different. She would not treat her child the way her parents had treated her. She would not withhold love and kindness and all the things that made a person feel good. Now, as she stood at the window, she wondered, *Why she hadn't kept her promise?*

Chapter Three

The sounds of children laughing and playing slowly began to decrease. Every now and then, Tia heard the rumble of a car engine as it passed by the open kitchen window. Occasionally, the rumble would stop directly in front of the window, and she would hear the sound of a car door slamming. She would jump from the couch and stick her head out of the window, straining to see into the darkness. Always, she hoped to see a familiar shadow on the sidewalk below, and always, she was disappointed.

Her eyelids felt heavy, but they would not stay closed. Each time they began to droop, her stomach would growl and remind her that she had not had anything to eat in a long time. The two hot dogs she had eaten earlier—and endured soda-drenched hair for—had long made their way through her stomach, and she was hungry again.

She walked over to the refrigerator and pulled on the metal handle of the door. One of two screws holding the handle in place fell to the floor, causing the metal bar to swing downward, still hanging on by one screw. There was an almost empty jar of mayonnaise inside of the refrigerator, along with two eggs, and something in a pot that had black and green fuzz covering the top of it.

She took the jar of mayonnaise and placed it on the table next to the half-empty loaf of bread. She opened a cabinet drawer and took out a serrated knife. Reaching for the package of bread, she was startled by the medium-sized cockroach that scurried out from underneath it in search of another location where it could lie undisturbed.

After spreading what was left of the mayonnaise onto the slice of bread, she folded it in half, took two bites, and it was gone. Reaching for another slice, she noticed the same black and green fuzz that was on the food in the refrigerator also on the edge of the bread. She left the bread in the bag and went back into the living room.

The long, oval-shaped telephone sat on a wobbly wooden table next to the sofa. She picked up the receiver and listened to the dial tone. Then she began to push the buttons randomly, hearing a short beep each time she did. Suddenly, she heard three high-pitched tones—one after the other—and then the voice of a woman, who sounded like one of those talking dolls her mother had once bought her, said that her call could not be completed. She told her to dial the operator if she needed assistance.

Tia was about to ask what an operator was when a bell sounded through the receiver, and the voice disappeared. She continued pressing the buttons, one after the other, until suddenly, there was a real voice on the other end of the line, a man's voice.

"Operator," the male said.

Tia was silent.

"Operator, may I help you?"

"Hello?"

"Hello. This is the operator. How can I help you?"

"Um, your name is Operator?"

"No, my name is Ben. What's your name?"

"Tia."

"Tia, are you playing with the phone?"

"No."

"Is your mommy home?"

"No."

"How old are you?"

"Six."

"Is there someone else there that I can talk to? Is there a grown-up there?"

"No."

"Are you at home all by yourself?"

"Uh-huh."

"Where's your mommy, Tia?"

"She gone."

"Where did she go?"

"I don't know." Tia felt the rumbling in her stomach and added, "I'm hungry."

"You're hungry?"

"Uh-huh."

Ben quickly inhaled as if he were trying to suck back in the air that had, seconds earlier, drifted from his mouth.

"Okay. Just hold on, honey," he said as he high-lighted an area on the computer that showed the address where she was calling from. "I'm going to send someone over to your house, and we're going to get you something to eat, all right?"

There was silence on the other end.

"Tia?"

"Huh?"

"Did you hear me?"

"Uh-huh."

"Okay. So, here's what I want you to do." He paused for a second. "Are you listening?"

"Yes."

"Don't hang up the phone, okay? You can just lay it down if you want to, but don't hang it up. Can you do that for me?"

"Yes."

"Good. And when the doorbell rings, go to the door and ask who it is before you open the door." He paused, giving her time to take in everything he was telling her. As a telephone operator, he had been trained to provide all information to the caller in a simple and straight-to-the-point manner. Now, all of his training was being put to the test. He continued speaking slowly.

"Now, here's the important part, Tia. Are you listening?"

"Yes."

"After you ask who it is, come back and tell me what they said, and I'll tell you if you can open the door, okay?"

"Okay."

"Good. So, somebody's already on their way over to your house, and while we're waiting, can you tell me what you're supposed to do when they ring the doorbell?"

"Ask who it is."

"That's right. And then what?"

"Tell you what they say."

"Excellent. Good job, Tia."

She felt like jumping up and down, dancing even. Instead, she continued to sit by the window and wait just as she had been doing earlier. She talked with the operator and told him how she wished she could wake up her baby brother and tell him the good news. She told him how happy she thought her mother would be, knowing that someone was bringing them something to eat.

***

Her eyelids had begun to grow heavy again, but she would not fall asleep. She could not fall asleep. And then she heard it—the sound of a car door slamming. Not once, not twice, but three times. And then she heard the doorbell ringing. It may as well have been the sound of angels singing, causing subdued emotions to rise from beneath their confinement of a malnourished existence, to greet with anticipation what she thought would finally be . . .

"The doorbell's ringing," she shouted into the telephone receiver.

"Okay, go see who it is," the voice on the other line answered.

Tia ran down the stairs. "Who is it?" she shouted through the door.

Having been briefed that there was only a six-year-old in the house and what instructions had been given to her, one of the officers answered, "It's a policeman."

Tia ran back up the stairs and grabbed the phone. "It's a policeman," she said between breaths.

"Okay," Ben breathed a sigh of relief. "Hang up the phone and go ahead and open the door."

"Okay, bye."

She ran back down the stairs and opened the front door. There were two men, each dressed in the same blue uniform and hat, each with the same wide, bulky belt around their waist. One was slightly taller than the other was, and behind them was a woman carrying what looked like a small suitcase. None of them were carrying any bags of food unless, Tia hoped, there was food in the suitcase the lady was carrying.

"Hi," Tia sang out.

"Hello there, little lady," the taller of the two men in blue answered. "Is your mommy home?"

"Nope, she'll be back later. Are you a policeman?"

"Yep, I sure am," he answered.

"Is anybody here with you, sweetie?" the woman with the briefcase asked.

"Nope, just my baby brother."

"Well, we're just gonna come in and take a look around and make sure you and your brother are okay, all right?" the shorter man in blue asked.

"Okay," Tia said, backing away from the door. "Did y'all bring me something to eat?" she asked as they started up the stairs.

"I didn't bring anything with me, honey," the lady with the suitcase answered. "But I promise you'll get something to eat in just a little while, okay?"

"What about my momma? Can we get her something too?"

"Well, I'll tell you what—since your mommy's not here right now, we'll get you and your brother something to eat and find a nice safe place for both of you until your mommy comes home. How does that sound?"

"How will she know where I'm at?"

"Oh, don't worry about that. We'll leave her a note, okay?"

Tia was hesitant, but the gentleness she saw in the woman's green eyes made her feel like she could trust her. "Okay," she said. "What's your name?"

"My name is Ms. Cee," she smiled. "But you can call me Missy. I came with these two nice policemen to make sure you and your brother are all right." She sat down on the sofa. The liquid from the bottle of cola that Ida had thrown earlier was still embedded within the fibers of the cushion, causing a damp feeling underneath her. She immediately got up and with one hand began searching for a dry section while she reached out to Tia with her other hand.

"Here," she said, "come sit next to me for a minute."

Tia sat down and watched as one of the policemen began opening cabinets in the kitchen while the other one looked into the bare refrigerator. Their attention was soon drawn to the bassinet in the corner, where they noticed the small, emaciated frame lying still inside of it. One of them pulled out a square black object and began talking into it. Ms. Cee got up and went into the kitchen as well. When she returned to the living room, the paleness of her face reminded Tia of a friendly little ghost that she saw on television whenever she watched Saturday morning cartoons. As the woman sat back down on the sofa, Tia said, "I'm hungry."

Missy looked at her, and it seemed to Tia that her eyes were now sad and tired. "I know," she said. "I'm going to take you to a place where you can stay at for a while and get something to eat. Okay? Would you like that?"

Tia nodded her head. "Where will me and my brother sleep?" she asked.

"Well," Missy began, "you'll have a bed all to yourself."

"What about my brother?"

She chose her words carefully. "Your brother is already . . ." she stumbled, ". . . I mean, he has a place to sleep."

"Where?"

"Well, he's sleeping with God, now," she said quickly, and patted Tia on the thigh.

"With God?" Tia frowned.

"Yes," Missy's voice cracked. "With God."

"Why?"

She struggled to keep her voice steady. "Why, what, honey?"

"Why is he sleeping with God?"

"Because God decided to take him up to heaven to live with Him. He's happy up there."

"Is that why he don't cry no more?"

Missy stiffened. "That's why, honey," she said softly.

"I want to be happy. Can God come and take me, too?"

Missy felt the heaviness in her heart. It was not something new. It had been growing there ever since she'd begun her career as a social worker for the Child Protective Services fifteen years ago. She had seen many things through the years, and every time she had to walk into a home that was not fit to raise a child in, every time she had to remove that child from its parents, was another added weight to the load she was already carrying. Now, the burden was complete, and it was too heavy. It was too much to bear.

She sighed, "Well, you have to wait until it's your turn, sweetheart."

"When will it be my turn?"

Missy did not want to continue with this conversation. It was enough that she had had to tell a child that her sibling was dead in the first place.

"It will be your turn when God is ready," she said, and in anticipation of Tia's next question, she quickly added, "and no one knows when that will be except God."

The tears came quickly for Tia. "I want my brother!" she cried out in sheer anguish.

And then the heaviness, complacency, and stagnation in Missy's heart created a tear that was too wide to mend, and she began to cry too as she put her arms around Tia.

"I know you do, honey, I know you do. It's going to be okay."

Missy began rocking her back and forth as she continued to whisper words of encouragement and wondered which of them needed to believe it the most. She was tired and disillusioned. Tired from carrying that burden in her heart, tired from the realization that the little girl she was holding in her arms would one day be a part of the next generation, and she was now going to have to grow up with the awful memory of having been left by her own mother in a house with a dead baby lying just a few feet away.

She continued rocking her gently. How much longer would she accept feeling this way before she finally said no more and quit this profession? Her job was to investigate any claims of child neglect and/or abuse. And through the years, she had begun to develop a great disdain for the justice system that only seemed to work in favor of the children a small percent of the time. Most of the time, they were shuffled from parents to shelters or safe houses to foster homes, then back to parents again, only to have the parents repeat their pattern of abuse that caused the children to be taken out of the home in the first place.

Yes, there were some happy endings, but those were the exception. For most, this shuffling activity would continue until the child turned eighteen years old. Then, without adequate counseling or therapy, the abused-child-turned-adult would be released into society and confronted with comments like "get an education" or "get a job and make something of yourself." She stopped rocking.

How could someone make something out of himself or herself if all their life they've been shown by irresponsible adults—who, themselves, lacked proper upbringing—that they are nothing? She loosened the grip she had unconsciously formed around Tia's waist.

Missy looked around the room and noticed there was now, along with the two police officers, an investigator who was writing on a pad of paper as he performed a visual examination of the dead body. He then began to examine the surrounding area, taking pictures and writing down more notes as he went along.

"The place I'm taking you to is a very nice place," Ms. Cee said, "with really nice people. You'll be safe, and you'll get a bath every night, and plenty of food to eat."

"Lunch too?" Tia's tears were subsiding.

"Lunch too."

"What about my brother? Will he get food to eat up in heaven?"

"Yes, he will," Missy said softly. "God takes care of babies." She remembered a scripture from the Bible that she'd read many times: "Come to me, all you who are weary and burdened, and I will give you rest." *And anybody else if we let Him*, she reaffirmed to herself.

The small apartment had become crammed with people. Some of them were wearing white rubber gloves, and each time the flash from the camera went off, Tia jumped. Two more men arrived dressed in white jumpsuits, and Missy knew they were there to wrap the body and remove it.

"Come on, honey," she said. "It's time to go."

Tia held Missy's hand as they made their way through the crowd, down the stairs, and out to the car that sat waiting halfway down the block. The warm, humid air surrounded her, but she shivered as they walked the distance to it.

As she climbed into the backseat, she thought she heard her mother calling her name. But when she turned to look, all she saw was a trail of darkness following the car as it began its voyage into the night.

She couldn't make out the shadows swiftly passing before her as she looked out from the passenger window, but her heart skipped a beat when she saw a familiar yellow arch sitting on top of a building off in the distance. The car did not slow down, and she slunk back into the seat. She began to suck her thumb. When was she going to eat? She wondered where she was going and if they were almost there. But most of all, she thought about her mother and hoped she would be waiting for her when she arrived.

Ida was on her way back home when she saw the ambulance and the squad cars parked in front of her house. Halfway down the block, she could see a white woman escorting Tia out to a car, and she began yelling out Tia's name while running toward the house. By the time she made it to the steps, the police officers were waiting for her with their questions and handcuffs ready.

"Are you the mother?" one of the officers asked.

"Yes, I am," she answered in between short and heavy breaths.

"Ma'am, are you aware that one of your children is dead?"

Ida thought about the hundred dollars she had accumulated that night. She thought about all the things she had done and tried not to remember what she'd felt while she was doing them in order to get what she'd needed. But the nausea in her stomach began to rise, and all the dollar bills in the world were not going to be able to settle it.

She turned sideways and hunched over. If only he could have held on a little longer! The foul-smelling liquid spewed out of her mouth as the police officer jumped backward. She had the money now! She had enough to buy food and milk that would get all three of them through until the end of the month! She gasped for air before the next round found its way onto the ground. Exhausted from the liquid heaves and other activities no woman should have to engage in, she sat down on the curb next to the squad car.

She held her breath. "Where's my daughter?"

"She's being taken to a safe place for the night."

"Where?" She stood up. "A shelter?" She could not keep her voice steady. "A foster home? Where?"

"Might be either one, ma'am. But I'm going to need you to calm down, turn around, and put your hands behind your back."

"For what?" She was screaming now. "I just went to get some money so I could feed my kids! Do you know what I had to do to get this money?"

"Ma'am," the officer raised his voice, "you left two kids alone in the house with no food, and one of them is dead." He snapped the second handcuff around her slim wrist. "We're going to have to take you downtown." He led her, struggling, to the backseat of the squad car. "Watch your head getting in," he said.

Ida smirked at the irony of going back to the area that she'd just come from, and she couldn't decide which was worse—going downtown to sell her body for money or going downtown to sit in a jail cell charged with the death of her baby. As the squad car drove away, she looked up at the window across the street, and just as she suspected, there stood her mother, a distant shadow, doing nothing as always.

Chapter Four

The first thought that entered Mavis's mind when she opened her eyes was of Tia. She turned to look at the small digital clock on the nightstand and wondered where they had taken her granddaughter the night before. It was now six-thirty in the morning, and everything had finally settled down. It had been quite a night. The sound of car doors slamming on and off had awakened her first. She had gotten out of bed to see what all the commotion was about and discovered not only an ambulance parked in front of her daughter's house, but several police squad cars as well. What had Ida done this time?

"Henry, wake up," she said, turning toward the bed.

"I am awake."

"Well, why are you just lying there? You know we got to be in church in two hours."

"What's happening across the street?"

"Nothing now."

"Did she ever come back home?"

"Yeah, she did. And they took her away too, screaming and acting a fool. She really cut up when they brought that baby out on the stretcher. I don't know why. She never cared—"

"Stretcher?" Henry interrupted his wife. "What do you mean stretcher?"

"I mean the stretcher they took into the house."

"Lord, I hope the baby's going to be all right," Henry said, almost whispering.

Mavis looked down at her husband. "Why are you so concerned about the baby?"

Henry could feel her eyes piercing his back. "What are you talking about?" he said.

Ignoring his question, she continued analyzing his body language while she spoke. "Look like the baby was dead. The whole thing was covered with one of those white sheets."

"Lord have mercy." Henry closed his eyes and sighed. What had Ida done? Is that why the baby had been so quiet the last time he had been there? Was he dying then? Or already dead? Ida had said he was sleeping, and he'd thought nothing more about it. Was she so messed up in the head that she'd gone and killed her own child? He'd always thought of the baby as *her* child. He'd never been convinced that it was his. But just the same . . .

"Didn't have no business with those kids anyway," Mavis's voice continued as she walked to the other side of the bed where Henry lay facing the wall. "Leaving them alone at night. Stumbling down the street in those little dresses, looking like a prostitute. I know she's my daughter and all, but if she didn't act like such a fool, she could have asked me to watch them instead of leaving them alone like that. Now look what's happened. Lord knows, I should have called the police on her myself."

Henry kept his eyes closed. He knew that what his wife was really complaining about had nothing to do with how Ida raised her children or how she dressed. He knew that she was jealous, and had always been jealous, of the attention he'd shown Ida when she had lived in their house. He believed that had been the real reason why Mavis had kicked her out the day after she'd turned eighteen.

Ida had only been twelve years old when he married Mavis. And even then, it had been obvious to Henry that Ida seemed to hold some sort of animosity toward her mother. Whenever he would try to ask Mavis about the tumultuous mother-and-daughter relationship, she would just chalk it all up to Ida being crazy, and then become irritated if he continued to ask questions.

In all truth, Henry liked the passionate feistiness he'd seen in Ida. She was, ironically, a lot like Mavis had been before they'd gotten married. But it had seemed to Henry that as soon as the wedding vows had been exchanged, the passionate Mavis he'd known— and had expected to *keep* knowing—slowly began to disappear, leaving him in a smoldering state of passion that, in his twisted way of reasoning, he had allowed to be reignited by his then seventeen-year-old stepdaughter. Now, this thing that had happened to her baby made him wonder if she wasn't a little crazy after all like his wife had said she was.

"Why are you looking like that?" Mavis was standing in front of him with both of her hands on her hips.

"Looking like what?" He hadn't realized he had opened his eyes.

"Like you just saw a ghost or something."

"Well, how do you expect me to look? You just told me that Ida killed her baby. Am I supposed to be smiling?"

"First of all, I didn't say she killed him. I just said they brought the baby out covered up. And second—"

"Yes, you did." He sat up on the side of the bed and jammed his left foot into his house shoe. "You said, 'the baby is dead, Henry.'" He forcefully stuck his other foot into the right shoe. "Now that's what you said."

"Right!" She leaned over him, her bosom almost resting on the back of his head. "So, I didn't say she *killed* him!"

"Well, if she didn't, who did?"

"I don't know. But what you need to do is get up out of that bed. You see what time it is? People are going to be wondering where we—you—are."

"They'll wait," he said.

"Probably. But you still need to get up and shower. You been perspiring all over the place." She pointed to the pillow that he had slept on. "Got that pillow soaking wet."

"Men don't perspire, Mavis; they sweat."

"Sweat is an ugly word. Makes me think of a pig. I like the word perspire."

He rubbed the stubble on his chin and sighed. Everything was ugly to her. "Sure would like to feel some butter," he said reaching up to pat her full behind.

"Butter's in the fridge," she said pushing his hand away.

Again, he sighed as his desire for his wife slowly began its descent back to a familiar state of nonfulfillment.

Mavis closed the bathroom door behind her. She pulled back the shower curtain and turned on the water. As she began to undress, she thought about Henry's request and wished that she could have obliged him, wished that she could call upon her desire to be close to him once again. But she had not held that desire in a very long time. The truth of the matter was that she did not love her husband anymore. In fact, she couldn't even say that she liked him all that much, so it stood to reason that she no longer enjoyed being touched by him sexually. Except right before *that* time of the month, and even that was just occasionally. Then, it wasn't so bad with him. She could even say it was pleasurable. But what was not so pleasurable, and far less tolerable, was the giving.

She could receive his advances well enough, but returning them was the problem. He wanted kisses and words of love during those times. And she just could not give them. He wanted all of her, demanded all of her. But she did not have all of her to give.

She wondered what had happened to the feelings she used to have for him. She wondered if they had somehow gotten buried underneath the past that she knew she was still living in. It was a past where she was still paying homage to all the wrongdoings inflicted upon her by her mother, father, and then her own daughter—all those who were supposed to have loved her. It was a past with no ending.

When she'd taken her marriage vows, she'd done so in earnest, or at least she believed she had. But somehow she had lost her understanding of this thing called love. Or had she ever really possessed it to begin with? After all, what had love ever really given her? What did she have to show for it? A childhood spent with dysfunctional parents. A boyfriend who disappeared as soon as he found out she was pregnant with Ida, and then Ida herself who turned out to be a disappointment to her like everyone else had been in her life.

No, she couldn't make herself be tender and loving and passionate like Henry said he wanted, needed. And she sensed that, even if she had those emotions still in her, it would take so long to dig them out that by the time she got to them he would no longer be interested in receiving them.

She adjusted the temperature of the water, and then stepped into the shower stall. She immediately reached for the bar of soap and began to lather the washcloth. She felt the dimples in her large thighs as she scrubbed them, and she was reminded, again, that her fifty-four-year-old body had seen better, leaner days.

Her fondness for anything chocolate, combined with a lack of physical activity, had led to her almost doubling her weight in the twenty-four years they had been married. To make matters worse, Henry would make comments about the increase in her weight from time to time. And this would irritate her to no end. She knew she could stand to lose some weight. She had eyes. She could see! And she didn't need him reminding her! She lowered the temperature of the water. *And he had the nerve to want some of this, this morning!*

She moved in closer toward the showerhead until the warm water was drenching her face. It had been a long time since she'd cried. But here, on a Sunday morning in the safety of the shower, she closed her eyes and let the tears flow.

Henry lay on his back listening to the water running in the bathroom. He was fifty-five years old, and his weight had practically remained the same throughout his twenty-four-year marriage. With the exception of the small pouch around his belly and the thinning hair in the center of his head, he did not look his age and was proud to say that he could still perform his manly duties whenever they were called upon. But it was not called upon nearly enough at home by his wife as it should have been. And, just like this morning, whenever he tried to offer it, it was met with rejection. A man had needs that could not go unmet. And since Ida was now out of the picture, he told himself that if his wife was not going to do what she was supposed to do, then he would just have to find somebody else who would.

Henry Dolittle was a third-generation Henry, and the grandson of a hardworking coal miner. He thought about his grandfather now, and remembered a conversation he'd had with him when he'd still been a little boy.

"You know, son," his grandfather had said as he'd scrubbed but never completely removed all of the black grime from beneath his fingernails, "there's a lot of value in a hard day's work. A lot of righteousness. The Bible tells us that if a man don't want to work, he shouldn't eat!"

"How come Daddy's hands don't look like yours, Grandpa? Don't he work hard too?"

"Uh-huh. Sure do." And Henry saw that his grandfather's speed in scrubbing his nails had increased. "He works hard, but in a way that God don't approve of . . . and neither do your momma, for that matter. And that's all I'm going to say about that!"

Throughout his youth, Henry often compared Henry Jr. to Henry Sr., and the contrast between the two did not escape him. His grandfather worked long and hard hours and always smelled like oil and grease. The truck he drove smelled like oil and grease, and even after he had bathed, the odor still lingered as if it was a permanent part of him.

His father worked long and hard too as the pastor of the First Presbyterian Church, and his efforts seemed to pay off the most. The car they rode to church in on Sunday mornings was always clean and filled with its own kind of oil. But it was the sweet, intoxicating kind that made the single women in the congregation giggle and carry on as though they were teenage girls. It was the kind of scent that kept Henry's mother in a state of insecurity and turned her into a private investigator.

She would go through his father's pockets and argue with him about his whereabouts after he'd come home until finally, she couldn't take it anymore and left. His father's oil was the kind that had other women quickly vying for the coveted title of the "pastor's *new* wife," and it would only take a few more years before the third-generation Henry would also discover a way to work hard for the Lord—his father's way—looking and smelling good while he did it.

Now, as the second-generation pastor of First Presbyterian Church on the east side of town, he had seen the size of the congregation dwindle down to half of its 250 members, and most of them were women and children. Still, he managed to support his family from the generous donations of the congregation who found him almost infallible.

He jumped out of bed, positioned himself on the floor facedown, and began his morning ritual of push-ups. He thought about the sermon he would be preaching in a few hours. He had titled it, "The Wages of Sin," and had planned to use Ida as an example of the consequences that come from living a life full of unrepentant sin. He was going to compare her nameless soul to a chapter in the Bible, the book of Judges, which told the story of how Samson, caught up in the sin of fornication with Delilah, lost his strength, dignity, freedom, and ultimately, his life.

He would warn the men in the pews—young and old alike—not to be led astray by a pretty body or a pretty face. He would urge them to take heed and remind them of what the apostle Paul said in Second Corinthians 11:14, ". . . Satan himself masquerades as an angel of light." Then, he would close his sermon with a few scriptures from the book of Proverbs and remind them that to give in to the enticement of lustful fornication could mean a lifetime of regret and exposure to the wrath of God. He thought about Ida and what had happened to the baby and decided he'd emphasize the point that even with repentance there could still be consequences to deal with.

He was aware that his message would not get through to many of the men in the congregation. He knew that preaching alone would not hold up against the lust of the flesh. It was a battle that had to be fought by the Lord. It was a battle that he had lost. For he had lusted over Ida's body. He had dared to taste her forbidden fruit, and it had been good, and sweet, and ready for the taking. Yes, Lord, he had sinned. But he would not reveal that to the congregation. All he could do was ask God to forgive him and admit that he had been weak, so weak, in fact, that he had kept going back for a taste of that forbidden fruit over and over again.

When he got to the forty-ninth push-up, the running water in the bathroom stopped, and the door opened. He watched Mavis walk across the room; the movement from her buttocks caused the tiny brown bears on her blue terry cloth robe to jump up and down with rhythmic precision. He wanted to be one of those bears. Didn't she understand? He *needed* to be one. He was too young *not* to be one. He quickly finished the last push-up and sat up.

"So, what do you plan to do about your granddaughter?" he asked, his breathing slightly labored.

"What do you mean what do I plan to do?" She stopped rubbing the moisturizing cream on her face and looked at his reflection in the mirror. "I don't know where they took her. And anyway, Ida never even let me see the girl. That child don't even know who I am."

"Maybe it's time she did."

She returned her attention back to her face and vigorously rubbed another layer of cream into her skin. "Yeah, well, like I said, I don't know where they took her."

He stared at her back for a few seconds. "You could find out."

"Yes," she gave him a look of disdain. "And you could go get in the shower. We're going to be late."

"Is there any hot water left for me?"

"Plenty."

"You know," Henry said, "all you have to do is call the Department of Human Services and tell them who you are. They should be able to tell you something."

"Yeah, but will it be something I want to hear?" Mavis asked stoically.

Henry got up from the floor and headed toward the bathroom, his desire null and void. Yes, he was going to have to find another woman to satisfy him. But it wouldn't be hard. His lips formed a crooked smile as he closed the bathroom door. The congregation was full of them.

Chapter Five

Tia had not slept much last night. She had arrived at the new house and was told that she would be staying for a few days with the man and woman who lived there. There had been a bed and food waiting for her. Missy, the lady who had taken her from her home, had kept her promise. After she'd finished eating, Tia had been taken to an upstairs room at the end of a hall. Her mind was a flurry of questions. How long would she have to stay here? Where was her mother? Did she know she was here? Would she come for her?

"You're going to get some sleep now," Missy had said wearily as she climbed the stairs with her.

But how could she sleep? She wanted to go home. She wanted to cry. Especially when the lady who lived there gave her a pair of pink and white pajamas to put on. But she would not cry. She was determined not to. And anyway, that was the thing her mother disliked most, hearing her cry. So, she slowly undressed and climbed into the cold and unfamiliar bed.

Sleep was not peaceful. When she finally closed her eyes, it was against her will, and she dreamed about her mother.

"Momma, can a mouse fly?"

"Some do."

"How come they don't have wings then?"

"They don't need no wings. They so little they just glide through the air like birds."

"I wish I could fly. But not like a mouse. Like a bird."
"Hmm."
"I would fly all over the world. But first I would fly to Cinnati and find my daddy."
"It's Cincinnati, and hush. Your daddy don't want no bird for a daughter."
"Do he want me?"
"Be quiet now and go to sleep."
"Momma."
"What."
"Little girls have dreams too, don't they?"
"Yeah, but it don't do no good."

Daylight filtered through the shaded window as Tia surveyed the small room. There was one window to the left of her with beige curtains that partially concealed a white window shade. On the floor directly in front of the window lay a rectangular brown rug with orange stripes running through it.

In the corner next to the window stood a wooden three-shelf bookcase filled with various types of books, some big with hard covers, others small and soft. Many were stacked on top of each other, and most of them were brightly colored. Her eyes traveled the length of the wall to a small door that stood partially open, and she could see the edge of a bathtub, white and shiny, just past the door. Continuing along the same wall, she saw a hanging picture of a brown-skinned woman holding a baby. The baby was looking up into the woman's eyes with one arm outstretched in midair.

There was nothing else to look at in the room except for the tall door that she had entered through the night before. It was now closed. She glanced back toward the bookcase, and a bright purple and yellow book caught her attention. Particles of dust danced on the sun's rays as she pulled the book down from the shelf. It had a picture of a tall, yellow bird waving its hand. The purple, she discovered, was actually a tall building situated directly behind the bird. She began flipping through the pages, stopping only on the ones that contained a picture of the tall, yellow bird.

"How long will she be here?"

Startled by the sound of the voice, Tia quickly closed the book and returned it to the shelf. The voice belonged to a man and was very close to her door. Her mind quickly resumed its flurry of questions. *What now? Who was that talking?* She hadn't seen a man last night. *Where did he come from?* She sat perfectly still in the middle of the bed, watching the door, waiting.

The night before she had sat on the edge of the couch in her living room, immobilized with fear and afraid to speak. Her mind replayed the image of the bottle of cola flying toward her, its contents smashing against the wall. Now, here she sat on this strange bed, in this strange place, immobilized with fear once again.

She heard the doorknob click, saw it turn, and heard the creaking of the hinges as it slowly opened. A stream of light rushed past the tall shadow that stood in the doorway and entered the room. Then the shadow spoke.

"Good morning, Tia. I'm Greg."

"Good morning," she said almost in a whisper.

"It's time to get up now."

Tia said nothing.

Greg turned on the bedroom light, and she could see him better. He was very thin, and the color of butter. His head was completely bald, and he walked with a limp. He smiled when he spoke to her, but there was something about his smile that she did not find comforting. She looked down at the rustled blanket on the bed.

He stood over her. "You don't remember me from last night?"

She shook her head.

"Well," he said as he walked past her into the bathroom, "it was late, and you were tired. I'm Cora's husband." He stopped in the bathroom doorway and turned. "You remember her, don't you? The lady that gave you something to eat last night?"

Tia nodded.

"Good." He winked at her. "I'm going to give you a bath since it was too late to give you one last night, okay?"

"I can give my own self a bath." She had finally found her voice.

"I bet you can. How old are you again?"

"I'm six."

"Okay. Then I'll just run the water for you and stick around to make sure you're okay."

He went into the bathroom, and she heard the water running.

"Come on," he said.

She hesitated before going into the bathroom. He sensed her reluctance and walked out of the room, closing the door behind him.

"I'll wait for you out here, okay?"

"Uh-huh," Tia mumbled.

She walked into the bathroom and looked up at the ceiling. There were no cracks in the paint, and she did not see it peeling anywhere. She took off her pajamas and put one foot into the tub, quickly removing it.

"It's too hot!" she yelled.

"Oops," Greg said, opening the door. "Let me add a little cold water to it."

Tia stepped back, placing her arms in front of her body in a crisscross fashion.

"Here, try it now."

She put one foot into the tub. The water was warm now, and she could tolerate it.

"Is that better?"

"Uh-huh," she said, as she put her other foot into the tub, and then lowered herself into the water.

"Let me wash your back for you."

He scooped up handfuls of water and let it run down her back. Once, twice, the third time she did not feel the warm water on her back, but instead felt the roughness of his large hands. She wanted to tell him to stop, that she did not like the feel of his rough hands, that she did not like the feel of any of this. Instead, she sat perfectly still and imagined herself to be a block of ice, surrounded by this tubful of warm water. Only she would not melt. She would just sit there and concentrate on the rapid beating of her heart.

"Greg!" she heard a woman yelling from beyond the bedroom door. "Greg, where are you?"

He jumped at the sound of his name and quickly removed his hand from her back.

"Be right there, Cora!" he called back as he dried his hands on a towel. "I'll have to give you a bath another time," he said smiling.

Seconds later, the lady Tia remembered seeing last night entered the bathroom and asked if she needed any help.

"Umm, can you wash my back?" she asked as her heartbeat slowly returned to a slower pace.

"Sure, baby," the woman smiled. "Hand me the washcloth."

She gave Cora the cloth and hunched over as the woman gently scrubbed her back in circular motions.

"Who is that man?" Tia asked.

"Who, Greg?"

Tia nodded.

"Oh, he's my husband."

"Does he live here?"

"Well, yes, honey, he does because he's my husband."

"How long is he going to live here?"

Cora smiled. "Well, since he's my husband that means he lives here all the time."

Tia's heartbeat began to quicken. "How long will I be here?"

"We don't know yet, honey. But you can stay as long as you need to."

"No, I have to go home as soon as my momma comes to get me." She thought about the rough hands of Cora's husband. "And I don't need to take anymore baths."

Cora stopped scrubbing her back. "Of course you do," she said. "Don't you want to be clean?"

"No, I want to go home," she said as droplets from her eyes became intermingled with the foamy bath water.

Cora swirled the washcloth around in the warm water, then lifted it back up to the nape of Tia's neck, watching as the water chased the soap film down her back and into the tub.

"It's going to be all right," Cora said softly, wondering why the little girl didn't want to take any more baths.

"No, it's not," Tia moaned. "I want to go home!"

Chapter Six

It was almost a week later, and Ida, sat, confined to the county jail having been charged with negligent homicide in the death of her two-month-old baby. Bail had been set at $25,000, but it didn't matter. She knew she couldn't make bail whatever the amount was, and she certainly wasn't going to ask Mavis *or* Henry for anything.

When her preliminary hearing came in a few weeks, she was going to plead guilty, waive her rights to a trial, and ask to be sentenced on the same day of her conviction. She just wanted to get it over with . . . much like this therapy session the judge had ordered her to attend during her initial appearance in intake court.

The therapist, Dr. Nothingham, sat behind her desk, her lips pressed tightly together until they appeared to form one thin line across the lower half of her face. She sat still, pen and paper in hand, waiting for Ida to start talking.

"Emotions can get a person in trouble sometimes," Ida said. "*Most* of the time," she continued as she looked around the room. "In fact, anger is a lot like love."

"How so?" the therapist asked.

"Well, they both make people do some really wild things, you know? I mean, people have been beaten, killed, even sent to prison because of those two funky emotions."

"Which one of those emotions would you say caused you to end up here? Anger or love?"

Ida ignored the question and continued. "They say that the opposite of love ain't hate, but indifference. Indifference. I been thinking about that, and that's what I am. I'm indifferent. I don't care. You do me wrong, expect to get done wrong. I don't care who you are!"

For the first time since entering the room, Ida looked directly into the eyes of the therapist. They reminded her of a winter afternoon in January when the sky is blue, and the sun shines bright, yet everything is still frozen to the core.

"Have you always felt this way?" the therapist asked.

Ida leaned forward and let her arms rest on her slender thighs. She looked down at the dark blue carpet covering the floor. "Long as I can remember," she said, not wanting to divulge too much information. She did not want to get into how she came to be the way she was. There was no reason for her to explain in detail how she had been taught indifference through many beatings at the hands of her mother. The bottom line was that she had grasped the concept well, and had embraced it because it was the only thing that she could embrace. Never did it run away from her, let her down, or reject her. Time after time, it always allowed her to enter. So, she embraced being indifferent, and that suited her just fine.

"Is there anyone in your life right now that you love or want to love?" the therapist asked in a voice that was void of all compassion.

Ida chuckled. "Are you serious?"

"Yes, I am," the therapist said, maintaining her stoic composure.

"Then the answer is no," Ida said.

"Is there anyone that loves or wants to love *you?*"

"Man, you just keep the questions coming, don't you?" Ida rubbed a brown spot on the carpet with the sole of her shoe. "I wouldn't know," she said, then added, "not really. I mean, my mother never wanted me, and if she did she had a funny way of showing it."

"What do you mean?"

She shrugged her shoulders. "I don't want to talk about it."

"What about your father?"

"What about him?"

"Did he show love toward you?"

Ida stared hard at the therapist. "It's kind of tough to show love toward somebody you ain't never met."

"Tell me about your baby."

Ida flicked an imaginary piece of lint from her county-issued pants. "Ain't nothing to tell. My baby's dead."

"And how do you feel about that?"

"I don't want to talk about it. That's how I feel." Her right foot began to shake as she looked past the therapist to the cracks on the pale white wall behind her.

"And your little girl?" the therapist persisted.

"She'll be all right."

"How can you be sure?"

"Because I am." Ida glared at her. "Next question."

The therapist ignored Ida's intimidating glare and continued. "So, what I'm hearing is that you're feeling abandoned and unloved. How do you feel about having to deal with those feelings?"

Ida sighed heavily as she uncrossed her legs and shifted her position in the chair. Why was this lady asking her all these stupid questions? Didn't she just tell her how she was feeling?

The therapist was staring at her with those cold eyes, and Ida wondered if she had her own problems to deal with. Maybe that's why she wasn't listening to what she had just told her. And maybe that's why her eyes were so cold.

"I know the county's not paying you big money for this mess," Ida said. "I need a cigarette."

"Well, you know we have a no smoking policy inside the building," the therapist hesitated, "but Ida, can you answer my question?"

Ida knew a little bit about body language, and if what she had discovered through the years was correct, then she was just wasting her time here anyway—in this room with this woman—surrounded by all of her achievements hanging on a wall, sitting stiffly in her leather chair with her arms *and* legs crossed, nodding every now and then, asking questions that were supposed to encourage Ida to understand herself better, knowing that she would still be paid for her day's work whether Ida talked to her or not. Ida stood up. Why had she stayed this long?

"I gotta go," Ida said. "This ain't for me."

The thing with the cold, blue eyes said nothing, did not even stand and escort her to the door. But then again, she didn't have to. The guard was standing just on the other side, waiting for her.

Chapter Seven

Mavis sat at the mahogany dining-room table holding the thick, white envelope in her hand. The paper shook slightly as she read the red stamped letters in the upper left-hand corner: *Mailed from the county jail.* Above the letters was Ida's name, followed by a series of letters and numbers, then the address, city, state, and zip code. The envelope was postmarked August 1st, one week after Mavis had watched police officers put Ida, handcuffed and screaming, into the back of their squad car. Why was she writing to her? She and Ida had spent the last year living as strangers, estranged from one another. There had been no communication between them other than the name-calling Ida would occasionally yell at her window in passing. Neither had been welcomed in the other's home, and Ida had refused to allow her to see her own grandchildren. Why was she sending this letter? What would Mavis be accused of this time? She slowly tore open the envelope and removed its contents.

"You know, twenty-four years of feeling unwanted can do funny things to a person. I just had a meeting with a therapist, and she wanted to ask me all these questions, like who do I love, who loves me. Stuff like that. And you know what I told her? Nobody! That's right, Mama. Nobody. Including you. Don't sit there and pretend like your feelings hurt. I ain't mad at you. Probably because I ain't much to love anyway. But like I was saying, this therapist was really cold, like

she just didn't have no feelings. I guess that's her job,
though. Anyway, I didn't tell her much. I really didn't
trust her. But then I was thinking, I don't trust nobody
either. I guess that makes me more like you than ei-
ther one of us wants to admit, huh, Mama?

"Oh yeah, say hi to Henry, I mean your husband.
And tell him I said I'm sorry about the baby. He'll
know what I mean. So, Mama, look like you don't
have to worry about seeing me no more. I know you
wasn't anyway, but I'm gonna be gone for a while.
The public defender man say I could get 10–12 years,
so I guess I'm gonna be right where you said I should
be. Hope you happy. Ida."

Mavis was not happy. What in the world kind of
crazy mumbo jumbo was this girl talking about now?
She had done the best she could with Ida, but look
at what she'd had to work with. The Lord had surely
cursed her the day she gave birth to Ida. She was just
like her daddy from the get-go—no good.

Mavis had been eighteen years old when she'd gotten pregnant with Ida, and when her father found out
she was pregnant, he'd put her out of the house—while
her mother stood by and did nothing. She'd gone to the
father of her unborn baby, but he wanted nothing to
do with her as well. She ended up living in a shelter for
a while, eventually applying for, and receiving, county
benefits.

The benefits had been enough for her to rent a small
one-bedroom apartment in an impoverished section of
the city. Six months after Ida had been born, Mavis had
managed to get a job as a customer service clerk in one
of the retail shops located in the downtown mall. She
earned just enough to keep them in that small apart-

ment, and it was furnished with only a few basic pieces of furniture—all purchased from the Goodwill.

It had been a lonely life for her. An only child, estranged from both her mother and father, she wondered if that had been how Nelson Mandela must have felt, having been imprisoned in South Africa at the time for opposing apartheid. But even he had not been completely alone; there were fellow prisoners and letters from home she imagined he must have received. She had no one.

She rarely socialized because she would always be faced with another dilemma—who would watch Ida? The woman who watched her during the day so that Mavis could work was reimbursed by the county and had a day care operating from her home. Mavis knew she certainly would not want to turn around and watch Ida at night as well . . . especially since she would not be reimbursed for any nighttime hours.

The years went by, and Mavis resigned herself to simply working and making sacrifices for her daughter. But her daughter, then eight years old, had begun to get on her nerves. And Mavis found herself becoming impatient with her on a much more frequent basis.

It was the little things, like squeezing the tube of toothpaste from the middle instead of the bottom. Putting the roll of toilet paper on the cylinder holder backward so that Mavis would have to pull the 2-ply sheets from behind instead of pulling them from the front.

She had grown tired of seeing her daughter come home from school every other day with dirt stains on her plaid, corduroy bell bottoms or the shoestrings from her black-and-white Buster Brown shoes dragging on the ground behind her as she walked. How many times had she reminded her about tying her shoes?

She had come to the conclusion that Ida just didn't listen. She just didn't pay attention. So, Mavis began using her hands to do what her mouth had previously done. A slap on the face would remind Ida to stop talking with her mouth full. A shoe to the side of her head would encourage her to stop playing and pick up her clothes. This went on for a few more years, and then Mavis met Henry.

He had been preaching at an outdoor tent revival, and she'd been captivated by the intense look in his eyes. He'd been dressed in a pair of nicely creased faded jeans with a casual, short sleeve white linen shirt. But it was the words he had spoken that impressed her.

"Are you lonely, afraid, feeling like the whole world is against you?"

It was as if every word he'd spoken had been meant specifically for her. She had been feeling all of those things for a very long time when she'd been drawn to that tent thirteen years ago.

"Feeling like no matter what you do nothing ever seems to get better!" He'd stated that as a fact rather than a question. "You try to do right, but your wrong keeps doing you!"

There had been handclapping and "amens" spilling out into the street as she walked to the grocery store with Ida. She had no intentions of stopping at the tent, but found herself there anyway. Once inside, she could not keep her eyes off him.

"But I know someone who can fix it, praise God! I know someone who will carry the load for you! Jesus Christ said in Matthew, chapter 11, verses 28 through 30, 'Come to me, all you who are weary and burdened, and I will give you rest. Take my yoke upon you and learn from me, for I am gentle and humble in heart, and you will find rest for your souls. For my yoke is

easy and my burden is light.' Amen!" he'd shouted, and
the crowd had been in agreement with him.

"Stop trying to fix it by yourself. Stop trying to live
life apart from the one who sacrificed His life in order
that you"—he had pointed his finger out toward the
crowd—"might have life eternal! John 3:16 says, 'For
God so loved the world that he gave his one and only
Son, that whoever believes in him shall not perish but
have eternal life.'

"But you have to do more than just believe, people.
You have to trust and obey. You have to put Him on!
Just like a parachute . . . If you're in a plane, and that
plane is going down, and you look at that parachute,
and you believe it's a parachute, but you don't put it
on . . . How much good do you think your belief in that
parachute will do you?"

Most of the crowd had hollered out the answer,
"Nothing! That's right!"

"Listen," he continued, "we're all sinners. We come
into this world with a sinful nature already residing in
our souls. Romans, chapter 3, verse 10 says, '. . . There
is no one righteous, not even one.' Now, some of us
lean more toward one type of sin than another. Some
of us don't have any preferences for the types of sin we
commit. But we all have one thing in common! We're
sinners!"

Mavis had stood listening, unable to move as he had
begun to preach the Gospel of Jesus Christ. "The only
difference between you and me," he said, "is that I'm a
saved sinner by God's grace. But you can be saved too!
Listen, things go better with Jesus! You need to secure
your eternal future while you still have time. I know
some of you can relate to what I'm saying. I know because God created you with a conscience that you keep
trying to quiet by talking loud, laughing hard, having
sex, listening to loud music, using drugs, alcohol . . .

anything, anything at all. But it's really not working, is it?"

The crowd was quiet.

"You need to surrender yourself to the Lord, people, and have faith! Paul said in Romans, chapter 10, verse 17, 'Consequently, faith comes from hearing the message, and the message is heard through the Word about Christ.'

"Hebrews, chapter 11, verse 6, says, '. . . without faith it is impossible to please God, because anyone who comes to him must believe that he exists and that he rewards those who earnestly seek him.' Before God can help you, you have to want to be helped. Then you have to admit to God that you are a sinner in need of His forgiveness.

"Acts, chapter 2, verse 38, says, '. . . Repent and be baptized, every one of you, in the name of Jesus Christ for the forgiveness of your sins. And you will receive the gift of the Holy Spirit.'

"Confess Jesus Christ as Lord and Savior! Matthew, chapter 10, verse 32 through 33, says, 'Whoever acknowledges me before others, I will also acknowledge him before my Father in heaven. But whoever disowns me before others, I will disown him before my Father in heaven.'

"So, come now, people." He had stepped away from the podium and had both of his arms outstretched toward the crowd as the choir behind him began to sing. "Come on now before it's too late! Tomorrow is not promised to any of us! Paul said in Hebrews, chapter 3, verse 15, '. . . Today, if you hear his voice, do not harden your hearts . . .'" He held up his Bible and shook it in the air. "Today, people! Today!"

And on that day, with Ida in tow, Mavis made her way up to the altar and answered the call of salvation. She had received Jesus Christ into her life and was baptized the following Sunday morning at the First Presbyterian

Church. She was added to the church's membership and never missed a Wednesday or Sunday service. She became Pastor Dolittle's favorite admirer, which did not go unnoticed by him, and one year after responding to Henry's offer of salvation, she responded to his offer of marriage and said yes.

Ida had been twelve years old then and already out of control. No amount of whippings—God had sanctioned this form of punishment in the form of Proverbs 13:24, which told her that to spare the rod was to spoil the child—invoked a change within her. And having been born-again, Mavis could no longer cuss her daughter out and feel righteous about it. But if she slipped from time to time, she felt the Lord had understood

Henry, however, had never reprimanded Ida. He had never taken a stand with Mavis. In fact, it seemed to her that he had never taken a stand at all when it came to her and Ida. And as Ida grew older, her body blossomed into that of a young woman's, and still, Henry had never seen fit to explain to her why it was inappropriate for her to parade around the house in front of him without a bra on.

The image came back to Mavis; Ida strutting around the house, the excessive movement underneath her shirt clearly indicating she was without a bra. Then, as if that hadn't been bad enough, she had begun to sit on Henry's lap as if she were a five-year-old. And again, Henry had said nothing. Mavis would have to remind Ida in a stern way that she was too big to be sitting on her husband's lap and threaten another whipping if she did not get up.

Henry did not agree with the way she treated Ida, and Mavis did not appreciate him disagreeing with her. As a preacher—never mind a man—she thought he should have taken a stronger stance with Ida. Maybe he just hadn't wanted to hurt Ida's feelings. She, on the other hand, had had no problems hurting her feelings, and more, if need be.

Soon the phone calls had begun. Teenage boys would call the house at all hours of the day and night wanting to speak to Ida. This is when Henry had finally spoken up, and on more than one occasion, she heard him angrily telling Ida that she had better put an end to all of those phone calls, particularly the ones late at night.

"Why?" Ida had asked. "They ain't for you."

"You better watch your mouth, girl. You ain't grown yet."

"That's what you think."

Henry would stand there watching the backside of Ida as she sashayed away, not saying another word. Mavis would stand there too. Watching Henry. Trying not to think what she was thinking: Why did her husband always let Ida have the last word? And why each time did he just stand there watching the back of her retreat with that look on his face? She knew what that look was. It had a name, and she had tried to justify it by putting the blame on Satan for using her daughter to create that look that showed itself on the face of her husband each time he watched his stepdaughter walk away.

It was after these times that Henry would come to her for intimacy. Only it would not be intimate. It would be without passion, no soft words spoken, no tender caresses, and certainly not the look that she'd seen in his eyes when he'd watched Ida.

Still, Mavis had grown weary of trying to refuse his advances and soon realized that she could get to sleep a lot earlier if she would just give in to his request. And so she did. She believed it was not really her body that he craved, but just an urge to satisfy his own desires. She had made an unspoken, un-agreed upon pact that she would have intercourse with him purely to satisfy

his most basic needs and to fulfill her wifely commit-
ments . . . nothing more.

So, during these occasions, she would stare up at
the ceiling until her mind drifted off to some unknown
peaceful place, a place where nothing could penetrate
its barrier, and Henry, with all his moaning and groan-
ing and movements, could not touch her when she went
to this place. Sometimes she would immerse herself so
completely in it that she would not realize that the bed
had stopped moving, and he had rolled over to his side
and appeared to be on his way to a peaceful place of
his own. She never knew how long he had been on top
of her—in order to know that, she would have had to
forfeit her peaceful place to keep track of the time. She
only knew she couldn't stand for him to touch her and
how uncomfortable it was for her afterward trying to
sleep as close to the edge of the mattress as possible.
Had she always felt this way when it came to sex?

Henry was the only man she'd ever been sexually
intimate with other than Ida's father. And she could recall little about their one-time tryst that had ended up
with her being pregnant and kicked out of the house.
She could recall some sense of satisfaction on her part
when she'd slept with the young boy, knowing that she
was behaving in a way her father had not approved of,
but had the satisfaction been sexual?

Mavis looked down at the letter that she was still
holding in her hand and began crumbling it into a
medium-sized ball. *"Tell him I'm sorry about the baby.
He'll know what I mean."* But what *did* she mean?
Slowly, she began to smooth out the folds in the paper.
What kind of tricks was her daughter up to now?

Chapter Eight

It was midday as Tia sat on the floor in front of the television set turning the dial from channel to channel. There was a talk show on. She stopped briefly to view a woman and her scantily dressed teenage daughter sitting on the stage.

The woman's daughter was condemning the audience for criticizing the way she was dressed. A man stood up and asked her what she was trying to prove by coming out of the house half-naked, to which she replied, "My freedom."

There was a clapping of hands from a small portion of the audience, and then another man stood up and asked, "How does your father feel about the way you dress?" Before the young girl could answer, her mother volunteered the information that her father was not a part of her life. The audience was silent, and Tia changed the channel.

She stopped again to view a commercial of a man pulling into his driveway. A little girl came out of the front door and ran to give him a hug. A woman followed behind the little girl, and the three of them, smiling, walked into the house. When was her mother going to come smiling for her?

Tia didn't know how long she'd been at this house with Cora and Greg, but Greg was still trying to hug *her* and she didn't like it, and Cora was still making her take a bath every day. So far, she'd had seven of them.

She turned the channel again, and there was the big yellow creature she'd seen on the cover of the book she'd been paging through in the bedroom. But this time he did not hold her interest. Her mind was still picturing the previous scene of the little girl running to meet her daddy in the commercial. Where was *her* daddy? She'd tried getting the answer to that question from her mother, but had not succeeded. She was always given the same answer: "I don't know where he is." Tia would always follow up with a question about his name.

"His name is Frankie, Tia," her mother would say. "Now stop asking so many questions."

She tried concentrating on the yellow creature that now had several boys and girls forming a circle around him as they sang a song. She recognized the tune but did not know the words, so she began to hum softly along instead.

"What's that you're watching?" the tall, butter-colored man asked standing behind her.

He startled her, and her back stiffened as she remained silent.

He continued, "Oh, you're watching that educational channel. Good for you."

She remained silent.

"I bet you miss school, huh?"

"I don't go to school," she said softly.

"No?"

She shook her head. "I was supposed to go, but my momma didn't take me."

"Hmm," he said, rubbing his chin. "If you stay with us we can take you to school."

Ignoring his statement, she asked, "Where's Ms. Cora?"

"She went to the store," he said smiling. "She'll be back."

Tia wished he would stop smiling. She wished as hard as she could that Cora would walk through the door at that very minute. She did not like the way his eyes turned into skinny strips of blackness when he smiled or how his long, crooked teeth would not stay inside of his mouth.

She walked back to the couch and sat down. "When is my momma coming to get me?"

"I don't think your mother will be coming for a while," Greg said, sitting down next to her.

She scooted her small frame away from him. "Why not?"

"Because she's in jail."

"For what?"

"For being a bad mommy." He patted her thigh.

She stiffened at the touch of his hand just as she had previously done when she'd been in the bathtub and he had made the attempt to wash her back. She wanted to push it away, but instead did nothing.

"What did she do?"

"Well, for starters, she didn't treat you very nice, now, did she?"

"How do you know?" she asked, frowning.

"Because that's what the lady who brought you here told me."

"Well, when she gets out she'll come and get me."

"Don't you want to stay here with me and Cora? We love you," he said. "I love you."

His hand was on her thigh again, but this time he was rubbing it, and she could not make herself look at his face. She concentrated on his fingers, long and slender with nails that were rough and yellow. Moisture began building up in her eyes. As she blinked, a single tear escaped and landed on the back of his hand.

"Oh, don't cry," he said, putting an arm around her shoulder. He let it rest heavily there, and she could smell the stench of underarm odor.

She cried even harder now. It was her fault that she was in this place, her fault that her mother was in jail. If she hadn't talked to that man on the phone, all of those strange people would not have ended up at her house. She had just wanted something to eat, and he had said he was sending food, not strange people who would take her away from her mother. She continued crying, covering her face as she did so. Where was her daddy? Where was Cora? Why did this man have his arms around her? She tried to get up from the sofa, but he hugged her even tighter.

"Where are you going?"

"I want to go home," she cried.

"You can't, sweetheart. Weren't you listening to me? There's nobody at your house. Your mommy's in jail. "

"No, she ain't," she said while struggling to free herself from his uncomfortable hug.

"Just calm down, little lady. You ain't stronger than me."

"Let go of me!"

"Okay, okay. Just calm down," he said, finally releasing his grip. "I'm not going to hurt you. I just wanted to let you know that I love you."

"I don't want your love," she said as she ran for the front door.

Once outside, she raced down the concrete steps and stopped. Where was she running to? Which way was home? She turned to look up at the front door. It was closed, and the man was not in sight. She sat down on the last concrete step with the palms of her hands pressed firmly into the cement. Like a runner waiting for the signal that would indicate the beginning of the race, she maintained her position, looking back at the front door from time to time. If it opened, that would be her signal.

She looked up and down the block and discovered that the house was one of only three other houses on that block. There was a lot large enough for another house to sit on that separated the house she was staying at from the other. And what had once been a field of grass was reduced to mostly dirt with litter strewn about. The house sitting on the other side of the lot had all of its windows and doors boarded up, with big letters and symbols painted on its white frame.

The third house and the entrance to the main highway were on the other side of the street. It was a small brown and yellow house that reminded Tia of the houses that she had often drawn with her crayons. Its front door stood perfectly in the middle with one small window on each side. The brown paint on the frame of each window had begun to peel revealing a yellow layer underneath, and there was a round window on the top half of the house that reminded her of a mirror whose glass had been cracked. Its frame too was peeling. The cement walkway leading up to the house had various cracks in it that allowed unsightly weeds to surface and flourish underneath the sun's rays.

As she continued looking at the house, the front door suddenly swung open, and a small black-and-white puppy made its exit. An old woman followed behind the dog as it sniffed around in the yard, and then lifted its hind leg up to a tree. After it had finished, it continued sniffing around the yard until the woman gave her thigh two quick pats, and it quickly returned to the house, entering through the door she held open for it.

Tia noticed the picnic table sitting on the side of the house and tried to picture the woman and her dog sitting there. She imagined she would be eating a sandwich or maybe a bigger meal while her dog enjoyed a bone or whatever it was that dogs got to eat.

The house where she had been taken to looked a lot like the house across the street. The only difference was that there was no peeling paint or broken window. She began searching for cracks in the cement to compare with the house across the street when she heard the front door being opened. Her heartbeat quickened as she leaned forward, preparing to run.

"Tia." It was the voice of Cora.

She turned her head in the direction of the voice. Cora stood looking at her. "What's wrong?" she asked.

"I want to go home."

"Why don't you give it a few more days here? Give yourself a chance to get used to us."

"I can't."

"Why not, honey?"

Tia didn't know why. She only knew that she did not like Greg. And she did not like sleeping in that bed, or wearing those pink pajamas, or sitting on that couch or—with the exception of having food to eat—anything else about being there. This much she knew. She didn't really mind being around Cora. But Cora was not her mother. And she wanted to go home.

"Are you hungry?"

Tia looked up at the sky. A thin, white streak of smoke stretched across the pale blue background. A flock of birds made their journey across the land, each one parallel to the other with one lone bird forming the tip of the unison. She closed her eyes and pretended that the warm breeze she felt was caused by her own movement through the air.

"Tia."

It was difficult for her to pass up the opportunity to eat, so she agreed to come inside for lunch. "But then," she said, "I have to go."

She ate her lunch—a ham sandwich and potato salad— watching Greg from the corner of her eyes as he sat at the table eating with her.

"After lunch you can take a nap," Cora said as she put the containers of food back into the refrigerator, "and maybe you'll feel better when you wake up." She walked over to where Tia was sitting and patted her shoulder. "I have to go to work, but Greg will stay here with you."

The food in her mouth became immobile. She tried chewing but could not get her teeth and tongue to co-operate. All attempts to swallow became futile, and she had to take a gulp of milk to push the food down in order to talk.

"I can't take a nap," she said on the verge of tears. "I told you I have to go."

"Come on, now," Greg said, "you sure you don't want to stay? Cora went out and bought all this food for you. *And* you've got your own room. You sure?"

Ignoring him, she continued, "Can you call that lady and ask her to come and take me home?"

"Well, Tia," Cora sighed, "if that's what you want. I can call her, but I'll tell you right now, honey, you won't be going home. There's nobody there."

"My momma's there."

"Remember I told you already, Tia," Greg said. "Your mommy's not at home. Where did we say she was?"

Cora glared at Greg, who smiled back at her.

"I'll call the social worker," Cora said gently. "But just so you know, sweetie, she'll probably send you to another home just like this one."

"Just like this one?" The shrill sound of Tia's voice filled the kitchen. Her eyes widened.

"Just like this one," Cora said, wiping her already clean hands across her apron.

Tia could not bear the thought of having to be around another man like Greg. And what if the next lady was not as nice as Cora was? This was all the more reason why she had to go home, and one way or another she would. Maybe she could take some food with her, but she was determined not to spend another night in this house.

"I still want you to call her," she said to Cora.

The ringing of the telephone interrupted Mavis's thoughts. She placed the letter from Ida on the dining-room table and walked across the room where the phone sat.

"Dolittle residence."

"Hi, my name is Ms. Cee. I'm a social worker with the Department of Human Services. Is this Mrs. Dolittle?"

"It is."

"Mrs. Dolittle, I'm calling about your granddaughter, Tia."

"How did you get my number?"

"Your daughter, Ida, gave your name and number to one of the police officers."

"Continue."

"Well, the reason I'm calling is like I said, about your granddaughter, Tia." There was a pause, and then she continued. "Tia has been staying with a foster family, but she's having a hard time adjusting. I just received a call from the foster mother who said that Tia is insisting on being taken home. Now, the foster mother said she tried to explain to her that there was no one at home to care for her, but she refuses to stay. Are you able to care for your granddaughter? And if so, would you be willing to?"

"Well, I don't know." Mavis was careful of the words she spoke. She saw no need to reveal all of her business to this stranger on the other end of the phone. She bit her top lip. Why had Ida given the police officer her name and number? After all, she'd deprived her of being a grandmother for many years. And only now that she was in trouble, she needed her.

"I think it would really be good for Tia," the social worker was saying. "She needs to be with family."

"I'll have to think it over and talk to my husband about this."

"I understand, Mrs. Dolittle. How about if I call you tomorrow, and you can let me know then?"

"That'll be fine."

"I'll also give you my number just in case you have any questions. I can be reached between eight A.M. and five P.M. If I'm not in my office just leave a message on my voice mail, okay?"

"I'll do that." Mavis noticed the trembling of her hand as she wrote down the seven numbers. She hung up the phone and tried to imagine what it would be like to have another child in the house after six years. She did not attempt to fool herself. She knew she didn't want the responsibility of raising another child, especially after the terrible job she'd done with Ida. Still, how could she say no and keep a clear conscience?

Chapter Nine

Tia sat on the living-room sofa next to the social worker and listened intently.

"Well, Tia, there's a possibility that your grandmother might be willing to take custody of you."

Possibility? Might? Those words didn't sound reassuring to Tia. "What does custody mean?" she asked.

"That means you'd be able to live with her," the social worker continued. "But she has to talk it over with her husband—your granddad."

Tia frowned. "What's a granddad?"

Ms. Cee exchanged glances with Cora. "Well, let's see," she spoke slowly. "A granddad is usually your mommy's daddy. You know. Like your grandmother is your mommy's mother. It's the same thing, only he's a man so he's the grand*dad*. Does that make sense, sweetie?"

Tia nodded. "I don't know who my grandmother is," she said softly.

The social worker sighed. *There was that weight again.* "Well, you might know tomorrow."

"Tomorrow?" Tia could feel the panic beginning to rise in her throat again.

"Yes, your grandmother told me she would let me know tomorrow. Do you think you can stay here just one more day, Tia?"

She shook her head violently.

"Just *one* more day, honey?"

Although her head was down, she could feel *him* staring at her. She imagined him with his teeth bared and his eyes slanted, waiting along with everyone else in the room for her to answer. She looked toward Cora and asked, "Do you have to go to work today?"

"Yes, baby, I do. But Greg will be here with you. He'll take good care of you."

"That's right," he said. "I won't let anything happen to you." He touched her shoulder, and again she cringed.

"I still want to go home," she whispered.

"I know you do, sweetie, but we have to wait for your grandmother to call us."

"Can I go to work with you?" she asked Cora.

Cora smiled—it was the first time Tia had seen her smile—and rubbed Tia's back. "No, baby. I'm sorry, but they won't let me bring any children to work with me."

"So, you'll stay with us one more night?" Greg asked.

Tia said nothing.

The social worker stood, looking at Cora and Greg. "She'll be all right," she said, then motioned with her hands for them to call her if they had a problem. She bent down and gave Tia a hug. "You'll be all right," she whispered. "Cora has my number if you need to call me, okay?"

But it was not okay. Tia sat quietly as Cora walked the social worker to the door.

"Looks like it's going to be just you and me, kid," Greg said smiling.

She looked at him and frowned as she got up from the sofa and stormed out of the room.

"I got a call from some social worker who's supposed to be handling Tia's case," Mavis said to Henry as he sat on the living-room sofa.

"What'd she want?"

"She wanted to know if I'd be willing to take custody of Tia."

"What'd you tell her?"

"I told her I'd have to think about it and talk it over with you."

"What's there to talk over? I already told you what I think you should do."

"So you don't have a problem raising another child?"

He arched his eyebrows. Raising another child? What was she talking about? As far as he was concerned, he hadn't raised the first one. "No, I don't. She's your granddaughter, not some stranger off the street." Although she was only six, he hoped she would be like her mother, Ida. And bring some sort of life into the mundane existence that he shared with his wife.

"I also received a letter from Ida today."

"And what did she want?"

"I'm not sure. She went on and on about how I never loved her, and how I don't have to be bothered with her anymore now that she's locked up in jail."

Henry was silent.

"She also said to tell you that she was sorry about the baby. She said you'd know what she meant." Mavis waited for Henry's response as he slowly bent down and pulled off his shoes.

He said nothing, but he felt her staring at the back of his neck. Still avoiding her stare, he sat up and simultaneously reached for a cigar.

"Don't light that in here, Henry. You know I can't stand the smell."

It was a good thing—her protesting the lighting of his cigar because he feared his hands would tremble, and that might give her a reason to question him further about Ida's comments.

"So are you going to tell me?"

"Tell you what?"

"What did she mean? About the baby."

He took a deep breath, steadied his voice, and turned to look at Mavis. "I don't know what she's talking about!" he said with the best look of indignation he could conjure up. "You know how crazy Ida can be sometimes. What's wrong with you?"

She stood staring at him, slowly placing her hands on her hips.

"Go ahead and make that call," he said as he got up from the sofa. "And turn on the air. It's hot as hell in here."

"There's nothing wrong with me," she said as he walked away. She frowned. *But there's going to be a whole lot wrong with you if I find out you had something to do with that baby of hers.*

Chapter Ten

Tia spent the rest of the day in the bedroom. She fell asleep for a while, then awoke disappointed that the sun was not shining through the window to indicate a new day had come. How would she make it through the night? She turned on her side and felt the pressure from her full bladder. She did not want to get out of the bed and had decided to stay right where she was until daybreak or Cora or the social worker arrived. But each time she changed positions, the pressure threatened to release itself at any moment. She had no choice but to get out of the bed and go to the bathroom.

It was dark in the room, but the thin stream of light filtering in from beneath the door made it possible for her to see just enough to make it to the bathroom. Once inside, she closed the door softly, turned the rectangular knob to lock it, and turned on the light. Maybe she could be safe in here. But there was nothing but hard ceramic surrounding her, and the thought of spending the night in this tiny space was not very appealing. She flushed the toilet and made her way back to the bed.

The rumbling sound coming from her stomach told her that she had a new problem; she was hungry. She had not eaten since the afternoon when Cora had made lunch. She stared at the door, listening for any sounds that would let her know if Greg was still up, and if so, where. After a few minutes of silence, she tiptoed across the floor, and then stopped at the door to listen again. Still no sounds. She opened the door slowly and peered first to the left, then to the right. Still tiptoeing, she went down the carpeted stairs and walked through the living room. It was dark except for the light from a street lamp outside that produced a rectangular pattern across the floor. She turned to make her way toward the kitchen and was startled by his form.

"What are you looking for?" Greg asked, standing in the hallway, blocking the only entrance into the kitchen. He reminded her of a monster she'd seen in a cartoon once. It had been tall and skinny and bald with arms that touched the floor and banana-shaped eyes.

"Nothing," she said.

"Nothing? Come on, now. Nobody looks for nothing at twelve o'clock at night. What were you looking for?"

"I'm hungry," she said with as much courage as she could muster up.

"Oh. You're hungry. Guess that's probably because you didn't eat dinner, huh?"

It was hard for her to answer because her heart was beating much too fast, so she said nothing.

"Tell you what. You be nice to me, and I'll be nice to you."

He continued blocking her path as she stood at eye level with the belt around his pants. How was she supposed to be nice to him when she didn't even like him?

She found her voice. "Never mind," she said softly, turning to go back upstairs.

"Never mind?" He grabbed her arm. "But you haven't been nice to me, Tia. And I thought you were hungry."

"I'm not anymore," she said trying to wiggle out of his grasp.

"Now, now, you don't want to go to bed because if you did I wouldn't have caught you tiptoeing around down here, would I?" He pulled her close to him.

"Let go!"

"Come on, I'm not going to hurt you. I just want to give you a kiss."

"Stop it!" she screamed, continuing to twist her body in an attempt to free herself. But he was too strong. She felt the warmth from his breath as he spoke.

"Come on now. Just one kiss."

"Stop it!" She was crying now.

"Go on, girl," he said as he released his grip and pushed her back into the living room.

"Leave me alone!"

"What? You yelling at me? Girl, don't you know I'll whip your little behind?" He unbuckled his pants belt and pulled it off as he came toward her. He raised his left arm up into the air and out of instinct, she drew both of her arms up in a cross to over her head. The belt caught her on her side and back, and she curled her body into a ball, anticipating the next hit. Instead, she felt his foot kick the lower portion of her back, and she let out a whine.

"Get up!"

But she could not move. Her fear paralyzed her, and she was afraid to uncover her face.

"I said, get up!"

Just as he bent down to grab her, the telephone began to ring. He hesitated before turning and heading in the direction of the phone, and suddenly, Tia found it in her to move. She stumbled to a stand and ran up the stairs, back to the bedroom. She did not stop until she had entered the bathroom, closed the door, and turned the rectangular knob to the lock position again.

Her breathing came rapidly, and she could feel herself trembling. She wished she could call the social worker, but that was out of the question because she would have to go back downstairs to use the phone, and she didn't know the number anyway. She resigned herself to staying in the bathroom for the rest of the night, sitting on the floor with her back against the bathtub.

The tears, though still present, had stopped, had turned themselves inward where they would remain hidden deep inside of her, forming a pool of icy waters that would soon freeze over. As she sat on the tile floor, her breathing became less labored and she was aware of the throbbing sensation in her back and on her side. She sat watching the doorknob with vacant eyes, and this was the way Cora found her several hours later.

Part Two
Chapter Eleven

2000

The year 1999 had come and gone like any other year, making way for its numerical successor, 2000. There had been no big bang of destruction to mark the beginning or end of time as so many had predicted there would be. No nuclear warfare, no food and water shortages (except for what was caused by those who stockpiled canned goods and water based on the predictions of others who knew no more than they did).

Life continued on as it had been. And now, during this first month of the New Year, Tia stood at the window contemplating the life that had begun to grow in her. She rubbed the slightly detectable pouch on her stomach. If she didn't do something soon, it would become quite noticeable over the next six to seven months.

By her calculations, she was two-and-a-half-months pregnant. If she continued with the pregnancy—which she was not going to do—the baby would be born in the same month as she had been born eighteen years ago. Geoffrey, the father of her unborn baby, didn't want her to have an abortion and had been refusing to give her half of what it would cost to get one. She hadn't seen him since she'd last asked for the money two weeks ago, and now here he stood at her door. She decided that this would be the last time she would ask him for the money.

Time was running out. If one more week passed, she would begin to show, not to mention the price for the procedure would increase. Plus, she knew that if she didn't get it done soon she would have to explain to her grandmother why she was putting on weight. And Lord only knew what she'd do if she found out she was pregnant.

"Hello," Geoffrey said, almost singing the greeting as he walked past her and situated himself on her living-room sofa. "How have you been doing?"

"I'm doing fine," she answered, thinking how quickly his smile would vanish when she gave him the news of her decision. "But I'll be doing even better when I'm not pregnant anymore."

She watched his facial features, waiting for the curve of his mouth to turn downward. But nothing happened.

"So, you've decided to go ahead with it, huh?"

"Yes, I have."

"Tell me again," he said still smiling, "why do you want to get rid of it?"

Ignoring his question, she continued. "I need your half of the money."

"Why, Tia?"

"Geoffrey, we've been through this. I can't have a baby."

"Yes, you can."

"No, I can't. I'm eighteen years old, and I am not ready to be a mother. Besides, my grandmother would kill me!"

"But I'll be here to help you. It won't be that bad. You'll see."

She looked at him and wondered why he was telling her this lie. He wouldn't be there for her any more than her own father had been. And she was not going to be abandoned by another man again.

"Look, Geoffrey, if you really want to help me just give me the money."

"I can't do that. You want to do the wrong thing."

"That's easy for you to say." She was doing her best to keep the volume in her voice from rising. "You're not the one who'll have to face my grandmother. You're not the one who'll end up all swollen and fat. And you certainly won't be the one who'll have to take care of it day and night!"

"Hold up," he said, raising his hand in the air. "I said I'd help you, and I meant it!"

"No, Geoffrey. I just can't have a baby right now."

"My offer still stands," he said calmly. "We could still get married."

"Married? Are you crazy? You ain't getting ready to ambush me! Talk me into having this baby, and then you vanish into thin air. Uh-uh, I am not the one! I only see you once or twice a month as it is. And now you want to talk about marriage? I haven't even met your parents. Don't nobody in your family even know about me!"

"I could introduce you to them."

"Yeah, right! I can see it now. You take me home and say, 'Momma, this is Tia. She's pregnant, and we're gonna get married—eventually.'" She laughed sarcastically.

"Well, I can't give you the money."

"Yeah, that's because you're cheap! You don't want to marry me. You just don't want to give up the money. But that's okay. I'll get it one way or another. And you're either with me or you ain't."

"I ain't."

"Then you can leave," she said, walking to the door and opening it.

She had finally succeeded in making that smile of his disappear. He slowly walked out the front door and closed it gently behind him. She stood there waiting for the trembling in her bottom lip to subside. She almost did it. She almost cried. But like the winning tackle in a football game, something hard and solid jammed itself into her wall of emotions, blocking all exits and entrances.

Geoffrey had been a senior who was graduating from Willington High School the same year that Tia was beginning. He had been her first sexual encounter, but he had not been her last; she had experimented with two other boys at the same school while she continued to see Geoffrey. She would often skip classes with one boy or the other during her sophomore and junior years without anyone finding out. All she had to do was be on time for the first marking period so that she wouldn't be marked absent by the teacher. Then she would sneak out of the building and meet up with whichever boy she had been sleeping with at the time.

During her senior year, she stopped cutting classes to sleep with other boys. She stopped sleeping with other boys at her school altogether. But she continued to see Geoffrey, and they continued to do the same things that she was no longer doing with the other boys.

Back then, it had never occurred to Tia that what she was doing could have ended up with her getting pregnant. She hadn't even thought about that. She hadn't cared. Her concern went no further than the boys she used for her own self-gratification.

In her mind, it was a trade-off. She gave them what they wanted, and they gave her their attention—however short-lived and conditional it might have been. But Geoffrey had cared about her becoming pregnant because he'd always worn protection whenever they'd done anything. The one time he didn't use anything was the one time she got pregnant. Now, as with everything else in her life, she would have to make yet another decision on her own.

She had just gotten her income tax refund check, and she was planning on using that money for a security deposit on her own apartment—whenever she found one. Now, it would have to be spent on getting the abortion.

She pulled the card from the clinic out of her pocket and looked at the phone number printed in the upper right-hand corner. Without hesitation, she picked up the phone and began dialing.

Chapter Twelve

There were about thirty-five chairs in the two adjoining waiting rooms, all of them taken. She walked up to the counter and gave the receptionist her name. She told Tia to have a seat, if she could find one, and listen for her name to be called. Tia found a corner to stand in and surveyed the scenery around her.

There were women of all ages and colors. She wondered if some of them might be married, mothers already who had more children than they could handle. Some of the women wore heavy makeup and tight, revealing clothing. Some looked angry; some were engaged in idle conversations with each other that were interrupted with short, soft giggles every now and then; and some of them looked just like her, solemn-faced and young. One such girl sat in a chair across from Tia, holding the hand of another girl sitting next to her. Both girls were silent, making eye contact with no one.

Tia shifted her weight from one leg to the other. When would the receptionist call out a name so that somebody would get up and she could sit down? Then, as if she'd heard Tia's wish, the receptionist grabbed a folder and called out a name.

"Bethany." The receptionist was calling the women on a first-name basis only for the sake of confidentiality.

A middle-aged woman who had been sitting next to the teenage girl got up, and Tia quickly took her seat. The teenager turned to her and smiled.

"Sure is crowded in here."

"Sure is," Tia agreed, noticing the frightened look in the girl's eyes.

"I'll be glad when it's all over."

"Me too."

The girl spoke nothing about how she came to be in this clinic, nor did she mention anything about the absent male who was also responsible for her predicament. Tia did not speak of her circumstances either, but *her* absent male remained in her thoughts. Would she ever see him again? It didn't really matter. All that talk about marriage was just that—talk! She shifted in her seat. She wasn't about to be fooled by that.

In all the time she had been seeing Geoffrey, he had never once mentioned marriage. Now when she tells him she's pregnant, he wants to get married! She stopped swinging her right foot back and forth. Forget about him! Just another man waiting to break her heart, waiting to leave her with a baby the first chance he got. Just like her father did with her mother.

An hour passed before her name was finally called.

"Tia."

She quickly got up and followed the receptionist to the end of the hall. They entered a small, brightly lit office, and the receptionist motioned for her to have a seat.

"Okay, Tia, I just have a few questions to ask. I know you've given this information already, but this is just to confirm everything, all right?"

"Okay."

"What is your age?"

"Eighteen."

"Mother's name?"

"Why?" She shifted in her seat. She didn't mean to sound defensive, but any questions pertaining to her mother automatically put her on edge. She had done a very good job of cramming what few memories she had of her way back into the corners of her mind, and that's where she preferred they stay. She did not want that area disturbed.

"We just need the name of your next of kin, you know, in case there's an emergency and we need to contact someone."

"Well, you won't be able to contact her. I don't know where she is."

"How about your father?"

"He's dead," she lied. But it really wasn't a lie. She had never known him, and as far as she was concerned, he may as well have been dead.

"Grandmother, aunt, uncle?"

She rubbed her forehead. The last person on earth she would want contacted would be her grandmother. Mavis had made it clear to Tia that when she graduated from high school and turned eighteen she would have to move out. Well, she had turned eighteen six months ago in June—four days after graduating from high school—and her grandmother was now regularly asking her about when she would be moving.

Tia knew that if her grandmother was to find out about the pregnancy and the abortion, all asking would stop, and she would probably be put out on the spot. She frowned. That was the kind of relationship she had always had with her from day one—distant and cold. Many times, Tia had felt like a stranger, an unwanted guest in her home. She wondered if Ida had felt the same way growing up with her as well.

The receptionist was staring at her, waiting for an answer.

"Just put down Monica. Monica Davis."

"And how is she related to you?"

"A friend."

"Okay. Do you have any physical disorders?"

"No."

"And how did this happen?"

"How did what happen?"

"How did you become pregnant?"

"Obviously I didn't use any protection."

"Yes, that is obvious," the receptionist said dryly, "but what I'm asking is why. Did you not have anything? Did you forget? Do you experience problems when you use birth control?"

Tia crossed, and then uncrossed, her legs. "None of the above," she answered.

The receptionist gave her a long stare from above the dark brown rims of her eyeglasses. "So, how will you prevent this from happening next time?"

"There won't be a next time."

"Okay." The receptionist gathered the small stack of papers together, tapping them on the desk. "You can go back to the sitting room now. The nurse will be calling you shortly."

"Shortly" turned out to be another twenty-minute wait before the nurse finally came to the doorway and called her name. She led her up a flight of stairs with dirty gray carpeting covering them. They passed two women sitting at a table, and then entered a small dressing room. There, she was instructed to change into the robe that she'd been told to bring with her earlier.

As she pulled the thin paper curtain to the dressing room closed, she could hear the upbeat chatter between the two women she'd just passed. They too were clothed in robes, waiting for their turn. Cheerful. As if this was some sort of social gathering they were attending. How could they be so happy at a time like this?

She pulled back the curtain, left the dressing room, and took a seat at the table with the two other women. They looked at her and smiled. She did not smile back but turned away as the nurse approached them.

The nurse began explaining to the three of them what was about to happen. She told them that it would not be too painful, and that the stomach cramps they would feel afterward would diminish within fifteen to thirty minutes. Then it would be all over. Tia stared into her lap. *Such a small price to pay . . . or was it?* The nurse gave each of them a small, white pill to take, which she said would calm their nerves, and then the procedure would take place.

It was the waiting that almost drove Tia insane. She could feel herself just on the verge of anxiety. Were it not for the little white pill and its pharmaceutical ability to keep her calm, she felt she would have exploded. Why was it taking so long? Girl number two had been taken back into the room over twenty minutes ago. And she had yet to see girl number one emerge. Where was she? Did something go wrong?

"Tia." It was finally her turn.

The nurse led her to a room that was circular shaped with rectangular windows offering a view of the gray and cloudless sky along three of the four walls. There was a stretcher positioned in the middle of the floor. Crisp white sheets adorned it. A small table with stainless steel instruments sat next to the foot of the bed on one side. The doctor came into the room, and after a brief introduction, instructed her to lie down on the stretcher. She positioned herself on her back and stared at the plain white ceiling as she heard instruments being picked up.

Suddenly she felt a pinch in her uterus. *This is your fault, Tia.* She squeezed the hand of the nurse standing next to her and turned her head toward the window. *That's right. Go ahead. Look out the window. Enjoy the view while the doctor destroys what could have been prevented in the first place.*

She felt her heart betray her as the tears began to cross over the bridge of her nose and run down the side of her right cheek. In an effort to contain them, she returned her gaze to the ceiling. But it was too late. They had already found a release, a pathway out, and they would not be stopped. The nurse, without speaking, grabbed a wad of tissue and began gently wiping the accumulating moisture away from the center of Tia's neck.

Thirty minutes later, she sat in a recliner in the recovery room. The same nurse who had held her hand during the procedure and wiped her tears away gave her a glass of orange juice and a few cookies and told her she was free to go after that.

It was one o'clock in the afternoon when she left the clinic and started walking down Michigan Avenue. It was snowing, and the force from the wind pushed the flakes mercilessly into her face. The plastic supermarket bag that held her gown, robe, and a few feminine hygiene pads dangled from her wrist as she stuffed her hands into her silver parka.

The sky was still gray and cloudless and matched the mood she was in, but the cramping in her stomach had stopped. Now the familiar pangs of hunger took its place. She hadn't eaten since ten o'clock the night before—fifteen hours if she didn't count the juice and cookies—so she headed for the nearest restaurant four blocks away.

A gust of wind danced around her head until it found an entrance between the hood on her jacket and the back of her neck. The icy chill caused her to shiver, and she immediately pulled the hood over her head, tugging on the drawstrings tightly to create an airtight seal. She was tired, both physically and mentally. She was going to get something to eat, and then go home and go to sleep.

It was warm inside of the restaurant. She pulled off her hood and unzipped her jacket as she looked intently at the menu. She ordered a double cheeseburger, large order of fries, and a medium-sized soft drink. After paying for the meal, she took the tray of food to a small table next to a window.

Each bite of the burger was a delight with its smothered onions, crisp lettuce, and melted cheddar cheese topping. She popped the last french fry into her mouth, and then washed it all down with the soft drink. Finished eating, she reached for a cigarette in her coat pocket and also pulled out the pamphlet the nurse from the clinic had given her.

There was a list of dos and don'ts to follow after the procedure, and on the last page there was an anonymous questionnaire to fill out and return by mail. It wanted to know, on a scale from one to ten, with ten being excellent, how she would rate the "service" and how she would rate the staff in terms of professionalism, communication, and confidentiality.

She closed the pamphlet and sighed. What did it matter now? Their services were offered, and she'd accepted. It was all in the past. Time to move on.

"Excuse me, but you can't smoke in here." A tall man with a dress shirt and tie on was standing in front of her. The name tag he wore said he was the manager.

She stood up and began putting on her coat. As she opened the door to leave, she saw the bus that would take her home pass swiftly by. She sighed and wished she had better timing.

Chapter Thirteen

"Tia, is that you?" Mavis hollered from the kitchen.

"Yeah, Grandma, it's me."

"What are you doing home this early? Didn't you go to work?"

She sighed as she turned her head from side to side, trying to relieve the tension that she felt in her neck. It really was none of her business why she was home early. "Yes, I did go to work, but I started feeling sick so I left."

"Humph. You need to be keeping your behind at work. The end of the month is almost here, and you're going to need all the money you can get." She stood in the hallway staring at her. "You haven't forgotten what I told you, have you?"

"Don't worry. I'll be out by then."

Mavis turned to go back into the kitchen. "Oh, I'm not worried," she said over her shoulder. "I'm not worried at all."

Tia was as eager as Mavis, maybe more so, to move out of the house. In the twelve years that she had been living with her, her grandmother had never missed an opportunity to remind her that she had to be out by the time she turned eighteen. If she could have left sooner she would have, but she had only recently found a job, working part-time at the Burger Hut, and had begun saving as much of her paycheck as she could. Having to pay for the procedure today depleted a huge chunk of her savings, and she had no idea how she was going to come up with the first month's rent and security deposit for an apartment by the end of the month.

There had never been any closeness between the two of them, but she was hoping that if she just did what her grandmother wanted her to do and stayed out of her way, maybe she would allow her to stay a little longer.

From the very first day that Tia had come to live in her grandmother's house, she sensed that she was not really wanted. When she did something that bothered her grandmother she would have to listen to her complain.

"Tia, I'm sick and tired of having to say the same thing over and over again to you. I did the same thing with Ida, and I am not going to do it again!"

This would then lead into Tia's behavior being compared to that of her mother's. "You just like your momma," she'd say, "but Lord, help me, because you ain't getting ready to worry me to death like she did."

Tia was sick and tired of a few things too . . . especially of being told how much like her mother she was, and how she would never amount to anything. *I'm not like my mother,* she thought, *but if you want me to, I can be.*

Henry, on the other hand, seemed to have found a way to escape the wrath of his wife. Most of the time he would be in another room working on a sermon or just sitting in his easy chair not saying much.

It was as if they lived two separate lives, each occupying the same space, yet in their own private little world. Tia could not ever recall them actually sitting down and talking *to* each other. The only thing they did together was attend church on Wednesday evenings and Sunday mornings. And even that they did in semisilence.

She might have felt sorry for Henry had he not looked at her in such a way that made her feel uncomfortable. It was the same type of discomfort she remembered feeling at the foster home with the tall, light-skinned man. Did her grandmother notice how Henry looked at her as well?

When she had been younger, Henry would always try to get her to sit on his lap. "Leave that girl alone," Mavis would say. "She don't want to sit on your lap!"

And she had been right; she hadn't wanted to sit on his lap. But he would eventually have his way by offering her two dollars if she would. He would smile at her with his even white teeth, but there was nothing in his eyes that told her he was a nice man. There was nothing to trust. Still, his offers of money began to entice her, and from time to time, she would climb up on "Grandpa's" lap and pretend to enjoy sitting there.

Sometimes when Mavis was not in the room, they would play a game he called "horsy," telling her that the horse was an old, tired horse and could only bounce slowly. Afterward, with the two dollars in her hand, she would climb down from the old broken down horse and make her way to the corner store to spend it all on penny candy, giving little thought to the firmness she always felt beneath her while she sat on the preacher's lap.

She frowned. *Let him try that mess now and see what happens!*

Mavis walked out of the kitchen and sat down at the dining-room table. She wondered why she felt so tired. Her weariness was not so much physical as it was mental. She was not happy. She could not even say that she was content. She had asked the Lord many times why.

Why did she feel this way? Had she not given her life over to Him? Did she not try to worship Him day and night? Didn't she incorporate Him into every single thing she did and thought? What then was the reason for her weariness? What was wrong with her?

She did not try to deny the fact that she no longer loved her husband. Still, she managed to perform her wifely duty, even though it filled her with disgust. She had even managed to remain by his side all these years in an effort to be a good Christian woman, but inside of her, there was only emptiness, and she knew it.

She knew it while she sang hymns on Sunday morning. She knew it while she read scriptures from the Bible on Wednesday evening. She was aware of it while she shook hands with other members of the congregation at the end of each service. No matter what she was doing, she could not seem to erase the nagging feeling that there was something missing, something wrong. Was it passion? Had she allowed herself to become so self-contained, so nonemotional until she'd smothered all feeling out of her own soul? Was God trying to tell her something? Had she made a mistake? She tried to analyze her situation from the beginning.

She began with Ida and wondered what the real cause of her only daughter's misfortune was. What could she, as a mother, have done differently? Should she have been less stern and more loving? Her soul stirred with a fleeting twinge of guilt. Was that it? And if so, shouldn't she be redeemed since she had taken in Tia? But every time she looked at Tia, she saw Ida's face.

They lived in the same house, but just as it had been with Ida, they seldom communicated. And when words were spoken, they were quick and to the point, holding no real substance.

It had begun to bother her, living in the same house with two people with whom she could not talk, could not relate to. There was Henry, whose cravings she could not fulfill, and who, she suspected, was probably getting his satisfaction elsewhere. And then there was Tia. She had known the responsibility that would come along with raising her, and she had not been there for her emotionally like she should have been.

Mavis was painfully aware of her shortcomings. It had cut through her like the sharpest of swords every time she allowed herself to see the pain and confusion in Tia's eyes. Still, she had been unable to extend herself to her granddaughter. The unspoken words of comfort would rise up in her and get stuck in her throat each time she tried to speak them. She had been unable to extend any type of emotional comfort to Tia. And it had become easier to just stop looking at her, to turn the other cheek and just wait. Wait for the day when she too, like her mother, would turn eighteen and leave.

But then what? What would she have left? Henry? She hadn't looked to Henry for anything in quite awhile. And neither had he looked to her lately. He had begun sleeping on the couch one or two nights a week, and she told herself that that suited her fine. But what didn't sit well with her was the way she often caught him staring at Tia with that "look" in his eyes.

It was a look that she vaguely remembered seeing long, long ago, when the two of them were younger, when that look had been directed at her, when she had welcomed it. Now, they barely made eye contact. And when they did, there was nothing in his eyes that made her want to keep looking into them.

She heard his heavy footsteps climbing the stairs, heard the key being put into the lock. And as the slow creaking of the door hinges announced his entrance, she felt the presence of a strange disappointment flood her being.

It was automatic—like a thermostat programmed to react to the environment. She didn't know who had programmed her or if she had programmed herself, but that's how it was. It was a feeling of dread, and it was the only emotion she felt, had allowed herself to feel, in a long time.

One minute she was sitting in her own private, unhappy world. The next thing she knew, he was coming through the door, and she had to camouflage her sadness. She couldn't even be miserable in peace, and this upset her even more.

"What's wrong now?" Henry asked.

"What?" She did not turn to look at him. "What are you talking about?"

"You. Sitting here in the dark. No TV. No music. Just sitting here. What's wrong?"

"Why does something have to be wrong with me, Henry? Can't I just sit and enjoy the quiet from time to time?"

"Yeah, but you have all day to do that. Why do you wait until I come home to start your meditating?"

"Well, excuse me! I didn't know my sitting here was going to disturb you that much."

"I didn't say it disturbed me." *Here we go again,* he thought. "It just seems like every time I come home here lately, you're just sitting at that table looking like you just lost your best friend or something. Why don't you lighten up a little?"

"Maybe if I had a reason to I would."

He tried to smile, but the furthest he got was simply pressing his lips together. "I tried to give you one, but you don't want my reason."

She got up and headed toward the stairs. "You right about that."

He looked at her behind as she climbed the stairs. It was getting to the point that whenever he looked at her, he didn't really see her, only the increasing width of her body pushing through whatever pieces of clothing she had on. He could count two thick rolls of flesh surrounding her waist, and the front of her looked as though she was two-thirds of the way through a pregnancy.

He really didn't mind the extra weight as much as she thought he did—as much as he may have implied that he did. Her breasts were still nice and full and the best-looking thing on her body . . . whenever he got to see them, and he wished he could see them more. He wished he could squeeze her whole body, but she was so uptight that he could barely brush up against her without her pushing him away.

When they actually did engage in intercourse, not only did she act like she was doing him a favor, but she acted like she was dead as well. And she may as well have been. So, he had resigned himself to just getting the bare essentials from his wife in order to fulfill his natural, God-given desires. But she was not in his head during these times nor was she in his heart. He would fill his head with images, real and imagined, of women smaller, prettier, and younger than his wife. And his heart . . . he just left empty.

He picked up his briefcase and headed toward the dining-room table. Once situated, he opened his large white leather-bound Bible and began flipping through the pages. The edge of each one was trimmed in a shiny, goldlike material, and countless highlights and red markings covered many of them. He had another sermon to prepare. As he looked up the stairs in the direction of the bedroom they sometimes shared, he knew just what the title of it would be: "Wives, Be Loving Unto Thine Husband." He sighed. *Because if y'all don't, somebody else surely will.*

Chapter Fourteen

People are always taking chances and risks, and when the risk backfires, they wonder, *Why me?* This is what ran through Ida's mind as she sat in the small cell reserved for those who refused to follow the rules at the Taycheedah Correctional Institution, which was located an hour and twenty minutes outside of Milwaukee County.

It was the state's largest maximum and medium-security prison for women, housing more than 700 inmates. Out of that number, 130 were on Ida's unit, and one of the many rules was: No Fighting.

"But I was minding my own business, and she stepped to me!"

"You know the rules, Ida," the guard said, "Let's go."

Ida threw up her hands as if to surrender, and then said, "Let's go then. And I guess I'll be going again and again. Because if anybody thinks they're just gonna step up to me, they got another think coming."

"Yeah, yeah, tell it to the walls. You'll have plenty of time."

The walls constituted the cell that the guards placed her in, a windowless cubicle big enough to contain a steel basin on one wall and a toilet bearing the same identical steel coating underneath it. On the opposite wall was a wooden plank with a thin mattress lying on top of it. That was it. There was nothing else in that space. She sat down on the makeshift bed and stared at the gray cement walls.

It had been twelve years since she'd been incarcerated, and it seemed like very little had changed within her, including her memories. Not even time could change the memories of her mother—whose only emotions ever displayed toward her had been of anger or disapproval—or the memories of growing up without a father. His absence had produced an almost constant unfulfilled desire in her that had led her to repeatedly choose the type of men who had spoken a lie each time they told her they loved her.

And then there were the memories of her children, both living and dead. Dead. How could she ever forget *that?* Her mind drifted back to the day she delivered her baby, him.

"Push!" the nurse was yelling. "I can almost see the baby's head! Come on, you can do it!"

Ida wiped the moisture from her forehead and let out a moan. She knew she could do it! She'd done it before, and if the nurse would just shut up, she'd do it again!

"Okay, rest for a minute. Catch your breath."

Ida couldn't decide who needed to catch their breath more, she or the middle-aged nurse standing at the foot of the bed concentrating intensely on what was between her legs.

"Doctor Moore is on her way," the nurse said to the area between her legs.

"I can't wait!" Ida screamed. "It's coming out now!" And so she pushed with all her might, pushed until it felt like her flesh was being ripped apart. She pushed until it felt as if all of her internal organs would come out, right along with the baby—pushed even though the hot, searing pain threatened to render her unconscious. It was unbearable, the price of little pleasures.

"The head is out!" the nurse yelled again. "The worst part is over. You did good."

She tried to relax and catch her breath. The moisture on her forehead continued to congregate into small beads of fluid, separating themselves, one from the other. She didn't bother to wipe them away. She didn't bother to do anything except wonder why the nurse thought she had done good. She was twenty-four years old with two children, no husband, and no job. How was that good?

She bore down once more, and the newborn made its entrance into the world. It was a boy. The nurse gently placed him on top of her stomach, but Ida's instinct was not to hold him. As far as she was concerned, this baby was just a reminder of a man that she knew did not love her. She looked at the baby briefly, its mouth open, making sounds that demanded his desires be met, but all she remembered was gathering him in her arms and handing him back to the nurse standing beside her.

Her mind returned to the present as she got up and walked over to the bars. The steel felt cold and hard when she wrapped her fingers around it. She had never planned for her baby to die. That had never entered her mind. But she had now come to understand that it had been her inability to care for or about the infant that had blinded her to what should have been obvious—that he had been slowly starving to death.

She thought about Tia. Ida had been eight months pregnant with her when she walked across the stage to receive her high school diploma. She could still remember how the satin fabric of the red graduation gown had clung to her stomach with every step she made.

She thought about how she'd stood in the corridor after the ceremony impatiently scanning the sea of heads around her as she looked for the brightly colored fedora Henry had worn, and the swirled updo that would be sitting on top of her mother's head. They hadn't been hard to spot. Henry's six foot four-inch frame had hovered over almost everyone else, and right behind him was Mavis with that always present look of disapproval on her face. She had begun to make her way toward them when Brianna, one of her graduating classmates, cut into her path.

"Hey, girl, we did it," she'd said enthusiastically. "We graduated!"

"Yep," Ida had replied.

"Are you coming to Frankie's party tonight?"

"Nope. My feet are killing me."

"Ah," Brianna had sounded disappointed. "Bring some house shoes to put on. You can still go," she insisted.

"Nah, I'm going home. I'm tired," Ida had lied. How could she tell Brianna that the real reason she would not be at Frankie's party was because he had broken her heart? How could she tell her that he—the father of her unborn baby—had abandoned her?

"Okay," Brianna had said as she walked away smiling.

Ida could remember how she'd kept smiling too that day. She smiled to keep the tears from forming in her eyes. They had been tears of disappointment because not only would she not be at Frankie's party, she knew she would not be anywhere else with him.

He had lied to her, had told her that he loved her and would be there for her after she told him that she was pregnant with his child. When she'd mentioned the possibility of an abortion, he'd said—and this is the part she remembered clearly—"The choice is yours, but if you do, I can't guarantee I'll still feel the same way about you."

So, for the sake of love, she had decided to have the baby. And just as she'd completed her eighth month of pregnancy, Frankie had decided that he was too young to be a daddy after all and had made plans to join the air force right after graduation.

She'd thought about giving the baby up for adoption, but she clung to the hope that maybe he'd change his mind after she'd given birth. That had never happened. The only thing that did change was her love for him. It changed to hatred, and she hated him so much that even she could not realize how destructive it had become to her and the little girl they had produced.

Now, it had been twelve years. Twelve years since they'd taken Tia away, and in all the time she'd been locked up she'd never received a visit from either Tia or Mavis. She squeezed the bars as she pressed the side of her face against them. Tia would be all grown up now. What did she look like? How did she sound? What kind of personality did she have? After being raised by Mavis, there was no telling what kind of person she had grown up to be.

She closed her eyes tightly. One thing she was sure of; just as she had hated her own mother, Ida was sure that Tia hated her. And it had been this belief that had kept her from ever writing Tia a letter—not one—in twelve years. She opened her eyes and stopped squeezing the bars. Then she walked back to the bed and sat down.

Inhaling deeply, she called out, "Guard! I need some paper and a pencil!"

A few minutes later, the guard handed Ida two yellow sheets of 8x11 paper and a pencil.

"Don't make this a habit," he said.

"Thanks, appreciate it," she mumbled.

She stood looking around the tiny cubicle until her gaze stopped at the cot that was her makeshift bed. She removed the thin mattress from it, placed it on the floor, and then sat down on top of it. She placed the sheets of paper on top of the now exposed wooden base of the cot and thought about what to write. She had no idea of what to say or how to say it. She was tired, so she began with that.

I am tired. I am tired of fighting to forget the past. And always losing. I am tired of trying to be happy. I can't be happy in here. But I am still here alive. If you want to call being in this hellhole alive.

We had a preacher come in last Sunday morning. He told us a story from the Bible about a man named Daniel and the lions' den. And about how Daniel got thrown into a pit with some lions, but he prayed to God and nothing happened to him. I'm probably leaving something out, but you know the story. I think he said the story is about belief and faith in God. Made me think for a minute. I guess you could say I'm in a lions' den. But I can't remember the last time me and God had a talk.

Anyway, I don't sleep so well at night. But who could? And I ain't mad about you not coming to visit me. But you could have at least let Tia see me. I know I wasn't no kind of a mother, but she still was my child. So, anyway, I don't want to run out of paper so let me finish.

I saw the therapist, and she wanted to call me depressed. She wanted to give me some pills to take, but I told her I ain't taking no pills. Now get with that! She said I was depressed because I had an unhappy childhood. I told her, no kidding; tell me something I don't know. Another example of being overpaid. So, anyway, I'm not seeing her no more. I don't like the way she looks at me, and like I said, she ain't telling me nothing I don't already know.

So, I don't know whose fault it is that I never knew my daddy. And I don't know whose fault it is that me and you never got along. I just don't know. But I do know I'm tired of trying to figure it out. And it really ain't gonna get figured out on this little piece of paper. But you know what's funny? In all the time I been here, I ain't cried once. Ain't that something? Not once. I don't laugh too much either. But it's a whole lot harder to cry than it is to laugh.

So, anyway, I'll save this other sheet of paper for later in case you decide to write back or maybe let Tia write. Oh, I forgot. She's grown now, ain't she? Well, maybe she can send me a picture. Bye, Momma.

Ida.

"Momma," she whispered. It was a word that she had not used in years. She put the pencil down and tried to block out the shouts from the other inmates. The only thing she wanted to hear was the sound of her own voice as she repeated the word that had been so seldom used by her.

Chapter Fifteen

Tia stood in front of the house with hunched shoulders as she waited for her high school friend, Monica, to answer the doorbell. She looked out at the gray sky, and it seemed to her as if the sky had remained that color ever since she'd had the abortion two months ago. Just as she had expected, she hadn't heard one word from Geoffrey since the day she'd told him to leave. She had begun to feel restless and had decided to pay Monica a visit.

"Hey, girl," Monica said as she opened the front door.

"Hey," Tia said looking down at her. Monica was all of five feet tall, but she insisted on telling everyone she was five feet two. That was actually Tia's height, and she would remind Monica of that, saying that if they were actually the same height they could look each other straight in the eye instead of Tia having to look slightly down at her whenever they stood next to each other. Monica would just laugh and dismiss the comment with a wave of her hand in the air.

Tia studied the back of the shorter girl's hair as she walked into the living room.

"Did you dye your hair?"

"Yeah. Well, actually, you haven't seen me in a while. This is a redo, and I got it cut." She turned to face her. "You like it?"

"Yeah, I do." She fingered her friend's short curly hair. The cinnamon color glistened and was a perfect complement to her caramel-colored complexion.

"It goes real good with your skin tone," Tia said, "but I think it might be too light for me. Anyway, I have to work on one thing at a time," she said pointing to the short dreadlocks she had begun to grow. She stood studying Monica for a few more seconds. "It kind of makes your face glow." She smiled. "Unless that's from something else."

Monica put her finger up to her lips and looked toward the hallway that led to the kitchen. "Ma's home."

Tia mouthed the word, "Oh," and sank down into the brown leather sectional in the living room. She looked at the furniture that was color coordinated in maroon and various shades of brown. An occasional speck of dark green or burnt orange popped out of a pillow or picture hanging on the off-white walls. Suddenly, she felt sleepy.

"So what's up?" Monica asked.

"Nothing much."

"You ain't heard from Geoffrey?" Monica asked as she plopped down on the sofa next to Tia.

"Nope. And I'm sure I won't. But I'm not surprised. That's why I did what I did in the first place."

"Men." Monica shook her head. "You just can't trust them. They always disappearing on you when things get tough."

"He wasn't about nothing anyway," Tia said, browsing through the channels on the television set. She stopped on one channel to listen to the scratchy, soulful voice of a black woman singing about a lady with too much emotional baggage.

"You see that?" Monica said pointing to the screen. "She should be calling that song Bag Man, because they the ones always doing something to make the lady end up with all that baggage."

Tia sighed. She knew where Monica was heading. She knew her friend believed the same things about men that she did, only Monica adhered to her beliefs much more strongly than Tia clung to hers. Sometimes Tia got tired of hearing her complain about black men.

She had grown weary of hearing her use the few bad relationships she'd had with men as an excuse to bad-mouth them all. It was always the same conversation every time the two of them got together, a ritual being performed, and Monica seldom wavered from her belief that black men were all the same.

Tia did not want to have that conversation today. She wanted to talk about something positive, something different, but it was too late. Monica was up and running.

"Yeah, they ain't no good."

"How would you know?" Tia asked. "It ain't like you been with all of them."

She looked toward the hallway again. "I been with enough," she whispered under her breath.

And maybe that's the problem, Tia thought. At first, she had been an active participant in the degrading process because firmly rooted in the back of her mind were her own bad memories of both emotional and physical abuses that she'd been subjected to at the hands of various men of color.

For starters, she had never known who her real father was. Then, there had been the man at the foster home who had beaten and attempted to molest her. After that, there had been Henry and his little horsy game that he liked playing with her from time to time, and which she now knew had not been a good game for him to play with her. And now, she was adding Geof-

frey, her ex-boyfriend, man-friend—whatever he had
been—to the list.

But a part of her had its doubts, and these doubts
were slowly beginning to win her over. Secretly, she
wanted what she suspected Monica wanted—someone
to love her. *Is that too much to ask?* She had to fight
off the cynical side of her that wanted to answer: *Of
course, it is.*

Not only did she want to feel loved, but she wanted
to be able to recognize it when she did. She wasn't sure
she even knew what love felt like. So, how would she
recognize it when and if it ever did come around?

The woman on TV with the scratchy voice continued
singing. Now, she was singing about the lady with too
much baggage missing her bus.

Tia looked at Monica. "Remember when you used to
get all excited about going to a movie with Chris, and
y'all would catch the bus?"

"Aw, Tia, come on, now. You know I was just a kid
back then." She waved her hand in the air. "That was
kid stuff. I bet you I won't be catching any more buses."

Tia laughed.

"You can laugh if you want to, but when I get to college, I'm gonna get me an older man."

"And y'all still gonna be catching the bus."

"Uh-uh. You'll see. He's gonna have a nice car, a nice
house, and a good job."

"How's he gonna have all that if he's still in college?"

"Well, he will after he graduates. That's why I'm
gonna get me an older one. It don't make sense for both
of us to be broke, do it?"

They both shared a laugh before Tia's expression
turned serious. "You want to get married?"

"Yeah, she do," Monica's mother answered for her as
she walked into the living room carrying a tall pitcher

of water. Her petite frame and stature were almost identical to her daughter's, and Tia could see a glimpse of how Monica would look when she turned fifty years old.

"Oh, hi, Ms. Whitley," Tia said.

"How're you doing?" she did not wait for an answer, but continued, "Don't pay no attention to all that complaining Monica be doing. She always finds something wrong with a boy."

"No, I don't," Monica said defensively.

"Yes, you do," her mother said over her shoulder as she began slowly pouring the water from the pitcher into a potted plant next to the sectional. "If they don't call you like they said they would, you get an attitude. If they call you every day, you think they're moving too fast and they must be up to no good. But, you already know what I think."

Monica said nothing.

"What do you think, Ms. Whitley?" Tia asked.

"I think—no, I *know*—that all her complaints are really just a cover-up."

"Not again, Ma!" Monica said, rolling her eyes.

"A cover-up for what?" Tia asked. She wanted to hear it from someone far more experienced than Monica.

"A cover-up to protect the real issue," she said as she made her way to another plant that resembled a small tree sitting in front of the window. "Now, this plant is what they call a Money Tree," she said. "Somebody from work gave me this. It's supposed to be a symbol of good fortune." She smiled. "I don't know about all that, but it's pretty, and it don't require a lot of care. It likes a lot of sun, though."

Tia looked at the sky again. The gray color remained. "I don't think it's gonna get any of that today," she said.

"Yeah, I think you're right. Anyway, like I was saying," she continued standing at the window, "the real issue with Monica ain't even about the little boys she calls herself dealing with. It's really about how society has conditioned her. And not just her; you, me, all of us," she said, waving her hand in the air.

"Conditioned to what?" Tia said frowning.

"To seeing all black men, boys—let's just say the black male species—in a negative light."

"Always the philosophical one, ain't you, Ma?"

"I'm telling you, you better stop that, girl. And stop saying 'ain't.' You're getting ready to be in college, now."

Tia smiled at the older woman.

"Now, let me lay this on your mind," Ms. Whitley continued in a raspy voice. "Here's the truth. Some men are up to no good. It doesn't matter what color their skin is. Just like people, you got some decent ones, and you got some not-so-decent ones. Now get that through your head! Why do you want to put a permanent label of distrust on all of the black men? Just for being black? Ain't that what society tries to do?"

"Mama, stop saying, 'ain't,'" Monica whispered as if she were singing a lullaby.

Her mother rolled her eyes. "I *ain't* the one going to college."

They all laughed before she continued. "Now, let me tell you something. If you find yourself a strong, kind, honest, God-fearing black man, then guess what?" She didn't wait for an answer. "You got a beautiful thing. And I happened to have had a beautiful thing."

Monica raised her eyebrows. "But how are *we* supposed to find that, Mama?" she asked

"That's how Memphis was." She continued, ignoring the question. "We were married for fourteen years, and we'd still be married now if he hadn't died. I remember how he used to fix me breakfast and serve it to me in bed. Sometimes he would wash my hair for me. And he used to always hold my hand whenever we went walking somewhere.

"But don't get me wrong now," the radiance that had begun emanating from her face died down. "He had his flaws, too. But he was the only man, the only person really," she hesitated, "who I would allow to tell me about myself and set me straight when I started acting a fool." She looked at Monica. "And you know it's true."

Tia looked on as Monica sat silently nodding her head. Like Tia, Monica had never known her real father, and when she was two years old, her mother had married Memphis. He had become the only daddy she had ever known. As far as she was concerned, he *was* her real father right up until the day he died from a heart attack when she was sixteen.

Suddenly, without warning, Monica's mother curved her thoughts back around to answer the question Monica had asked her earlier. "Now, how are you supposed to find that? That's a good question. I'll have to get back to you on that one."

Monica sighed.

Tia laughed. "I think you're right, Ms. Whitley."

"Of course, I am. I know Monica. She's got trust issues."

"And you don't?" Monica directed her question at Tia.

"I don't what?"

"You don't have trust issues with the guys you've been out with? And it ain't been that many."

"I'm not saying that—and it's been more than you. I just agree with your mama. You should probably give them the benefit of the doubt. Just like you would anybody else."

Monica tilted her head to the side. "How do you know who I would and wouldn't give the benefit of the doubt to?"

Tia rolled her eyes.

"Well?" Monica was waiting for an answer.

"Look," Tia said in exasperation, "I'm just trying to help you out."

"Girl, please," Monica said, dismissing Tia's statement with her hand as if she were shooing a fly away. "Why don't we just let somebody with more experience than you do that, okay?" They both looked at Monica's mother, who took that as her cue to speak.

"Let me ask you this, Tia," Ms. Whitley began. "How many men would you say you've trusted in your life—your short, young life, I might add?"

"Amen." Monica whispered. Tia shot her a quick glance, and then answered.

"Well, I trusted Geoffrey, kind of, sort of."

"Humph!" This time Monica didn't mumble.

"Okay, well, I wanted to. But it was hard, you know? But I tried to."

Monica let out a snicker.

"Forget you, Monica."

"How come it was so hard to trust him, Tia?" Ms. Whitley wanted to know.

"Because he only came around when he wanted to . . . you know."

"Have sex," Ms. Whitley said looking straight at her. Tia shifted in her seat. "Yeah," she answered.

"And I bet you didn't want to do that, huh?" Monica asked with a smirk on her face.

"That's not the point. The point is that's the *only* time I saw him."

"Well, you got a mouth, don't you?" the older woman asked. "You know how to say no, right?"

"Nah," Monica offered, "she don't know how to say that, Mama."

"Sometimes I did feel like saying no, but he was always trying to pressure somebody," Tia said.

"Hmm," Ms. Whitley frowned. "That's not good," she said.

"Yeah, I know. But I don't have to worry about him anymore."

"What?" Monica's mother put down the now empty pitcher of water. "You kicked him to the curb?" she asked.

"Uh-huh."

"Okay, then," the older woman concluded, "now you need to just slow your little self down. Get to know who you are."

"Uh-huh," Monica chimed in.

"Monica, be quiet," her mother said. "You in the same boat she in."

"Maybe." Monica winked at Tia. "But at least I can swim."

"Shut up," Tia said as she playfully swung out at her friend. The laughter coming from the three of them filled the room. It filled the empty space in Tia's heart as well. But she knew it was only temporary. She knew that after the laughter died down, she would be left with a lingering quietness. It was the kind of quiet that held no peace, the kind of quiet that she could not seem to escape from.

Tia looked at Monica's mother and thought about her own. Ida had been convicted of negligent homicide, and the judge had sentenced her to twelve years. This was the twelfth year, but Tia had no idea when or if Ida would be released.

The only reason Tia knew her mother was still in prison was because of the envelope that had come addressed to her grandmother with Department of Corrections: Taycheedah Correctional Institute, stamped on it. Her grandmother had never mentioned the contents of the envelope. And Tia, not knowing how to ask about the mother she barely remembered, found herself stuck in her own prison of increasing indifference. She'd convinced herself that the motherly love and recognition she'd never received from Ida hadn't mattered at all. As far as Tia had been concerned, it didn't make a difference whether Ida got out next month or never. She didn't know the woman. Ida was a total stranger.

Now, sitting here looking at the two generations before her, she felt a sudden tug at her heart. She wished she had more memories of her mother other than the fading ones from when she was six years old. She needed to feel connected to something . . . to someone.

Chapter Sixteen

Tia had no idea where she was going after she left Monica's house a few hours later, but she knew she didn't want to go back home to a place where nothing was waiting for her and no one would be glad that she was even there.

She caught the city bus downtown to her favorite bar. It was a dark, dingy, hole-in-the-wall where no one ever asked her to show proof that she was old enough to be there. It was the same script, only a different actor. Her, sitting at the bar looking considerably older than her eighteen years; him, watching her for a while, and then asking her if she'd like to dance. A few dances later, he was buying her a drink and engaging in small talk with her.

Although she did not want to be alone, she had planned to finish her drink and go home when he began to talk about the fantastic view he had from his apartment. She suggested they go there, and he had quickly agreed. Now, here she stood, checking out the view of Lake Michigan from the twenty-seventh floor. He had not lied. The view was fantastic.

"Give me another hit," Tia said to the stranger sitting on the floor next to her.

The man passed the marijuana cigarette to her and slowly closed his eyes. The sound of Marvin Gaye's "Sexual Healing" played softly in the background.

"How long have I been knowing you?" he asked.

She looked at her watch. "I'd say about three-and-a-half hours."

"Is that all?"

"That's all," she said without releasing the smoke that she'd inhaled.

He leaned back and closed his eyes again. Tia sighed and returned to the drug-induced contentment that now took over her mind. She looked around the apartment. It was a large studio located on the twenty-seventh floor of a high-rise apartment building on the east side of town. It was the sort of place that she could live in simply because of the panoramic views it offered of the downtown area.

She walked over to the window and watched the activities that took place along the shore as the sun began to set. There were men and women jogging up and down the sidewalk, bicyclers trailed one another along designated paths, and dogs were taken for walks while their owners trailed behind on roller blades.

As dusk approached, the scenery took on a different view. City lights twinkled for miles, and all seemed right with the world. She could have stood at that window forever just thinking, except she didn't want to think anymore. She didn't want to remember; not about her mother who still sat in the state penitentiary for starving her baby brother to death, or the father she'd never known, or the constant emptiness she felt inside. She didn't want to concentrate on any of these things. *So what's left?*

"You feeling all right, baby?" The man was standing behind her with his arms around her waist.

"Uh-huh," she lied.

Her thoughts returned to her mother, and she told herself that she was not to blame for what had happened. There was just too much pressure on her mother to raise the two of them by herself with no man around to help. She refused to believe that her mother had deliberately let her brother starve, yet she could recall many days and nights when she, herself, had sat on that old tan and white sofa fantasizing about all the different kinds of food she would eat if she could.

She remembered the night she made the phone call and how she'd told a stranger that she was hungry. That was the night that had changed her entire life. But it hadn't been her fault. If her father had been any kind of a man, he would have never abandoned her. He would have loved her and cared about her well-being. He would have seen to it that his daughter had enough food to eat and whatever else she needed.

But her father hadn't been a man, had he? If the truth be told, he hadn't loved her either. And this was the other thing she was having trouble dealing with. How could he not have loved her? She had loved him, sight unseen. But he had rejected her. Now, she had no choice but to reject him as well.

The stranger turned her around and placed his mouth over hers. *Why hadn't her father loved her?* He squeezed her tightly as he continued kissing her. *She'd needed him. Why hadn't he been there for her?* He led her to the sofa, and for a while, the void in her soul became nonexistent. Her memories about her mother disappeared, her questions about her father subsided, and all thoughts ceased . . . for a while.

It was almost dawn when Tia turned the key in the lock and let herself into her grandmother's house. She tiptoed to her bedroom and softly closed the door. In the fading darkness, she became fully aware of the returning void inside of her. It would not stay filled.

She crawled into bed. How long would she have to feel this way? When would someone come and take it away permanently?

The man she'd met a few hours ago hadn't been able to do it. When would she be loved? She turned on her side. And how would she know if she was? She switched to her other side. What was love all about anyway? Slowly, she drifted off to sleep as the answers to her questions remained hidden.

A few hours later, the sound of her phone ringing jarred her from a deep sleep. With her eyes still closed, she reached out for her cell phone. "Hello." Her voice was a whisper.

"Tia?" It was Monica.

"What?"

"Are you sleeping?"

"I was. What's up?"

"It's Saturday. Let's go out."

Tia rolled on her side and stretched. She opened her eyes, thinking that all she really wanted to do was stay right where she was, in that bed, and not move.

"I really don't feel like going out, Monica."

"Come on, Tia. It's ladies night. You know what that means."

"I'm tired, Monica. I just got in this morning."

"What? This morning? Where were you?"

"Out."

"Out? All night?" She was quiet for a second, and then added, "What's his name?"

"Why?"

"What do you mean, why?"

"Just what I said. Why?"

"Because I want to know. I know it wasn't Geoffrey, was it?"

"Yeah, it was," Tia lied. Monica didn't have to know *all* of her business.

"I thought you were through with him."

"Yeah, well, I don't want to talk about that right now."

"Okay, then," Monica said. "Well, let's go out tonight. I got my mama's car."

Tia sighed. "Okay. But I'm not staying long. I'm tired."

"You should be."

"What?"

"I said I'll pick you up at ten."

"Yeah, right."

Tia sat up and placed the phone next to the small digital clock on the nightstand. It was only four-thirty in the afternoon. She had plenty of time to go back to sleep. She didn't need to give much thought to what she would wear later that evening. That was not a real concern. The primary thought that kept running through her mind was how tired she was of always feeling unwanted by the people who were supposed to want her.

Her father hadn't wanted her, her mother *didn't* want her, and her grandmother just wanted her out. She fell back onto the bed. Something was going to have to change. She couldn't live with these feelings for much longer. She dozed back off to sleep thinking it would be better if she just never woke back up.

Chapter Seventeen

Mavis sat downstairs in the easy chair with her legs elevated. Dusk was approaching as she pressed the buttons on the remote control. Although she could feel her stomach growling, she had no desire to eat, yet the hunger pangs would not relent. She knew that sooner or later she would have to go into the kitchen and fix herself something to eat.

The occasional sound of papers being shuffled about in the next room let her know that Henry was still working on his sermon for tomorrow's Sunday service. She thought about her own internal manuscript, a combination of self-will and determination that was supposed to alleviate the dullness in her and remind her to be positive. But she knew she hadn't been positive in a long time, and she also knew that the manuscript was all she had, and it was just not working, had never worked. Still, she feared that if she abandoned it, there would be nothing to live for. And she was so close to nothing already . . .

She loosened her grip on the remote control and changed the channel on the television set in front of her. The Saturday night news was on, and a reporter was giving an update on a collision between two Tokyo Metro trains that had killed five people. It didn't matter to her. Nothing seemed to matter to her; yet everything mattered.

She didn't want Henry touching her, yet she longed to be touched. She didn't know how to communicate with her granddaughter, so she told herself she didn't want to anyway. And then there was Ida, and a growing sense of guilt that hinted that she just might be partially responsible for her daughter, her only child, turning out the way she had.

Every night she got down on her knees and prayed to God to free her from her demons. *Tomorrow, let it be a new day*, she would pray. But, with each new day, the demons would arise, devising ways to keep her in turmoil. And there was nothing new about that. It had been going on for fifty-some years—most of her life.

Her heart was almost numb, and what little feeling there was left in it felt too heavy to keep carrying around. Every time she looked into the mirror she disliked what she saw. It was, to her, an image of a deep and long-standing sadness that, even when she tried to smile, would remain. She thought if she could just cry she would feel better, but she could not even do that. So simple a thing as a few small tears, and she could not even accomplish that.

She wished to God she could have talked to Henry, but she couldn't do that either. It was too late. He had to know that something was wrong with her, with this marriage, but his only solution was to try to have more sex. And she had been a willing participant, that much she remembered. But when did that part of her change? And why?

She closed her eyes and gently pinched the bridge of her nose. She could pinpoint the turn of events, her change of feelings, to the period when Ida had begun to grow into her teen years. Was it the looks Henry had begun to give her, or the looks *she* had given him?

Mavis rubbed her throbbing temples. She believed in God. She knew this much was true. Years ago she'd made her belief public on a crowded Sunday morning in the First Presbyterian Church. Answering the call to salvation given by the pastor who would soon be her husband, she had been baptized in the name of Jesus Christ for the remission of her sins. *But had she ever really put her trust and faith in Him? Had she ever really surrendered to Jesus?*

The volume on the television seemed far too loud. She reached for the remote control and turned the volume to mute. Slowly, she clasped her hands together and bowed her head.

Help me, Jesus. Forgive me for my sins. Bring me closer to you, Lord. Come into my heart and show me how to live a life that will be pleasing to you. I know I haven't been what I should have been. Change me, Lord. Please. Show me what I need to know. Lead me and let me follow. In the name of Jesus Christ I pray, amen.

The room grew darker, illuminated only by the light from the television screen. She knew what she had to do and part of it involved Henry. She opened her eyes and wiped the moisture away from her cheeks. It was time for the two of them to separate, and she would tell him so just as soon as he finished working on his sermon.

A few hours later, Mavis stood at the chrome kitchen sink drying the last of the dinner dishes. Henry walked past her to the refrigerator.

"Henry," she said over her shoulder, "I need to talk to you."

He stood still. *Talk?* That was an interesting concept since it was something they seldom did. "About what?" he asked.

"I'm not happy, and I haven't been for a long time." She took a deep breath. "I'm leaving, Henry."

He couldn't believe what he was hearing, and for once, he was not going to be so silent. "What are you talking about? Leaving? Leaving to go where?"

"Don't start yelling," she said as she continued rubbing the already dry CorningWare. "We don't even have to go in that direction."

"Well, what are you talking about then? I haven't been happy either, but you don't see me trying to leave you!"

"Really?" She pivoted around quickly to face him with the dish and dish towel still in her hands. "What would you call all of your little 'outside' activities?"

He was quiet. She had never made a direct reference to any of his extramarital affairs before. She had caught him off guard.

"You know what?" He pointed a finger in her face. "Maybe if you wouldn't have been so doggone cold and acted like you had *some* kind of feelings, none of those 'activities'"—he raised his arms and mimicked quotation marks with two of his fingers on each hand—would have happened!"

"And maybe if you wouldn't have acted like some kind of sex hound, I *would* have acted like I had more feelings." She knew that statement was not entirely true. She was beginning to accept the possibility that there was something not quite right about her own emotional state of being, but she was not about to admit that to Henry. He still had his wrongs, no matter what her flaws were.

He willed himself to calm down. "Okay, Mavis. I'm sorry." *How's that?*

"What's done is done." *Too late.*

"How long have you been thinking about this?"

"It's been awhile."

He continued scrutinizing her.

She returned her attention to the empty sink.

"I'm not going to beg you to stay," he sighed.

"That's good, because my mind is already made up." She folded the dish towel and hung it over the cabinet beneath the sink.

"Oh, and by the way," she said walking out of the kitchen, "I'm not *trying* to leave you. I *am* leaving you."

Henry walked out of the kitchen in the opposite direction toward the front door. He stepped out onto the porch and sat down on one of the two wicker and wrought iron rocking chairs. He moved his head from side to side as if he were watching a tennis tournament. There was really nothing to see, and occasionally, he would stop and just look straight-ahead.

It was late in the evening and most of his neighbors were already home and in bed, or getting ready for bed. He studied the street lamps that seemed to be strategically placed so that every fourth house had one placed directly in front of it. The metal chrome from the parked cars seemed to glow underneath the light, and it was difficult to tell which were been painted black and which were painted in other dark toned colors. In the darkness of the night, everything looked the same. He felt as though he were living in darkness as well.

He pondered where the future was going to lead him, knowing that, although he exercised daily, his body was beginning to catch up with his age. Now what? He stopped rocking. Put him in a nicely fitting suit and he would always be able to pull off his flamboyant ways, but if Mavis was leaving him, who would take her place? Not that she did much for him anyway, but that was not the point. He was used to her being there.

Now, who was going to want him with his stomach beginning to soften and round, and the muscles in his thighs beginning to relax with gravity? Who would want to be held in his flabby arms? He was getting old, and his wife was leaving him. If she was going to leave him, he wished she had done it years earlier, when he was still in his prime. He just couldn't understand it. Why now?

He'd cheated on her many times in the past, and she had not left; had never even spoken a word about it. Even when it was clear that she suspected something, she never followed up on her suspicions. She would just ask him a question or two, stand there with her hands on her hips, and stare at him silently for a few seconds before walking away. Just like she'd done that morning twelve years ago after they found out what had happened to Ida's baby. He could remember it as if it had just happened.

"Why are you looking like that?" she'd asked.

"Looking like what?"

"Like you just saw a ghost or something."

He remembered saying something like, *"You just told me that Ida killed her baby. Am I supposed to be smiling?"*

And there it was. That signature stance of hers. Looking down in front of him with her hands on her hips. Never speaking, just staring. And she'd done it again a week later after she'd gotten the letter from Ida telling her to tell him that she was sorry about the baby.

"So are you going to tell me?"

"Tell you what?"

"What did Ida mean? About the baby?"

He remembered the indignation he feigned when he answered her. *"I don't know what she's talking about! You know how crazy Ida can be sometimes! You said so yourself! What's wrong with you?"*

And that had been the end of that. Whatever she might have suspected, she never dug too deeply. Why? Even in matters concerning his faithfulness she still managed to keep herself distant. Unaffected. Why now, after twenty-four years of marriage, had she decided to speak on it at the same time she was telling him that she was leaving him? He couldn't figure her out. And that had been a large part of the problem with her. A huge part. Had she ever really loved him at all?

In the beginning, she gave her physical self to him willingly. But she never told him that she loved him unless he said it first. That had always bothered him, and when he would tell her how he felt she would just brush it off, telling him that he was being silly. Silly! He knew he was many things, but silly had never been one of them.

Henry saw headlights illuminating the street, heard the intrusive sound of a faulty muffler as a white two-door sedan made its way past the house. He looked up, then down the street again. All was silent, just as he had been throughout most of his marriage. Everything he'd done, he done silently.

He had quietly lusted over Ida until he had finally satisfied his desires. He had quietly seduced several other women, including his secretary, without ever feeling a need to admit his infidelities and betrayals to anyone. Now, sitting outside in the darkness of a cool April evening, he thought perhaps he should have. Perhaps he should not have remained silent, but should have let Mavis know just how dissatisfied he'd been with her lack of emotion.

Maybe he could have explained why he'd done the things he had, and if she would just stop being so cold he could stop doing them. But none of that mattered now. It was too late for maybes. What was done was done. She said her mind was made up, which to him meant it had probably been that way for quite some time. He was not about to beg her to stay. She was leaving, and that was that.

He stood up slowly, looking up toward the sky. It was not a starry night, but he managed to spot several twinkles of light separated by an unknown distance. He inhaled deeply and wondered why there had been so much distance between him and Mavis for so many years. Something had never been quite right in their marriage, and he had never known how to fix it. Instead of turning to God for the answer, he turned to other women.

He knew what the Bible said about adultery and deliverance from sin. Hadn't he preached on those topics many times? Hadn't he preached about the only one who could deliver us from the eternal consequences of sin if we would first confess our sins and repent?

Countless times he had quoted scripture, "So if the Son sets you free, you will be free indeed." He had preached it, yet had never gone to Jesus Christ for his own deliverance. He stepped inside the house and closed the door to the darkness outside. Tomorrow was another day. It was time to move on. And if God so willed, that's exactly what he planned to do.

Chapter Eighteen

The city of Milwaukee lies along the shores of Lake Michigan and is now host to a variety of cultural, art, and music festivals every year. It is eighty-three miles north, or south, of Chicago, depending on the departing location, and with a population of approximately 605,000 people, is the largest city in Wisconsin.

Throughout the year, televised campaigns run urging tourists to come and visit the city that has become known as "A great place on a great lake," where during the summer, tourists and Milwaukeeans alike can choose to rent a bicycle for the day or by the hour, go sailing, kite surfing, or choose from a variety of other activities. The shores of Lake Michigan are also host to a variety of ethnic festivals throughout the summer, including one of the largest music festivals that runs for ten days every year in June.

As with most cities, nightclubs are plentiful, as well as corner bars, taverns, and other establishments that feature both male and female dancers. The latter was what Monica and Tia were about to enter. It was Saturday night—ladies' night, and that meant the top male dancers would be featured.

"See, Tia, that's why I told you to be ready at ten o'clock," Monica said as they entered the New Wave Inn. A vibe of anticipation filled the air as red and blue neon lights circled the room. They made their way to a small table in the back.

"It's only ten-thirty, Monica. We're not late."

"Yeah, but now all the good seats are gone."

Tia sighed. This was exactly what she was talking about. If it wasn't one complaint, it was another. Monica was always complaining about not being able to find a man. Now here she was in what was about to become a room full of men, and she was *still* complaining.

"Some people just can't be pleased," Tia mumbled.

"What?" Monica yelled, cutting her eyes at her.

"Nothing." Tia hesitated, and then said, "What's wrong with you?"

"Nothing."

"Yes, there is."

"What are you talking about?" Monica stretched her neck upward, hoping to get a better view of the front stage.

"You know what I'm talking about. You act like you got an attitude."

"No, I don't."

"Yes, you do."

Monica turned to look at Tia. "No, I don't. I just can't see anything from way back here."

Tia pressed her lips together and looked around the room. The air was full of excited chatter and soft laughter that increased in volume as it got closer to showtime. She was not one of the excited ones. She was just tired. Tired of the noise, tired of Monica, and mostly, tired of men.

"Hurry up and start the show!" one of the women yelled.

As if the emcee had heard her, the stage lights began to dim, and a voice introduced the first dancer. The emcee said his name was Blue something, but Tia couldn't hear him, and she doubted that anyone else could either since they hadn't stopped yelling and clapping from the moment the lights had been dimmed.

His skin was the color of a Hershey bar, and his body looked like it had been carved out of stone. He was, of course, shirtless, and wore cowboy jeans with the seat cut out of them. The muscular build of his body was almost enough to hold her attention, but she found herself staring into his eyes instead. He looked at no one in particular as he moved around the stage, but would stop and lock eyes with anyone who was close enough to him screaming and waving money in his direction.

"Yeah!" Monica yelled out. She could hardly contain herself in her seat. It was as though she were dancing and the chair was her partner. Tia smiled at the thought.

Monica looked over at Tia. "What are you smiling about?"

"Nothing. I'm just looking at all these women acting like they ain't never seen a man before."

"Well, everybody can't get a man on demand," she cut her eyes away, and added, "like you."

"What's that supposed to mean?"

"You know what it means."

"No, I don't. Why don't you tell me?"

"Not now, girl. I'm trying to watch the show." She stood up clapping her hands above her head, dancing to the beat. "I'm going up to the front so I can get a better look. You coming?"

"No, I'll keep our table."

As Monica edged her way through the crowd, Tia opened her cell phone and looked at the time brightly displayed: 11:05 P.M. She decided she would leave in exactly one hour from the time now showing on her phone. She knew Monica wasn't going to be too happy about that, but that was too bad.

Unlike Monica, Tia had a job to go to in the morning, and she couldn't afford to call in and miss a whole day of pay. She was going to need all the money she could get because her grandmother was still asking her if she'd found a place yet, and she was sure the day was coming when Mavis was going to get tired of hearing her answer, "No."

A chime alerted Tia to a new customer at the drive-through window.

"Can I help you?" she asked through the speaker-phone.

"Yes," the customer answered. "I'd like a double cheeseburger with bacon and a small orange soda."

"Will that be all?"

"Yes."

"Pull around for the amount."

"Ma'am?" the female customer called out again.

"Yes," Tia answered sharply.

"Can you change that to a fish sandwich instead?"

Tia bit down on the inside of her bottom lip. She was tired. She'd ended up staying out with Monica much later than the one-hour time limit she'd given herself, and she blamed Monica.

Not only was the car Monica had picked her up in her only source of transportation home, she herself had become the designated driver when Monica had decided to start drinking. She couldn't leave Monica to drive herself home, and Monica would not leave until she had seen all six male strippers. By the time she'd dropped her off and driven herself home, it was almost three o'clock in the morning.

When her alarm clock had gone off four hours later, she'd hastily pressed the snooze button for an extra ten minutes of sleep and had decided then that that would be the last time she went out with Monica or anyone else when she knew she had to get up early for work the next morning.

She had wanted to call in sick, but the words of her grandmother were still in her head. *You haven't forgotten what I told you, have you?* Her grandmother wanted her out by the end of the month. How could she forget that? She had three weeks left, and she needed all the money she could get.

So, all day she had been dealing with customers who ate at the restaurant all the time and still couldn't make up their mind about what to order.

"Will that be all?" she said with unmasked agitation.

"Yes, that'll be it."

"Pull around to the first window for your total," she answered as she snatched the printed order from the cash register.

A midsized vehicle pulled up to the window, and Tia was surprised to see the silver hair and aged face that indicated *she* was the one who should be addressed as "Ma'am." "That'll be four dollars and seventy-nine cents."

She shivered as the woman handed her four one-dollar bills and began sifting through her coin purse for the exact change. It was cold outside. Too cold to be standing at an open window waiting for a customer to count out the exact change.

She slammed the window shut. Seconds later, the woman reached onto the passenger seat and grabbed a small pamphlet, and together with the change in her hand, stretched her arm out toward the closed window. Tia jerked the window open.

"Can I give you one of these?" the woman asked, smiling.

Tia took the pamphlet and flipped it over. The title read, *Is Something Missing?*

"Read it. It's lifesaving."

"Oh, okay," Tia answered, placing the folded paper next to the cash register as the woman drove off to the second window to collect her food.

She looked at her watch. It was two forty-five. Quitting time. She picked up the pamphlet the woman had given her, folded it into a small square, and tucked it into her back pocket. A coworker came to relieve her, and she quickly walked to the time clock and punched out. With equal speed, she turned the corner, stepped through the exit door, and slowly exhaled a breath of relief.

She pulled a set of keys out of her pocket as she walked to the car. This was the only good thing to have come from being out with Monica the night before; she had a ride home and didn't have to catch the bus.

She started the engine and let the car idle while she looked at the addresses she'd circled earlier in the rental section of the Sunday paper. Most of the one-bedroom apartments that caught her interest were out of her price range, and she tried to decide if she should go and look at the less attractive, but more affordable ones.

The thin red marker on the fuel panel let her know that there was less than one-fourth tank of gasoline left, and she would have to spend her last twenty dollars to put more gas in the tank if she was going to drive all over town looking at apartments. She let out a long yawn. Maybe she would just go home and get some more sleep. Then when she woke up, she would talk to her grandmother about letting her stay a little longer.

For the second time in as many days, the telephone jarred Tia from a deep sleep.

"Hello?" she whispered.

"Hey, what's up?" It was Monica.

"Nothing. I'm sleeping."

"Again? Every time I call, you're sleeping. What's wrong with you?"

Tia moved the phone away from her ear. "Stop yelling," she said.

"Well, what's wrong? You pregnant?"

"No, I'm not." *At least not anymore.*

"Didn't you have to work today?" Monica continued not altering the volume of her voice.

"Yes, I did," she set the volume on the phone to the lowest level, "and why are you talking so loud?"

"Uh, excuse me, but I'm not talking loud. I think you just have a hangover."

"You should be the one with the hangover. Remember last night?"

Monica laughed, and before she could answer, Tia said, "I'm just tired. I stayed out way too late."

"So, what're you trying to say?"

"I'm not trying to say anything. I'm saying it . . . I stayed out too late, then I had to get up early and go to work, and I'm tired."

"Well, you know we didn't have to stay out that long. If you were ready to go you should have said so."

"Yeah, right." Tia could have said more, but like her eyes, she kept her mouth closed as well.

"Let me call you back, okay?"

"Don't call me back. Just bring my mama's car back. She's about to have a fit."

"Can I bring it back later this evening?"

"Yeah. She don't have nothing to do. But just don't make it too late."

"Okay."

"Oh, and I almost forgot. Guess what Jake told me?"

"Who?"

"Jake. The owner."

"Oh, I didn't know that was his name."

"Uh-huh. And he told me last night that all he needed was just one chance with you."

Jake appeared to be between the ages of fifty-five and sixty years of age to Tia. The hair on his head was completely gray with a bald spot in the center that he tried, unsuccessfully, to cover by combing strands of hair over it. The size of his stomach could easily compete with that of a woman who was in her eighth month of pregnancy. There was nothing attractive about him except for the money he had accumulated from owning the club, and Tia was sure his wife—if she was smart— was managing that quite well.

"One chance to do what?" Tia frowned as she asked.

"You know."

"No, I don't know," she said finally opening her eyes. "And I don't want to know either. Why don't you go and take my place?"

"He don't want me. He wants you," she said laughing. "Anyway, I just thought I'd tell you."

"Well, I've been told. But I'll have to pass on that."

"I know you will."

They shared a laugh, and the conversation ended with Tia promising to return the car later that evening.

She flipped open her cell phone again and turned the phone completely off. Then she closed her eyes and turned on her back. Something inside of her was changing. A feeling, not like the other feeling that led her to the arms of first one man, and then another, not like the feeling that allowed her to sleep with a man the same night she'd met him. No, this was something different. This feeling hinted of disinterest, of giving up, of defeat. This feeling told her she was not doing something right each time she looked for validation through the touch of another man's hand or from the meaningless words they spoke. And the harder she tried to ignore it, the more persistent it became.

She could not hush-hush it away with flirtatious talk, loud music, laughter, or sex. She was aware of her need to feel secure, and finding a man to fulfill that desire had never been a problem. They were everywhere—in the mall, at the club, in the restaurant where she worked, on the bus, and even at the bus stop. The hard part for her was *keeping* a man because at some point, as always, she would begin to distrust them. Then, her desire to be loved by that particular man would start to disappear, and so would she.

Sometimes, it took months, other times only weeks, and with the stranger, only a night. She curled her body into a fetal position. Why couldn't she be loved? Why *shouldn't* she be? She had searched for it, watched for it, was eager to embrace it, and had tried her best to believe in it. But it had never come. She was going to stop looking for it. That was it. No more seeking. Her own father hadn't loved her. So why should she expect any other man to?

Still, those thoughts did little to erase the desires of her heart, and it occurred to her that maybe she was doing something wrong. Maybe there was something else out there that she should be seeking.

Chapter Nineteen

Mavis opened her eyes that Sunday morning to the faint, intermittent streams of sunlight shining through her bedroom window. Her ears took in the sound of raindrops pounding forcefully against her window-pane, and she thought it strange that the sun should be shining even though it was raining. She sat up and looked out the window.

It was the middle of April, and the last of stubborn patches of frozen snow had begun to melt, revealing muddy lawns underneath. There was always a period of ugliness before the beauty could shine through, a rejuvenation of sorts, and a transformation from barren bushes and soggy soil to an array of flowers bearing all the colors of a rainbow amid grassy, green lawns.

In between the rains, there were the warm rays from the sun nurturing the buds of flowers and trees, gently waking them from a long and frozen hiatus. Spring was a time for new beginnings, a time for starting over. It was a miraculous act of God that each season, a life that had been subdued by freezing temperatures was allowed to reemerge under the nurturing warmth of the sun and blossom just as vibrantly as it had the year before. It was His gift of rejuvenation that took place year after year.

As she listened to the rain, she thought about how to start her day. First and foremost, she closed her eyes and thanked the Lord for allowing her to see yet another day. It would not be easy—what she was planning to do. Nor would it be so hard as to make it impossible. She had not thought much about Henry and what he would have to say about her decision. His input didn't matter anymore—if it ever had. Her mind was made up. She was going to visit her daughter.

She had received the letter from Ida two days ago even though the date written at the top of it indicated she had written it months earlier. It didn't matter. What did matter was that Ida had referred to her as "Momma." That was a word she had not heard in years, and seeing it on paper, knowing it was written by the hand of her only child, caused a flow of emotions to be released from her heart.

She had to see her. She had not laid eyes on Ida for twelve years, and Mavis knew that the only reason it had been that way was because of the hardness of her own heart. The fact that Tia had never expressed an interest in going to see her mother, had never begged or pleaded with Mavis to take her to the prison, had made it easy for Mavis to maintain the rigid feelings she'd developed toward Ida. But now she was changing, and she had to try to put to rest all of the horrible, ugly feelings that remained between them.

Years ago, God had seen fit to give Mavis a child to nurture and love, and she'd messed that up. Even though Ida was no longer a child, Mavis felt like God was giving her another chance to redeem herself, to make it right. It didn't matter to her what may or may not have happened between Ida and Henry. It didn't matter if Henry *had* been that baby's father. She would never know because she would never ask. What mattered was that Ida was her only daughter, and she couldn't let this second opportunity to love her slip away again.

She did not know what she would say or how she would say it. Maybe they could just talk for a while. Maybe they could just be two people having a general conversation. She didn't know. But she did know that the Word of God told her that all things were possible with Him. She had heard it and read it many times through the years. Now, she was going to start living by it.

That Saturday night in the easy chair when she had cried for the first time in years was also the night she rededicated her life to Jesus Christ. She was not so foolish as to think all of her issues would be solved. What had happened had happened. There was no turning back the hands on the clock. Her spirit still felt weary, and her soul a little empty. But she was no longer trying to fight this battle alone. She knew she had the power of Jesus Christ—a power she had never truly called upon—growing within her. And she would not remain empty for long.

A verse from the Bible came to her mind. *"I can do all things through Christ who strengthens me."* And she let out a soft "Amen."

She remembered a passage she'd read months earlier in a Christian bookstore. It was really just a sentence, a declaration that had stayed with her: *"If you are confused . . . take that as a sign that you are not doing something right."*

Perhaps that statement had stayed with her because she *was* confused. About her marriage. About the difference between doing the right thing versus the righteous thing. Should she stay or go? All she wanted was some sort of peace of mind, but that did not seem to be a possibility as long as she occupied the same house with Henry. But what did God say about all things being possible with Him? Still, it had gotten worse.

They lived in the same house, yet seldom spoke to one another, and when they did, it was not in intimate conversation but in monosyllables.

"Dinner ready?"

"Yes."

"Turn up the heat."

"It is up."

"I'm going to bed."

"Good night."

Home was not a home anymore and hadn't been for quite some time. It was just a wooden and aluminum-sided structure that housed two, no, three, strangers. She hoped she could change that with Tia, but it looked and felt like it was too late to change things with Henry. She didn't even feel like trying. And he had stopped making sexual advances toward her completely.

Now, there was this rumor circulating that he was spending a great deal of time with the church secretary . . . more than what some of the sisters in the congregation felt was necessary. She didn't confront him about it because she didn't care. The opposite of love is not hate, but indifference. And it was this knowledge that led her to the conclusion that after she had made amends with Ida and Tia—or at least given it her best effort—she would make amends with herself and leave this man whom she did not love anymore.

She was fifty-four years old now, and if she was to have any peace of mind, any sense of serenity before she left this earth, she was going to have to leave Henry. She knew she should have left him a long time ago when she first caught that glimpse of desire in his eyes for her own daughter, Ida, who'd been a teenager at the time.

She could never prove that he'd slept with her, but Jesus spoke about lust in the Bible, and He was very clear on it. She recalled His words in Matthew 5:28: "But I tell you that anyone who looks at a woman lustfully has already committed adultery with her in his heart." She could have left Henry on those grounds alone, but instead, she tried to excuse his behavior away, justify it even by blaming Ida for being such a fast child. That had been her first of many mistakes in their marriage.

Then, when she began to dread the touch of his hands anywhere on her body, she considered leaving him again, but according to God's Word, that was not an acceptable reason for her to divorce him. Now, after twenty-four years of marriage, she had nothing to show for it except an ice-covered heart and a husband she didn't trust or love. She had to leave him if for no other reason than for herself.

The rain had stopped. She could no longer hear the pounding against her windowpane. But through it all the sun had continued to find openings between the clouds in which to make its presence known. She thought about the strange message in the letter Ida had sent from jail twelve years ago, "... *tell him I said I'm sorry about the baby. He'll know what I mean.*" What *had* Ida meant? Had she been trying to tell her that the baby was Henry's? And why hadn't she ever felt any sorrow about the death of the baby, her own grandson?

It was true she hadn't had a relationship with any of her grandchildren, but shouldn't she have felt some sort of sadness? *Tell Henry I'm sorry.* She shook her head swiftly. She couldn't think about that right now. She had to get up and get ready for church. So, she tried to focus on the sun's persistence instead, wondering if there would be another rainstorm before the day was over.

***

It was Sunday morning, and Henry sat at the dining-room table in front of his open Bible. Mavis had told him of her desire to leave him the night before. She said she was not happy and that God was giving her a chance to correct the mistakes she'd made in her life. But what did that mean? Yes, there was her estranged relationship with her daughter, and she wasn't exactly cozy with her granddaughter. But was she saying that he too was a mistake?

He had never thought about leaving her even as she had continued to gain weight year after year, even when she seemed to cringe each time he touched her sexually, and later, when she began to deny him intimacy altogether. Even after he had stopped trying to figure out why his own wife did not like to be touched by him, he had stayed. And now, she wanted to leave him.

She did not mention his infidelities as a reason, but he knew she'd been suspicious on occasion. And he could admit that he had been unfaithful more than once. But he had his needs, and if she had been doing her job—and doing it right in the first place—he would have never set his sights elsewhere, and that included her daughter, Ida. But the girl was always prancing around the house half-naked. What was he supposed to do? Act like he was deaf *and* blind?

He had grown tired of having to beg and plead for sex from his own wife. And when she did relent, it was only her body she gave to him. Her heart was never present. What was so ironic was that this was the first real conversation they'd had in months, probably years, and it was all about her wanting to leave him.

He closed his Bible. *Let her leave then,* he thought. She didn't care about him or his satisfaction. And he couldn't satisfy her. He had finally come to the realization that he would never be able to please her if she didn't want to be pleased. And it was evident that his wife most definitely did not want to be pleased.

She hadn't always been that way, though, and he struggled to remember how she used to be. Somewhere along the way, she'd begun to change. It might have been during the years when Ida had begun to mature and blossom into womanhood. It seemed to him that there had been some sort of jealous rivalry going on between mother and daughter. Maybe it had something to do with him. Maybe . . . Well, never mind. He was done with that. He was done with Ida.

One thing he could say, though, was that he had never touched the girl while she was still living in their house and under the age of eighteen. Oh, he had wanted to, but he knew Mavis was just waiting for the day when Ida turned eighteen so she could put her out. Lord knows he'd heard it enough times from her. So, while she waited for Ida to turn eighteen, he waited too. And the day she moved out was the day Henry made his proposition, and just as he had figured, Ida was more than willing to satisfy him for a price.

Several creases nestled themselves into his forehead as he tried to remember how much she had asked for. He thought it might have been around forty or fifty dollars a week. But whatever it was, it wasn't much. The girl was cheap. And after he'd found out what had happened to that baby, he had to agree with Mavis that she was crazy too. But he couldn't keep thinking about that. He had to clear his mind and be prepared for Sunday services.

He reopened his Bible to the section where the cloth bookmark lay. He had gotten up early so he could go over the sermon he would be preaching later that morning, and the last thing he needed was a distraction. If Mavis wanted to leave, he would let her go. There was always someone else.

He began reading the book of Matthew 26. He read verse 41—a verse he had read many times—and stopped as he felt a sadness creeping into his heart. The unexpected sensation increased as he read the verse again with conviction: "Watch and pray so that you will not fall into temptation. The spirit is willing, but the flesh is weak."

Chapter Twenty

The smell of cinnamon and nutmeg finally prodded Tia from a deep sleep. She was supposed to have gone apartment hunting after work, but she had been so tired from having stayed out late with Monica the night before that all she could do was go home and lie back down.

Now, she was awake, inhaling wafts of the sweet aroma as it made its way from her grandmother's kitchen to the upstairs, infiltrating any available space in her room. Those smells meant that Mavis was cooking Sunday dinner, which would include candied yams rich with butter and brown sugar, and seasoned to perfection with cinnamon and nutmeg. She turned on her side and inhaled deeply, this time taking in the tantalizing scent of baked chicken and dressing.

Instant hunger brought her to an upright position in the middle of the bed. She forced her body to turn, allowing her legs to dangle from the side of the bed momentarily before she stood up. After brushing her teeth, she made her way downstairs. Mavis was in the kitchen, stirring something in a pot in front of the stove.

"Hey, Grandma. Is that chicken I smell?"

"Well, it ain't pizza," Mavis answered without turning away from the stove.

Why couldn't she just answer a question without sarcasm? "And candied yams?"

"And candied yams."

"What else?" Tia knew from the different aromas what her grandmother was cooking, but she asked the question anyway. It was her way of trying to figure out what type of mood she was in, or rather, what level of sarcasm was in full force. And there were only two: Sarcasm Level One, which meant she had little to say, but when she did it was not pleasant, or Sarcasm Level Two, which meant she had much to say and *none* of it would be pleasant.

"Corn bread and macaroni and cheese."

Tia sensed a new sound in her grandmother's voice. It was hovering on the verge of being pleasant.

"Umm. Is it ready?" she asked reaching for a plate from the cabinet. "I'm about to starve to death."

"It's as ready as it's gonna get."

Tia turned her head sharply toward her grandmother's back. There it was again. That tone. It had less stress in it. To say she sounded happy would be going too far. But there was definitely something different.

"Ah, ah, ah," her grandmother said, waving her hand in the air, "put that back." *There,* she thought, *that was the grandmother she was used to.*

"Here," she said. "I already fixed you a plate. I figured you'd be getting up around this time."

Tia stood still as if her feet were weighed down with blocks of cement. Her arms did not know whether to reach out and take the plate or stay put at her sides, and so they stayed put.

"Here, girl," her grandmother stood before her, arms outstretched, holding the plate of warm food. "Take the plate."

"Thanks," was all she managed to say.

"You're welcome."

As she walked to the kitchen table, she smiled. She didn't know what was going on with her grandmother, but she was going to take full advantage of her good mood.

Her grandmother joined her at the table, and they ate their meal in silence. They were seated in an L-shaped fashion, with Tia facing the window and her grandmother facing the kitchen sink.

It was a good meal, too good to interrupt with words; plus, Tia needed more time to organize her thoughts. She had a case to plead, and she would have to present it well. Halfway through her meal, Tia spoke.

"This is so good."

"Uh-huh."

"Where's Henry?"

"Upstairs. Probably sleeping or whatever."

"He didn't eat?"

"Yeah, he ate."

"Uh, Grandma," she began, "I've been looking in the paper for an apartment, but you know, there really ain't nothing in there that's decent that I can afford."

"Uh-huh."

"So, I was wondering," she felt the moisture forming in her armpits as her heartbeat quickened, "if it would be possible for me to stay here just a little bit longer."

There was silence as her grandmother continued to eat.

"You know, just until I can save a little more money."

Mavis put down her fork and reached for the pitcher of tea she had steeped, and then chilled earlier. She poured some of it into a tall glass that sat before her, then raised the glass to her lips and took a long swallow. "Boy, that's some good tea," she said. She looked at Tia. "You can stay, but to tell you the truth, I don't know how long I'll be staying."

"What do you mean? Where are you going?"

Mavis got up slowly from the chair, taking her empty plate with her. Tia remained seated, waiting for an answer. Her grandmother walked over to the stove and helped herself to a second helping of chicken, yams, and corn bread.

"I said you can stay. That's the only answer you need right now, ain't it?"

"I guess," Tia mumbled. "If you say so."

"I do. Now finish eating before it gets cold."

But it was too late. Her appetite had just left her. What was going on? This was not like her grandmother at all; the pleasant attitude, the mysterious comment about not staying, and the concern about her eating. Was somebody dying? Was *she* dying? She started to tell her grandmother that if she wasn't staying, neither was she, but she forced a piece of corn bread into her mouth instead.

"You want seconds?" Mavis asked.

"Uh-uh," Tia said. "I don't think I can handle anymore."

Mavis said she didn't know how long she would be staying. But that was not entirely true. She knew what she was going to do, and it didn't involve continuing to stay in that house. Henry hadn't understood why she was leaving him, but that was too bad. She understood.

The night before, when she had been sitting in the easy chair praying for an answer, God had finally come through for her. She'd felt a strange sense of relief as she'd let the teardrops slide down her cheeks, and afterward, she could see things much clearer.

She recognized her situation for what it was. She had a marriage that seemed to produce only loneliness within her, an estranged daughter who was distant not just in terms of miles but in the heart as well, and a granddaughter living under her roof who she didn't even know how to talk to.

She had not reached out to her, or anyone, for that matter. She had not made any attempts to right any of the things that were wrong; not with Henry, who, by his own right, was just as guilty as she was. Or Ida, who was also not blameless. But that was not the point. They had all been wrong. Who was going to take the first step?

She could not escape the haunting guilt that she had not done right by Ida. And God forgive her, for while she had never used physical punishment with Tia the way she had with Ida, she had definitely allowed history to repeat itself by becoming emotionally unavailable to her in the same way she had been years earlier with Ida. It was time for a change. Tomorrow she would visit her daughter.

Chapter Twenty-one

It was a little over a seventy-mile drive to the Taycheedah Correctional Institution, and Mavis estimated she would be there by two-thirty or so in the afternoon. That was right at the beginning of visiting hours, and there would be time for the full three-hour visit allowed if it turned out that she and Ida had that much to say to each other.

She was not the only one making the trip. There were twenty-five to thirty other visitors, most of them female, standing in line ahead of her waiting to board the yellow charter bus parked on the lot of the minimart.

By the time she got on, there were only a few aisle seats left, and she chose the first one she saw toward the back of the bus. As she sat down, her hips pressed against the woman already seated by the window.

"Excuse me," she said trying to smile.

The woman smiled back and scooted closer to the window as Mavis tried to reposition the bottom half of her right side on the seat. This was something else she would work on after she left Henry. She would lose some weight.

The sun had briefly made an appearance earlier in the morning, but now the sky was overcast as the bus passed field after field of land. What would she say to Ida? How would she say it? She took off her sunglasses. How would Ida look after all these years? Would she be happy to see her? Or would she look at her with eyes full of hate? She didn't know if she would be able to handle being looked at like that. She could handle being looked at with empty eyes—Henry had conditioned her to that. But eyes full of hate were another story, especially by a child she had made so many mistakes with. Wasn't she full of enough guilt already?

The edge of the seat pushed into her outer thigh, and she began to feel uncomfortable. She tried to reposition herself in an attempt to alleviate the pressure. How would she start the conversation with Ida? She felt an apology would be an appropriate greeting after twelve years of not seeing her daughter. And maybe that would take the edge off any hostility Ida was probably still feeling. Yes, Mavis would indicate up front that she had been wrong. But then what? What would be Ida's response? Would she even have one?

The bus made a sharp left turn, causing all of her weight to shift onto the arm of the other woman seated next to her. It continued speeding along a gravel road, leaving an uproar of dust behind it.

"Sorry," Mavis said.

"We're almost there now," the woman replied.

The warmth on the bus seemed to close in around her. She wanted to take off her jacket, but instead, she began fanning her face and neck with her hand. She would suffocate if she didn't get some air soon. She took a handkerchief from her purse and began to dab at the moisture that was forming on her forehead. The reality of what she was about to do had set in.

"I'm going to see my daughter," Mavis said looking straight-ahead.

"How long has she been here?" the woman asked.

"A long time. Too long."

Immediately, Mavis wished she had not spoken. She did not want to have to answer the inevitable question of why her daughter was here. She was not prepared to tell the story. And she now felt implicated in the whole ordeal. After all, what kind of mother raises a child who has the ability to neglect her own child to the point of death?

The bus had come to the end of the winding dirt road. And Mavis thanked God that the woman did not ask any more questions. She began to wonder if she had made a mistake deciding to visit Ida. But it was too late now. The bus was slowing down in front of a long, steel gate that enclosed what looked like several large, multilevel dormitories.

The old brick buildings behind the gates were surrounded by massive acres of land amid a backdrop of trees and more land. Were it not for the top coils of spiked metal strips spanning the length of the gate, she might have thought she was preparing to visit a student on campus.

Everyone began gathering their belongings in preparation for exiting the bus, and there was complete silence. Mavis stood up and pulled her skirt away from the back of her thighs. Her legs felt weak, and she grabbed the back of each seat as she made her way to the front.

The cool spring breeze welcomed her as she stepped outside. It gave her a newfound sense of energy. Seasons changed, and so did people. She decided that however this visit turned out, she knew that at least she would be able to say that she had tried. She took a deep breath and looked at her watch. It was three o'clock. But that was okay. There was still enough time for her three-hour visit with Ida after she was checked in.

She walked toward the entrance and waited until it was her turn to walk through the metal detector. Once through, she joined the other visitors who stood in line waiting to be checked in after they had shown proper identification.

Mavis looked around the medium-sized room. Besides the huge window, metal detector, and gray walls there was nothing else to look at. Several plastic egg-white chairs were lined up in rows, and on the wall behind the last row were various plaques and notices hanging. She was not interested in reading any of them. She was only interested in seeing Ida.

Several minutes passed before she heard the strong feminine voice as it made its way to the back of the line where she stood.

"Please have proper identification ready!"

Mavis opened her purse and pulled out a laminated photo identification card from the state's Department of Transportation. She thought about sitting down on one of the plastic chairs while she waited for the line to move forward, but the possibility of somehow losing her place increased her anxiety. She wiped the palms of her hands on the side of her coat. The thought of having to wait any longer than she needed to would have been too much for her nerves.

A short while later she entered a room that was the size of a high school cafeteria minus the food counter. One of the guards led her to a rickety oak chair that was placed in front of a table covered in vinyl with random scratches etched all over it. There were two empty chairs on the other side of the table, and the guard indicated with his finger which side of the table she should sit at. He joined the other guard standing next to the two vending machines up against the cement walls, and they both maintained a standing position as they kept surveillance of the room.

The air inside was warm, but Mavis shivered when she saw Ida being brought in through the one entrance that also served as the exit. Her tall, thin frame moved slowly, and the bright orange top and pants she wore seemed to make the dullness in her eyes painfully obvious.

"Hi." Ida was the first to speak.

"Hi," Mavis replied softly. "How are you?"

The guard directed Ida to one of the two empty chairs on the other side of the table and returned to his standing position at the front of the room.

"I'm fine," Ida said sitting down.

There was silence between them as Mavis toyed with the locker key that had been given to her after she'd placed her coat into one of the lockers.

"How are things here?" Mavis shifted in her seat.

Ida shrugged her shoulders. "It's a prison. What else can I say?"

"Yeah, I guess so."

"How you been?" Ida asked in a detached tone.

"I could be better." Mavis looked directly at Ida. "I *could have* been better."

"Yeah, you could," Ida said without taking her eyes off her mother. She continued to study her face. Twelve years had not changed her much other than the extra weight.

"You look good, though," she said.

Mavis smiled slightly. "I'm glad you wrote me."

Ida was silent.

"Lord knows I didn't have the strength," Mavis continued, "or the courage to do it myself."

"That's not surprising." Ida inhaled, then exhaled deeply. "You know," she said, "I had planned to tell you that none of this would've happened if you wouldn't have been so mean." She frowned. "So . . . cold."

"Ida, I know—"

"Let me finish." She began tapping the tabletop. "But then I got to thinking. Because you know, a person can do a whole lot of thinking in a place like this. And I realized that maybe I had something to do with this too."

"Yes," Mavis said slowly. She wanted to remind her daughter that *she* was the one who let her baby starve to death. But intuition told her that was not the right thing to say. She had to choose her words carefully. She had not come this far to argue.

"Is it too late?" Mavis asked.

"I don't know. Is it? Is twelve years too late?"

Bits and pieces of other conversations taking place around them floated past Mavis's ears. She could think of nothing to say. She could not concentrate on an answer.

"Yeah," Ida continued, "you might be happy to know that I been having Bible Study with this Christian group that comes in on Sundays."

"Praise the Lord," Mavis whispered.

"Yeah, praise Him," Ida said.

Mavis heard the sarcasm in her voice and knew that the two of them would not be able to sustain a three-hour conversation. At least not this time.

"I'm sorry," she said.

"Really? Seriously?" Ida sat straight up. Her almond-shaped eyes appeared slightly bigger. "After twelve years?"

Mavis stiffened her back. "Yes. After twelve years."

"Well, I'll be darned," she said with eyes that still remained as dull as they had been when she'd first come in. "How's Tia?"

"She's okay, I guess."

"What you mean, you guess? She still lives with you, don't she?"

"Yes," Mavis sighed. "We don't have the closest of relationships."

"No kidding. How old is she now? Eighteen?"

"Yes."

"Does she want to see me?"

"I don't know. I haven't asked her."

"Well, can you tell her that I want to see her?"

"Yes, I can."

"*Will* you?"

"Yes, I will."

"Okay." Ida slapped both of her hands down on the table, and then motioned to the guard. "I guess I better be getting back."

The visit had barely lasted fifteen minutes. The guard walked up to the table, and Mavis realized there would be no good-bye hug that she had hoped for.

"Don't forget to tell Tia I want to see her," Ida said over her shoulder as the guard led her away.

"I won't," Mavis said trying to hide the disappointment on her face. She waited for the trembling in her body to subside, and then she slowly got up from the table. She walked over to the vending machine and put a single dollar bill into the slot. A bottle of spring water tumbled down to the opening, and she reached down to pull it out.

She made her way first to the locker to retrieve her coat, and then back to the waiting room. There was still two hours and forty-five minutes left before the other visitors would be done laughing and talking with their loved ones. It was going to be a long wait.

She took a seat on one of the plastic chairs and realized that she wasn't the only player in this game of waiting. Ida had been waiting for something from her for twelve years—probably more. And Tia had been waiting practically her whole life.

**

Mavis opened her purse and pulled out her minia-
ture Bible. She turned to Psalm 27:14 and read, "Wait
for the Lord; be strong and take heart and wait for
the Lord." And this time that was exactly what she intended to do.

Ida found it difficult to concentrate after the visit.
Her nerves were worse than they had ever been. She
found herself frequently gnawing away at the small
remnants of nail that remained on her fingers. And the
comments from a particular inmate were beginning to
irritate her.

"Quit biting your nails," the inmate said as they sat
under observation in the yard.

"Why? It ain't like they need to be long and pretty for
nobody."

"They don't have to be short and ugly either."

"Mind your business."

"I am. And part of my business is letting you know
that you getting on my nerves with all that nail biting."

"Ain't nobody telling you to look."

"It ain't like I can't see. You sitting right in front of
me."

"Close your eyes then."

"I got a better idea. Why don't you close that smart
mouth of yours?"

Ida felt the adrenaline rising, which, for her, meant
she was on the verge of losing all resemblance of peace.
It was mounting, and she needed to do something to
keep it at bay. It hadn't been that long since she'd gotten out of solitary confinement for fighting, and she
didn't want to go back before seeing her mother again.

Seeing her mother. That had been awkward, and odd as it seemed, all the animosity Ida had felt toward Mavis would not completely reveal itself once she was sitting in front of her. Face to face. At the end of the visit, Mavis had said she'd let Tia know that Ida wanted to see her. And she didn't want to do anything to jeopardize that visit. Ida stood up.

"What?" The other inmate stood up as well. "You wanna do something?"

"Yeah," Ida said. "I wanna do some jumping jacks. Or is that gonna get on your nerves too?"

The inmate maintained her stance as Ida walked to the other side of the yard and began jumping. *One, two* . . . her mother would try to bring Tia the next time; *three, four* . . . the next time . . . those words sounded pretty good; *five, six, seven, eight,* and for the sake of next time, Ida kept her mouth shut. She didn't want to do anything to jeopardize her release date, which was in six months. *Nine, ten.* "Lord, please don't let me hurt her," she whispered as she continued to jump up and down.

Chapter Twenty-two

Tia stood on the front porch smoking a cigarette. There was a slight chill that still lingered in the air as the sun played hide-and-seek with the clouds. Patches of straw-colored grass had yet to benefit from the rain that accompanied the spring season. But she knew it was just a matter of time before the colors of the season would begin to flourish. She shivered. When would she flourish? No one was caring for her, and she did not know how to reach out to anyone.

Monica kept trying to set her up on blind dates, but she had sworn off men since her last one-night encounter, and that had been months ago. Plus, if it was just going to end up being a physical thing, where would she be when that began to wear off? She couldn't even say she'd be back to square one because she would have had to make it to the next level in order to go back, and she didn't see that happening.

She exhaled a thin stream of white smoke, and like the smoke, wished that she could just evaporate into the air. It would be so much easier than trying to figure all this out. And then there was the latest out of character behavior of her grandmother.

After not having seen Ida for twelve years, her grandmother had all of a sudden decided to go and visit her, and then she'd had the nerve to try to get Tia to come along with her. Her grandmother must really be losing her mind! Why would Tia want to see the woman who neglected and abandoned her? She kicked a pebble off the porch. She couldn't stand Ida! She hated her! She hadn't seen or heard from her in all this time. Why change things now? What would be the point?

She lit another cigarette and tried to ignore the slight chill she was feeling from the cool midmorning air. She wondered if her grandmother had made it to the prison. She tried to imagine the two of them sitting across from each other, looking, or not looking, at each other. Talking, then not talking. Would there be tears? And if so, by whom? Who would be the first to cry? Or would they cry together? What would they talk about? Would they hug each other, or would there be bars to keep them separated still?

For an instant, she allowed herself to wonder what it might feel like to be face to face with her mother, and then with the same level of force she used to flick the burned out cigarette into a bush on the side of the house, she dismissed the thought from her mind. If her grandmother had seen her flicking a cigarette into her bushes she would have had a fit. But she wasn't there, was she? No, she was off visiting that other woman.

A few seconds passed before Tia stormed back into the house, slamming the door behind her. Later that evening, Mavis walked through the same door.

"Your mother wants to see you," Mavis said as she set her purse down on the living-room table.

"For what?" Tia's face became distorted as she tried to comprehend what her grandmother was saying.

"She said she misses you," Mavis said, as she slowly lowered herself to the sofa.

Tia arched her eyebrows. "Misses me?"

"Misses you," Mavis said unemotionally.

Tia was silent for a few seconds. "Well, I don't miss her," she said softly.

Mavis looked up at her. "But I'm not talking about you, now, am I?"

Tia began shaking her head slowly. "I don't want to see her, Grandma."

"I think you should."

"Well," Tia bit her bottom lip, "how was *your* visit?"

"It was okay." She pushed the back of her left shoe down and off with her right foot, then repeated the process with the other foot. "It was a little awkward, but that's to be expected after all this time. She's got a lot of bad feelings inside."

"Toward who?" Tia's eyes widened. "I know not me!"

"Did I say you?"

"Then who? You?"

Mavis stared at her. "Who else, Tia?"

"I don't know." She was biting her lip again. "I'm just asking!"

Mavis looked straight-ahead, to the outside, across the street to the duplex where Ida and her children had once lived. She let her gaze rest on the aging oak tree that half-obscured the address on the old house, and she just sat there, perfectly still, her hands resting in her lap, her shoulders slumped over from the weight of the visit.

To Tia, she looked like a statue, carved not out of stone, but out of cement. Solid through and through. After a few minutes Mavis spoke.

"I'm tired. I'm going to go and lie down for a while."

"Okay," Tia mumbled. But her mind had already begun to race. What went on at that prison? She took in a deep breath, preparing to ask the question before her grandmother got up. But then she saw the tears, silent at first, rolling down her cheeks. This statue of a woman, her grandmother, was crying. She began rocking back and forth, moaning softly, and the moisture began to build up in Tia's eyes as well. She tried to wipe the tears away just as quickly as they fell, but they would not stop. Everything had been fine. Why did her grandmother have to go and see Ida? Why couldn't she have just left the past in the past?

She looked down at her and felt an ache in the center of her chest. It grew in its intensity until it felt as though her entire chest was about to burst wide open. She could not resist the urge to place her hands on the tired woman's shoulders. It was a will not of her own. It was as if some force had taken over and lowered her hands until they were rubbing her grandmother's back. Then, without warning, the force took full command of her upper body, and she found herself bending down to hug her tightly.

"It's all right," she heard herself say. And the odd thing was—she had the strangest sensation that it would be.

Mavis reached up and gave Tia's arm a squeeze, and Tia stopped hugging her.

"Sometimes the past don't heal itself," Mavis said. "You have to go back and help it. That's why I'm telling you, you need to go see your mother."

Tia wiped her eyes one last time and shook her head. "Nah, Grandma," she sniffled. "I don't mean no disrespect, but you're wrong."

"No, I'm not. I know what I'm talking about. You can never look toward the future with yesterday's eyes."

"I don't want to hear it," she said, almost shouting. But even in her weakest moment, her grandmother still commanded full respect. And though the two of them had never been close, respect for her had been a learned behavior, and it was one that Tia could not relinquish.

"I don't want to hear it," she repeated as she walked away. But the words had already infiltrated her mind, and she knew that she *would* hear them over and over again.

Chapter Twenty-three

Tia lay on the edge of her bed thinking about what her grandmother had said earlier. What difference would visiting her mother make now? How *could* it make a difference? The damage done was irreversible. Still, those thoughts did little to quench the tug-of-war going on inside her head. If there could be no difference made, why did she feel so much anger inside?

She turned on the TV. It was ten o'clock, and the Monday night news was on most of the local channels. On one news station, a woman was reporting on a class action suit brought against Microsoft Corporation. The suit alleged that the company had abused its power of monopoly and had thereby gained victory over all its competitors. On another station, the results from a monthlong investigation into the Tokyo train accident that had killed five people back in March was still pending. She turned the TV off. The house was still and quiet, but the issues taking place under its roof were far from being settled.

There was an obvious change that had taken place within her grandmother, yet Tia was not sure of the cause. She figured out part of it and knew that it had something to do with Henry. Silent Henry. He was not sullen. He was just silent. In fact, he was almost what she'd call happy.

Sometimes she could actually hear him whistling from another part of the house. But why? He was not the whistling type. In all the years she had lived in that house, she had never heard him whistle. And then there was her mother. She sat up and turned on the lamp beside her bed. Had she just referred to Ida as her *mother?* She rubbed her forehead and looked at the folded paper lying next to the lamp. It was the pamphlet that customer had given her at the drive-through window two days earlier. It had been laying there ever since she'd taken it out of her pocket once she'd gotten home. She unfolded it and looked at it again. The title immediately caught her attention and she began reading.

John 14:6: "I am the way and the truth and the life. No one comes to the Father except through me."
Something Missing?

Is something missing in your life? Is there an emptiness in you that seems like nothing or no one can fill? Are you depressed, but trying to cover up your depression with smiles, sex, shopping, working all the overtime you can get? Or are you afraid? Are you desperately (while looking cool, of course) trying to find meaning in something while settling for the games people play with your heart and emotions?

Maybe you just keep trying to numb that empty feeling inside of you by drinking, using drugs, talking all the time, always on the run, or having sex that only feels good while you're doing it (maybe), but afterward, you are still left with that empty, so empty feeling.

Well, that emptiness you feel is the emptiness of your soul.

But there's someone who loves you and cares a great deal about you. His name is Jesus Christ, and He died to set you free from the emotional and physical prison you feel trapped in.

Since Adam and Eve sinned in the Garden of Eden, man has been separated from the loving God who created him.

Please come back to your Creator. He is waiting for you to call out to Him for forgiveness, help, peace, and comfort.

He is the only one that can fill your lonely heart and give you a measure of peace in the midst of your pain.

Have a talk with Jesus. Talk to Him like you would talk to a friend. Admit that you are a sinner in need of His deliverance and salvation (as we all are). Ask Him to forgive you of your sins and lead you in your Christian walk, and then make Him the Lord of your life. He will do it if you ask Him to.

"Salvation is found in no one else, for there is no other name under heaven given to mankind by which we must be saved" (Acts 4:12).

There is no sin so great that God will not forgive—but Satan wants you to believe otherwise. Don't believe him. Trust Jesus.

She kept the pamphlet in her hand, unable to deny its message. Something was missing in her life, and she had been trying to fill it with the very things it had mentioned. She'd never given God much thought, other than to wonder why He'd given her such a messed up life to live, and she'd certainly never thought about praying to Jesus Christ. She was just so tired of having nothing and no one who she could truly rely on.

For the first time since the abortion, she allowed herself to think about the baby that she had been carrying. If she had decided to keep it, she would have ended up with at least one person who loved her. But it was too late to think about that. It had been almost three months, and there was no taking back what she had done. She wiped her teardrops off the pamphlet. It was now a part of her past, and it had to stay there.

She looked at the last two lines on the pamphlet, *There is no sin so great that God will not forgive . . .* If God could forgive her, did that mean that He could also forgive her mother? And if so, did it mean that she too would be able to forgive her? Ten minutes went by before she flipped open her cell phone and began pressing the numbers.

Monica answered on the third ring.

"Hello." It wasn't a question, but more of a statement.

"Did I wake you up?" Tia asked.

"Nah, girl. I was just lying here looking at TV. What's up?"

"I have a problem."

"What? You need a man?"

Tia waited for the snickering to stop before she continued speaking. "No, I don't."

"What? You need two?" Monica laughed again.

"Quit playing and listen."

"Okay," she said as the last bit of amusement left her voice. "I'm listening."

"It's about what's-her-name."

"Who?"

"You know."

"Uh, no, I don't. Who are you talking about?"

"Ida."

"Ida?"

"That's what I said."

"Your mother?"

"If that's what you want to call her."

"That's what she is, ain't she?"

"Since when?"

There was silence between the two lines. And Monica had to admit that Ida hadn't been a mother to Tia in a very long time.

"Hello?"

"I'm here," Tia answered.

"So what's the problem?"

"She wants to see me."

"Really?"

"Really."

"And?"

"And I don't want to see her."

"Okay. So, what's the problem?"

Tia sighed. "It's my grandmother. She went to see her and came back talking all this stuff about how I should go and visit her too."

"Wow. That's a trip because I know how your grandmother can be."

"Yeah, I know, right? So, I told her I don't want to go see her."

"Well, then, you don't have a problem."

"Yeah, I do. Because she started talking about the future and something else. But then," Tia hesitated, "she started crying."

"What? Crying?"

"Yeah. And now I don't know. I mean, I ain't never seen my grandmother cry. You know, that's just something she don't do. So, now I don't know . . . Maybe I should go visit her."

"Well, maybe you should. I mean, what would be your reason for not wanting to?"

"Why should I want to? She ain't never done nothing for me."

"Maybe she wants to tell you she's sorry."

Tia was silent.

"You won't know unless you go."

"I don't know, Monica."

"Just go."

"What?"

"I said, go. Go see your mama."

"Just like that, huh?"

"Well, what else do you want me to say?"

"I don't know. I just wanted to run that by you."

"Well, you ran it by me, and I say, go."

"We'll see," Tia said softly.

As she closed the cover on her phone, she looked at the pamphlet still in her hand. *Was* Jesus the missing something in her life?

Chapter Twenty-four

Tia could feel the moisture trickling down the crease in the middle of her back. The palms of her hands were moist, and she kept pulling her ring finger as though she were trying to rub some invisible dirt from its skin. She had made a decision. Today, she was going to visit her mother.

She sat across from Monica at the kitchen table trying to think of a reason to change her mind. The clock on the coffeemaker read 12:05 P.M. Time was running out. If she was going to come up with an excuse, she had a little less than two hours left to do it. Otherwise, she would have to be on that bus.

She thought of one excuse after the other, but she knew she was not convincing herself. Monica had offered to make the trip with her. That was the kind of person she was, a chameleon of sorts, but when the chips were down, she always changed back into who she really was . . . her friend. Right now, she wished her friend would just be quiet. Her nerves were already like the ends of a live wire, jumping and jerking from the electrical power flowing through its copper veins. She had no idea what Monica was talking about, but every so often she muttered "um-um" or "humph" at what seemed like the right time. She picked up her cup of coffee and focused on the caramel cream color as she took a sip.

"So, anyway," Monica said, "I shook his hand, you know, just trying to be polite and mature about the whole thing. Well, you know how you shake a person's hand, and then you let it go, right?"

"Uh-huh."

"Well, when I tried to let go of his hand, I had to slide and pull it out, girl, because he was not letting go that easy."

"Humph."

"Uh-huh. And then when I had my fingers just about out, you know what he did?"

"What?"

"He had the nerve to take his thumb and rub it across my hand, girl."

There were a few seconds of sweet silence as Tia looked at Monica. Then, she realized Monica was waiting for her to respond. "So . . . What are you saying? You think he was trying to flirt?"

"Don't you?"

"Maybe." She massaged both sides of her forehead. "But you know you got to be careful not to read more into something than what's there."

"Yeah, I know. But people don't usually let their fingers slide like that when they let go of your hand. And especially a man."

"Uh-huh."

"I say he was giving me a message." She stopped for a second, and then added, "With his fine self."

"Pretty boy, huh?" Tia asked, trying to hide the indifference in her voice.

"Nah, I wouldn't call him pretty. He was more manly than pretty. Dark brown skin, short hair, looked like he had a nice little build, you know."

"Go for it."

"He's married."

"Oh, you left that one little piece of information out."

"Why do you think I was telling you about how he shook my hand?"

"Oh well," Tia said.

"Yeah, that's what I said too."

Tia looked at the clock. "What time is the bus leaving?"

"Two o'clock," Monica answered.

"It's twelve-thirty now. I guess I better get dressed, huh?"

Monica looked her up and down. "Yeah, you better get dressed."

"Well, let me go use the bathroom," Tia said. "This coffee's gonna hit me as soon as I get on that bus. And I am not trying to use no portable john."

"They're not portable johns," Monica corrected her.

"Well, whatever they are, they're nasty. And I'm not trying to use one."

"Yeah, I don't blame you," Monica laughed. "I'm not trying to use one either."

Tia got up and went into the bathroom. She didn't really have to use it. She just needed a few moments of silence. She needed to convince herself that she was doing the right thing by going to see her mother. She wished this day had already ended, or better yet, had never come.

"Hurry up, Tia," Monica yelled. "I have to use it too."

Tia flushed the unused toilet and listened to the forceful swirl of water as it rapidly became caught up in the pressurized vacuum, having nowhere to go but down. She listened to the settling exchange as a new volume of water replaced the old. She opened the door and looked at the clock one last time as she passed it on her way to her bedroom.

***

It was two o'clock, and the two of them stood in line waiting to board the bus that Tia's grandmother had gotten on days earlier when she'd made the same trip to the prison to see Ida. As it had been with Mavis, the trip took an hour and twenty minutes, and Tia had remained silent throughout the entire time.

When they got off the bus, Monica decided to stay behind and tried to convince Tia that everything would be all right.

"If you say so," Tia said. She tried to convince herself that the feeling of uneasiness she had was only natural—normal for someone who hadn't seen her mother in twelve years.

She made it through the metal detectors, then the front desk until finally she found herself sitting in a large, well-lit room with multiple sets of tables and chairs. She did not recognize her mother when they brought her toward the table.

"Hello," Ida said.

"Hi."

"How you doing?"

"Fine. How are you?"

"I'm doing all right," she waved her arms out and to the side of her, "all things considered."

Tia pressed her lips together and slowly nodded. A wave of heat traveled through her, and she could feel the moisture building up on the palms of her hands. She looked into the face of her mother. They were both the same medium shade of tan except for the dark brown crescent-shaped patches of skin directly underneath Ida's small, almond-shaped eyes. Her hair was pulled back into a short ponytail, and she wore a pair of silver, cross-shaped earrings that dangled each time she moved her head.

"So, I see you all grown-up now, ain't you?" The pride Ida felt as she surveyed her daughter quickly diminished when she looked into Tia's eyes. In them, she saw the pain caused by her twelve-year absence staring solemnly back at her.

"Yep," Tia answered. Her mind raced as she thought of something else to say, anything to keep from just sitting across from her in silence. "How old are you?"

"Thirty-six going on ninety." Her throat made a noise that sounded like laughter, and then quickly turned into a cough.

Tia noticed the crookedness of her front teeth as she smiled. And although her face held no wrinkles, she appeared much older than the thirty-six years she said she was. It was all in her eyes. They were sad and tired-looking eyes, and when she smiled, they remained the same. Tia tried to smile back, but the closest she got was a slight parting of her lips.

"So how's Momma been treating you?"

"All right." She picked at the edges of the already torn beige vinyl covering on the table. "She is who she is." She looked up then, and though she did not want to, her eyes recognized the anguish in the eyes looking back at her.

"I hope not."

Tia lowered her gaze to the tabletop where Ida had placed both of her hands. They were small with short, stubby fingers and nails that had been chewed down to the flesh. There was an upper case "T" tattooed on the middle finger of the right hand. "Well, she is," she mumbled.

"So, what are you doing with yourself? She told me you were working at a restaurant."

"I am," Tia rubbed the side of her face. *At least I'm not locked up in prison.* "For now."

"Well, at least you was smart enough not to have no kids."

"Yep." She brushed away an imaginary piece of lint from her pants. *You should have been that smart.*

"So, why do you keep holding your head down? You don't wanna look at me?"

She hunched her shoulders and felt another wave of heat. She wanted to ask her what had happened, what had started it all that had caused her to do the things she'd done and end up where she was. She wanted to ask her why, for twelve years, she had never contacted her. No letters, no phone calls, no birthday cards. Why? She wanted to scream it out. Just that one word. *Why?*

Then, as if Ida had been reading her mind she said, "I'm sorry."

And the last thing in the world that Tia wanted to happen was happening. Slowly and steadily, the tears rolled down her cheeks and landed on top of her pants.

"Tia, I'm sorry." Ida reached out to touch her face with the tattooed finger, but Tia inched back in her seat.

"Just stop," she said because with each apology her tears came harder and heavier.

"I'm so sorry."

And now, her shoulders were jerking, and it was too late to regain her composure. She took the palms of her hands and kept wiping the tears to the side of her face until she could see clearly enough to look straight into Ida's eyes and ask the question that she had repressed for twelve years.

"Why?"

Ida thought she had been prepared to hear that question. Thought she knew how she would feel when it came. Yet, when she heard it come out of her daughter's mouth, she felt like a bulldozer had just rammed itself into her heart. Her head dropped, and she had to grab the sides of the chair she was sitting on to steady herself.

"I asked myself that same question, Tia."

"I didn't ask you if you asked *yourself* that question. I asked you, 'why.'"

Ida slowly looked up. She felt weak. The pain was still reverberating in her heart. "Because I was stupid. Because I was young. Because I was misguided."

"For twelve years?" There was an icy glaze to her stare now.

"No. For six years. The first six years of your life. After that, I was here, mad at the world and full of hate." Ida looked at the two small fists Tia now had resting on top of the table. "I guess you must'a felt the same way too, huh?"

Tia ignored the question. "Hate for who?"

"My father, who I never knew. Your father, who left me while I was still pregnant with you. My mother."

Tia thought she saw a light flicker through Ida's eyes when she mentioned her mother.

"But that don't matter now," Ida continued, and the light in her eyes was gone. "You didn't have nothing to do with any of that. This is all on me. I made some mistakes, big time. I made some bad choices, and I been paying for them ever since."

She reached across the table and placed her hand on top of Tia's still balled up fist. An unfamiliar surge of warmth shot through Ida's veins. Tia jumped at the touch of her hand and slid her fist from underneath it. She'd felt something too. A brief connection made between the two of them.

"You reap what you sow," Ida said. "Ain't that what the Bible say?"

Tia stood up. "I have to go," she said.

Ida stood up as well and felt her heart separate into little pieces from the weight of this first visit. The guard walked over to the table.

"Thanks for coming," she mumbled as she headed for the door.

Maybe it was the bright lights in the visiting room or the stifling heat. Or maybe it was the coffee she'd consumed earlier. Whatever it was, it made her feel nauseated, and she almost did not make it to the bathroom in time.

A few minutes later, she was outside breathing in the cool, fresh air of spring. She fumbled through her purse until she found the unopened pack of cigarettes. She quickly pulled the plastic tab around the top until it lifted up, and with even more urgency pulled out one of the long white sticks. The lighter. Where was the lighter? In a near frantic state, she searched her purse again, this time feeling the oblong bulge at the bottom of the bag. She stopped just long enough to light the cigarette and continued walking quickly.

Monica had been waiting just on the other side of the fence and saw her coming. She could tell from the look on her face and the pace of her walk that the visit had not gone well. "What happened?" she asked.

"Nothing," Tia answered abruptly.

They stopped in front of the bus. The doors were closed, and the bus driver was nowhere in sight. Tia stood with her back facing the walls of the prison.

"Where's that bus driver? Ain't it time to go?"

"Not for everybody else," Monica said. "They've still got another forty-five minutes to go before visiting time is up."

"I knew we should've taken your car."

"Was it that bad, Tia?"

"Yeah, it was."

"What did she say?"

"She said she was sorry."

"That's all?"

"Yeah, that's all, Monica," her voice was getting louder.

"Oh."

"I need to get out of here. This is not for me."

"Just calm down, Tia. You—"

"Don't tell me to calm down. You're the one who told me to come in the first place!"

Monica wanted to tell her that, yes, she did tell her she should make this trip, but she didn't have to listen, but she knew that would only cause more harm.

"Yes, I did, but you can't go nowhere until the bus driver and all the other people come back."

"I need to go now." And for the second time that day she found herself crying again.

"We'll go soon." Monica took her by the hand and led her to a wooden bench that had been cemented into the ground just a few feet from the bus. "Come on, have a seat."

"She said she was sorry. Like that's supposed to make everything all better." Tia raised both arms into the air. "Like that's supposed to make twelve years go away. And what am I supposed to say? I forgive you?" She wiped what she hoped was the last tear away. "No." She sniffed. "It don't work that way. Sorry ain't good enough."

"I know," Monica said rubbing her back.

"No, you don't know, Monica!" Tia jerked away from her touch. "You really don't. You had a mother growing up!" She began pointing to her chest. "I didn't. Mine never wrote to me. She never sent me a card. She never called me. She never did anything. And it ain't like she didn't know where I was. She just didn't even try! And now she wants to say she's sorry?"

Monica wanted to tell her that maybe Ida really was sorry. But something in her warned her that this was not the time to speak on behalf of her friend's mother. She could not find the right words to say so she said nothing, hoping her silence—unlike that of Ida's for the past twelve years—would be of some comfort to her friend.

Chapter Twenty-five

Mavis stood up and wiped the sweat from her forehead. She had been sorting through items all afternoon, trying to decide which ones she would take with her and which ones she would leave behind or give to Goodwill.

She had brought a lifetime of memories down from her attic, a dress that had been worn by her only once or twice for some special occasion, a pair of shoes that had been worn with the dress. There were pants and other items of clothing all outgrown, outdated, or long forgotten.

She picked up a box, and the stale smell of mothballs greeted her as she opened it and removed a layer of tissue from around a purple cashmere sweater. It was still in good condition, and she wondered if Tia might like to have it.

Then there were the boxes of annual school pictures of Ida when she had attended McDowell Elementary School. In each picture something different was out of place. In her second-grade photograph, the collar of her shirt was turned up. In third grade, one of her ponytails had been unbraided. In the fourth-grade photo, there were loose strands of hair sticking up on her head as if they had received a charge of electricity and were ready to pass off that energy. What had she managed to get into from the time Mavis had combed her hair to two hours later when it had been time to take pictures?

That was a question she had asked many times and had never received a satisfying answer.

When picture day rolled around during Ida's fifth grade of school, after being sternly warned by Mavis not to mess up her hair, she somehow managed to miss getting her picture taken altogether. And there were no more photographs to be taken after that.

Mavis found a picture of herself standing next to Henry shortly after their marriage. She studied the face of the image staring back at her. The eyes seemed to be staring far off into the distance. What had she been thinking of? She could not remember.

She looked at the picture of Henry. He had seemed happy enough, much like he seemed now ever since she'd told him she was leaving. But there was something different. It was the whistling.

He had never been a whistler before, and now it seemed as though he was always whistling. He'd be in the kitchen silently getting something to eat until she walked in. Then, he would briefly make eye contact with her, turn away, and begin that silly whistling. Why? Was he trying to irritate her?

Other things he had begun to do *were* irritating her, like opening all the windows because he said it was too hot in the house. Just plain silly! It was early spring, and in Wisconsin, that meant the weather was still unpredictable, and temperatures rarely rose above forty degrees. Still, he would open a window, and she would close it as soon as he left the room. But this strange behavior of his was okay because she had put up with far worse during their twenty-four-year marriage. His days were now numbered, and she couldn't count them down fast enough.

She stopped what she was doing as the front door opened and Tia walked in. She studied her face, trying to find the answer to the question she had yet to ask. Finally, she spoke. "Well, how was it?"

"Okay."

The creases in her granddaughter's forehead told Mavis that the visit had probably not been okay. She waited as Tia sat down on the sofa as if she had just returned from a war in which she had been defeated.

"She asked me how I was. Said she was sorry. Stuff like that."

"And what did you say?"

"Nothing. I just listened."

"Just listened, huh?"

"Yep."

"So," Mavis started slowly, "do you think you might be able to forgive her?"

Tia shrugged her shoulders. The trembling in her bottom lip had begun again.

"If she can forgive me, then you can forgive her," Mavis added.

Tia looked at her grandmother. "Why does she have to forgive you?"

"She didn't tell you?"

"Tell me what?"

Mavis inhaled deeply. "I wasn't the best mother in the world. Looking back, I see I could have been different, nicer."

"That's the same thing she said to me. She said I shouldn't be blamed for anything. She said it was her fault, not mine."

"And she's right. Just like it wasn't her fault for the things that I did . . . or didn't do."

"What things did you do?"

"The same things that I *didn't* do with you."

"What?"

Mavis stopped fumbling around inside the almost empty box she had been holding and looked over at Tia. "When's the last time I gave you a hug?"

Many seconds passed before Mavis could no longer stand the permeating silence that convicted her. Finally, she spoke.

"The same things I didn't do for your mother are the same things I didn't do for you."

"Why?"

Mavis sat down next to Tia. "I never told you about my mother and father, did I?"

"No. You never told me about a lot of things."

The comment caught her by surprise, and she paused as the stinging pang shot through her heart.

"They drank a lot, both of them. My father drank the most, but my mother did her fair share too. They would get real mean when they drank, and I had to be careful of everything I said.

"I used to try to stay out of their way when they were drinking. But that was easier said than done because it seemed like my father would deliberately hunt me down just so he could start yelling and screaming at me. And if I didn't answer quick enough or with the right answer, there was gonna be hell to pay. And I paid it all.

"You see this little mark on my forehead?" She pointed to a small scar between her eyebrows. Tia had noticed it before, but had never asked about it.

"That's a birthmark, right?"

Mavis gave a short, quick laugh. "Yeah, that's a birthmark, all right." She paused, wondering if she should continue, then decided she would.

"He called me one day when I was about ten or twelve years, I think. I was sitting in my room just looking out of the window. I must have been daydreaming real hard because I didn't hear him. By the time I realized that he had been calling me, he was standing in the doorway. I turned to answer him, and he had something in his hand. And I'll never forget that look on his face. He looked like a wild animal or something.

"Anyway, the next thing I know . . . *bam!*" She gently slapped her forehead with the palm of her hand. "He had thrown the can of deodorant at me, and it hit me right upside the forehead."

Tia sat silent, waiting.

"That's how I got this mark. And that's a special day because that was the last time I cried. The very last time . . ." She paused, remembering the other night, and the tears that had begun to fall from her eyes after she had prayed to God for help. And then there was the other day after she had returned from her visit with Ida that she had cried again, this time in front of Tia. ". . . until recently," she said.

She wiped her hands on the side of her housedress and continued. "I don't know who I hated more, him for being so mean or her for never doing anything to protect me. And the sad part is, even after they both died, I kept right on hating them. All this time. After awhile, I think it just became a part of me, the hate, I mean. Every day. I was holding on to it. And you know that saying, 'God don't like ugly,' right?"

Tia nodded.

"Well, He sure don't like hate. But here I was praising the Lord on Sunday, and holding on to my hate Monday, Tuesday, Wednesday, Thursday, Friday, and Saturday. Look where it got me."

She decided to end the story there. She had told enough. There was no reason for her granddaughter to know about Henry and how she did not love him and now believed that she had never loved him.

"I'm only telling you this now, Tia, because I don't want to see you make the same mistakes. I don't want you to spend . . . no, *waste* the rest of your life hating your mother for all the things she never did. And that's what it will be, a waste, if you do.

"It's no good. It's a sin in God's eyes. And there's no way you can move forward. Have a talk with Jesus. If you want to be delivered, He can do it."

She stood up. "Scripture tells us, 'So if the Son sets you free, you will be free indeed.' And Lord knows we all need to be set free."

"Earlier you said you didn't know how much longer you'd be staying here, Grandma."

"That's right."

"Then can I ask you something?"

"Go ahead."

"Are you leaving Henry?"

"Yes, I am."

"Does he know?"

"Yes, he does."

"Why are you leaving him?"

"It's a long story. One I'm not going to tell you. Henry and me. We're not good together. Let's just leave it at that."

"When are you leaving?"

"It won't be very long. As soon as I find a place."

"How come he don't leave?"

"I didn't ask him to."

"Why not?"

She sighed. "It don't matter, Tia. I don't really want to stay in this house anyway. I don't need all this space. And besides, I'm going to have to find me a job." She walked back over to where she had left the many boxes of her former life. As she started rummaging through the items, she turned her head sideways and spoke.

"For the record, you can stay with me until you find your own place or . . . whatever." She waved her hand in the air as she said this, much in the same manner as her own daughter had done earlier with Tia during their visit.

Boxes were beginning to pile up. They lined the walls of the dining room and living room, and Henry could hardly turn a corner without rubbing up against one of them. They all had letters written on the outside of them to indicate which room their contents belonged in.

Some of them were marked, *LR* for the living room, *DR* for the dining room, or *K* for the kitchen. He passed what seemed like a multitude of letters blurring together until they all looked the same. What did it matter? The bottom line was that they all had one purpose, and that was to be carried out of his house into a new house of which he would not be occupying.

He stepped over several boxes in the kitchen as he made his way to the stove. There was a barbequed roast sitting in a pan on top of the stove along with a pot of mashed potatoes, and another pot filled with green beans. At least she was still cooking for him. He would miss that after she was gone.

He had come to terms with the separation. Since there had been no mention of a divorce, he had finally relented.

"If that's what you want, Mavis," he said. "I'm not going to stand in your way. I'm not going to make it difficult."

He'd told her earlier that he was not going to beg her to stay, and he meant it. He would have *preferred* that she stayed, but she had made it clear that she was leaving. So, he had no choice but to deal with it the best way he could. But these boxes were getting on his nerves!

"How long are these boxes going to be sitting around here, Mavis?"

"Until I move them," had been her answer.

"Well, you need to hurry up and move them. They're taking up too much space."

That's all he could complain about. The other space—the one in his bed that was now left empty every night—was no longer relevant. And other than the minimal amount of words they exchanged concerning the boxes, conversation between them had gone from being scarce to completely absent.

He had taken to whistling throughout the day in order to alleviate the uncomfortable situation he now found himself in. And he whistled now as he finished making his plate. There was just one problem with his newfound habit, and that was that it only worked during the day. After all, he mused, who whistles at night while they're in the bed?

He could have whistled in bed, though. He could have whistled all through the night since he was having an increasingly hard time falling asleep. And when he did, he would often wake up in the morning hardly able to catch his breath, his heart pounding as if it were trying to break free from the pericardial sac that enclosed it.

He needed his sleep. He still had a church to run. So to remedy the first problem, he turned to over-the-counter sleep aids. But he didn't know what he was going to do about the second problem concerning his heart.

Chapter Twenty-six

Tia was in a state of confusion. It seemed like she had a headache just about every day, and the unsettling feeling in her stomach refused to be calmed by antacids, pain relievers, or even laxatives. She just couldn't seem to think straight these days, and if her life depended on how well she concentrated, she would have been dead a long time ago.

For the third time this week, her register at the Burger Hut had come up short. Nothing much. Five dollars on Monday, two dollars and fifty cents on Wednesday, and three dollars yesterday. Her manager, realizing that something like this had never happened in all the time Tia had been working the cash register, wanted to know if something was wrong with her. She'd told him that she just hadn't been feeling well lately and apologized, telling him that she would be more careful.

It was all too much, these emotional changes. And everyone was deciding to have a change of heart all at once: her grandmother, her mother. Now, the move. What was going on? Were Mavis and Ida secretly scheming against her? Should she start watching her back? People just don't up and change like that.

She couldn't account for the actions of her mother since she barely knew her, but she knew her grandmother, and this behavior was out of character for her. Through the years, Tia had grown accustomed to her grandmother's cold and distant nature, and she just didn't know how to deal with this change.

Her mind was not the only part of her in turmoil. Cause and effect began to play their role, and her body was rebelling against the four-month long state of celibacy she had imposed upon it.

She had made a decision to wait for the right person and the right feeling. She just wasn't sure what the right feeling would feel like. But there was no mistaking the emptiness she always felt after being intimate with someone who she didn't love and who didn't love her. She knew what *that* felt like. And she didn't like it.

She thought of it as an uneven trade-off because the feelings produced from the physical act never erased that empty feeling she always felt afterward deep down inside of her. Still, her hormones surged through her body, then gathered momentum at specific nerve endings and, clustered together, tried to call an all-out war against her.

She did not know how much longer she could withstand their demands. She thought about reversing her decision to wait as she remembered what Monica had told her about Jake, the bar owner. Her hormones, as if encouraged by her weakening state, released another surge of superpower, and she decided to give him a call.

She agreed to meet Jake at a motel not far from the bar that he owned, but now she was having reservations. Not only was he a married man, but he was old enough to be her father! Had it really come down to this? She sighed as she stepped into the shower.

Maybe she should just call the whole thing off. She already knew she would gain nothing from this experience other than physical satisfaction, and even that was not guaranteed. She had gone without for four months. She could go longer, *would* go longer. And just as she had convinced herself, once again, that waiting was the right thing to do, her hormones, outraged by her decision, began racing through her veins, pounding out their opposition. She stepped out of the shower and dried off quickly.

As she returned to her bedroom she continued to have doubts. Should she really go through with it? She pulled out a long-sleeved white dress with small, black, irregular-shaped patterns that resembled a leopard's skin. It had a high neckline, and the cotton material clung to the curves of her small frame.

Even though her willpower had been overcome by the desires of her flesh, another feeling inside of her remained unsettled in an effort to gain acknowledgment. It hinted that everything about what she was planning to do was wrong. She looked at herself in the full-length mirror, and in defeat, walked out of the room.

It was after nine o'clock in the evening when she stepped out of the taxicab and knocked on his motel door. Jake opened the door, and the glow from a television set in a corner danced around the room. There were no other lights on as he greeted her with a hug, and then motioned for her to have a seat on the bed inches away.

"Whatcha' drinking?" he asked as he closed the door. And just the sound of his voice irritated her. It was neutral enough, she guessed. Neither high-pitched nor low, but why was he even talking? Why was she even there?

"Kind of dark in here, isn't it?"

"Sorry, I don't have that."

She looked at him in confusion. "Have what?"

"I asked you what you were drinking, and you said 'kinda' dark in here', so I'm telling you I don't have that kind of drink. Get it?" The protruding roundness of his stomach shook up and down as he laughed, and Tia tried to smile but she felt uncomfortable.

"You got any wine?"

She didn't like him. His upper arms sagged where muscles should have been, and there was too much hair on them. With a few more strands of hair added, she thought they would have a good chance of passing for gorilla arms. His mustache covered his entire upper lip, and she wondered how he ate without getting food caught up in it.

As he poured the wine, she let her eyes roam to the top of his head, stopping at the bald spot in the center that stood out like a tan cue ball polished to perfection.

"Is that the bathroom?" she asked pointing to a door adjacent to the television.

"Um-hmm."

She got up and walked over to the door. Once inside, she found the light switch, then closed the door behind her. She looked at her reflection in the mottled mirror. How could he be so hairy and still have that big bald spot in the center of his head? She adjusted the high neck of her dress and noticed the frown on her face. She took a deep breath, flushed the toilet, and returned to the sofa.

"Can we have some light in here?"

He was sitting on the sofa, waiting. "Sure." He reached for the lamp sitting on a rickety end table next to the sofa and gave the pull chain a quick yank. A bright light flooded the room, making it possible for her to see his short, thick fingers as he handed her a tall glass filled with white wine. Even his fingers had hair on them!

"So, Ms. Lady, how are you?"

Ms. Lady? "I'm doing all right," she lied raising the glass to her lips to keep from having to look at him.

"I'm glad we finally got together," he said as he placed his short, thick, hairy fingers on her thigh. "Tell me about yourself."

She tried to smile as her muscles stiffened in response to his touch. "What do you want to know?"

"Well, what do you do?"

"Right now, I'm just working part-time, living with my grandmother." She waved her hand as if swatting an imaginary fly. "You know. The usual stuff."

"What do you like to do?"

"I don't know. I go out sometimes with Monica."

Then there was silence. The kind of silence that speaks loudly, alerting both parties that they really have nothing to say to each other. It was the kind of silence that made her want to get up and leave.

"I like to party too," he said as she was rehearsing what she would say to make her exit. "I've seen some wild things in my day, let me tell you."

"Really?"

"Yeah. I had a girl once who—"

"I'm gonna have to go," she said suddenly. She stood up with the strap of her purse still dangling from her wrist.

"What's wrong? Did I offend you?" He touched her shoulder. "I was just trying to make conversation."

She stiffened her back. That was the best conversation he could come up with? "Thanks for the wine, but I just don't feel good."

"Well, why don't you stay here and lie down? I'll take good care of you."

Her hand was already on the doorknob. *I bet you'll take good care of you.* "No," she said. "I better go."

He stood surveying her from head to toe as if she were a piece of meat, seasoned, cooked, and ready to eat. And suddenly, that's exactly how she felt. Like an inexpensive cut of meat ready to be consumed, never to be thought of again until it was time for a new piece, and then it wouldn't be her because she would have already been devoured and digested. The thought made her feel cheap.

"You know what I'd like to do?" he said.

She opened the door. "No, but maybe next time," she answered as she walked down the vestibule. But there would be no next time.

Everything had been wrong from the moment she'd walked through the motel door—the dark room, the spotty bathroom mirror, the rickety lamp, and him . . . especially him. She shuddered. What was wrong with her? Why had she agreed to see him? She was still not sure of her actions, but one thing she *was* sure of was that her hormones would not win this war tonight.

"Next time make up your own mind," Monica said through the telephone receiver.

Tia looked at her phone in amazement, and then returned it to her ear. "I know you are not trying to say that you didn't have anything to do with it!"

"I didn't. I just told you what Jake told me."

"Well, if you wouldn't have told me, I wouldn't have thought about it."

"But who made the decision to see the man, Tia?"

"That's not the point. I—"

"I . . . I nothing," Monica interrupted. "Case closed."

"Yeah, you're right. It *is* closed."

Monica's laughter came through the telephone loud and clear.

"I'm gonna hang up this phone if you don't stop."

"Okay, okay," she said. Several more seconds passed before she regained her composure.

"Are you done now?"

"Yeah, but I don't know why you went over there anyway. He's old enough to be your father, *and* he's married. What were you thinking?"

"I'm thinking *you* should have gone over there."

"I told you, he didn't want me. He wanted you. And anyway, you know what I said. As soon as I get to college I'm gonna get me a campus man."

"Oh. Okay. Well, do me a favor then."

She snickered. "What's that?"

"Don't tell me nothing about nobody no more, okay?"

"No problem," Monica said, and the laughter started all over again.

Chapter Twenty-seven

"Why you looking so mad, Ida?" her cellmate asked.

Ida kept staring at the cement wall in their cell. "Who said I was mad, Belinda?"

"Uh, I know I only been sharing this cell with you for a month, but, those creases in your forehead and the way you keep your lips pressed together is a dead giveaway."

Ida did not respond.

"You had a visit from your mother and your daughter, didn't you?" Belinda continued. "What's the matter? Visit didn't go so well?"

Ida turned to look at Belinda. She was the third and youngest cellmate she'd had since she'd been at this prison. At the age of twenty-three, Belinda had held up a corner store on a bet. She hadn't even used a real gun—it had been one of those realistic-looking, plastic toy guns—but that stunt had gotten her a conviction of aggravated robbery along with a five-year prison sentence at Taycheedah. "Don't worry about it, okay?" she said.

"I'm trying not to, but I'm stuck in this cell with you so it's kind of hard not to notice."

"Well, if you gon' make it here," Ida said, "there's some things you better learn *not* to notice."

Belinda began organizing the few toiletries on the makeshift shelf for the hundredth time and tried to lighten the mood. "I need a man," she said. "That's what I need. That's what we *both* need."

"No, you were right the first time," Ida corrected her. "Because I don't need one."

"What? You gay?"

Ida looked at her and rolled her eyes. "Girl, you got a lot to learn."

"I was just asking. Anyway, I got a letter from my sister last week." Belinda held up an 8½x11 piece of paper. "She sent me this application to fill out, and once you do, your name gets added to a pen-pal list so that men can write to you. I'm gonna fill it out and send it back. You want me to ask her to send another one for you?"

Ida glanced over at the paper. "No." But she was torn between wanting someone and not wanting someone.

To anyone listening, she had given up on the idea of love and marriage. But secretly, she dreamed of a handsome man who had come to bring her only joy . . . no pain. Someone who would not use her, mistreat her, or lie to her.

Sometimes, in her imagination, he was tall and thin with a milk chocolate complexion. Other times, he was the color of light brown sugar with a muscular build. Sometimes, his hair was short and neatly trimmed; other times, he had long, well-maintained dreadlocks. But in all of them, he was always smiling, laid-back, and never, ever unpleasant about anything.

In her dream, he would take her hand, and they would go for long walks, or they would go down to the lakefront just to watch the sunset. They would face each other and talk about everything yet nothing in particular, and he, with eyes full of love, would gaze into hers. And she would not look away because her eyes would be filled with love also.

And she would not have to see the disdain reflecting from other people's eyes whenever she did manage to look into them.

She would no longer have to be assessed, judged, and dismissed by somebody else's eyes. In her dream, she would be a different person, a lighter person, no longer weighed down from the burdens of her own mistakes. She would be free, and smiles and laughter would come easy. Not like now, where there was really nothing to smile or laugh about at all.

The harsh sound of the bell signaled the closing of the cell doors. She lay back on her cot and watched the metal bars slowly come together until they met with a loud clang. She waited for the darkness that was about to ensue with the flick of a switch by the prison guard.

"You sure you don't want me to ask my sister to send another application?" Belinda asked again.

A lifetime of unfulfilled desires had changed Ida. It had made her want to give up. At least in her dreams, she was always in control and no one could ever hurt her. So, even if it meant the possibility of receiving a letter from a real man on the outside, she was too afraid to step out of that dream.

"I'll pass," she said as she closed her eyes momentarily and willed her dream back into the secret crevices of her heart.

The creases in her forehead returned as she tried hard not to dwell on what she had come to accept as her mistakes. It wasn't that she'd never loved Tia or the baby. It was just that they had needed so much of what she did not have to give. She had never hated Tia or even disliked her. It had been the situation that she was in that she'd hated.

It had bothered her beyond words to have to ration out food in order to make it stretch the full month. Hot dogs had been Tia's favorite food. And each day Ida had to tell her not to eat one because it was going to be her dinner the next night, was a day that another chunk of her pride disappeared.

Her spirit, as if there had been any whole pieces left of it, crumbled under the weight of her denial of her daughter's simple and natural request for food. But who could she have told that too? Who could she have turned to and admitted her inadequacies as a mother? Who would have understood and not judged her? It had all been too much for her to bear.

She was beginning to see things clearly now. And she realized that Tia had not been the source of her unhappiness and that the emptiness she had felt had been there long before Tia had been born.

It had been her inability to provide Tia and the baby with the most basic of needs that had gnawed away at her until, having no other form of knowledge about how to fix her problem, she had turned to the one thing that every male she had ever known had wanted: her body.

Since she'd never had a mother to tell her that she was worth so much more, she accepted the unspoken message from the men that she encountered who, through their actions, told her that sex was the only thing she was good for or good at. And she began using it to her advantage when she turned twenty, two years after Tia's father had abandoned her while she was pregnant.

She had turned to the oldest and what she thought was the easiest way for a woman to make money. And although she hadn't done it often—only when the food supply got dangerously low—each time she offered her body for sale only proved to increase her unhappiness along with the void that was growing inside of her.

She sighed heavily as she looked up into the darkness from her cell bed. She remembered the times she'd slapped Tia around when she'd been a child and imagined she must have felt the same way she'd felt when Mavis had slapped her around. Why had that thought never occurred to her before?

She remembered the fear she'd felt toward Mavis that had eventually given way to anger. And that anger had internalized itself and made it impossible for Ida to show any outward expressions of love toward anyone—including her children.

But she could not undo what had already been done. Yesterday was gone. She only had today, and maybe, tomorrow. She closed her eyes and made a quick, silent, and unfamiliar request. It was one sentence, one plea: "Help me, Lord, help me, please," she whispered.

Chapter Twenty-eight

Mavis had been going from room to room, lifting boxes, putting down boxes, unpacking items to determine which ones she wanted to keep, and then putting them back into the box again. The strain of the day was finally starting to get to her, and she sat down at the kitchen table to rest.

Although she hadn't given Henry a time frame about when she would be out of the house, she had given herself one. And the deadline was approaching. Her plan was to be out by the end of spring.

It was now May, and she had not even begun to go apartment hunting. She had not even begun looking for a job, for that matter. What could she do that someone would be willing to pay her for? She hadn't worked since she'd married Henry, and before then, the only jobs she'd held had been entry-level, minimum wage-paying jobs. Now, at the age of fifty-four, and no skills to speak of, who would be willing to hire her, and for what?

She thought about what skills she possessed that she could use to possibly make a living. She could cook. But she couldn't see herself—didn't even want to think about herself—slaving over somebody else's stove preparing meals for other people. She could sew. But sitting in front of a sewing machine for eight hours a day did not sound enjoyable either.

She rubbed her left temple, then placed her head on the back of the chair and closed her eyes. What was she going to do? Sewing was out. Cooking was out. Cleaning? Babysitting? What else could she do?

For a few seconds she allowed herself to wonder if maybe she'd spoken too soon about leaving. She was going to look a little foolish if she couldn't back up her words with action. Henry would just love that! But she wasn't going to give him that satisfaction. Not if she could help it.

The repetitive sound of water hitting the pavement outside caused her to open her eyes. She looked out of the window and followed the quick descent of the rain down to the cement where the surrounding grass and periwinkles waited for the life-sustaining liquid.

The yard in front of the house across the street had especially welcomed the rain with its straw-colored blades of grass finally beginning to show signs of resurrection as each rainfall left it a little less bland than the day before. That house belonged to both her and Henry, and it was where Ida and her children had once lived.

After Tia had been removed from the house, and Ida sent off to prison, Henry had hired a cleaning crew to come in and had had the house cleaned and fumigated from top to bottom.

The walls had been replastered where needed, and a fresh coat of paint applied throughout. They eventually rented it out to an elderly couple who had lived there until the husband suffered a stroke and had to be hospitalized. He never regained his strength, and his wife, being too old to care for him herself, had to put him in a nursing home. A short while after that, she too suffered a stroke, but her outcome was not the same as her husband's, and she died.

Mavis had found herself, once more, standing in front of her window watching a team of paramedics carry another lifeless body out of that house. And Henry, again, called in a cleaning crew, but afterward refused to rent it out.

"Just too much dying taking place over there," he said.

And he had been quick to remind her that it wasn't like they were losing any money by not renting it out because the mortgage had been paid in full. She hadn't been able to argue with him on that point. He was right. The mortgage had been paid off shortly after the elderly couple had moved in, and all they were responsible for paying were the property taxes on it at the end of every year. Although Henry had been adamant about not renting it out, he hadn't been ready to get rid of it by selling it. So, it stood empty for the past two years.

Then it came to her. The answer to her problem. If she could live in the house, she wouldn't have to worry about finding a job so quickly. The only thing she would have to worry about would be the utilities. By the time the property taxes were due, she was sure she would have found some type of employment. And since Tia would more than likely be moving with her, she could help pay for the utilities. They might be a little cramped as far as space was concerned, but it could work.

What would Henry say? She had never mentioned anything about money to him, and, of course, he had not offered to help her in any way. He would just have to agree with her. It was the very least, the very least he could do.

The rain continued to fall as she sat revising her plan. The longer she sat, the greener the grass surrounding the empty house appeared to become. And for the first time in years, she couldn't wait for Henry to come home.

***

Tia felt overwhelmed by everything. The boxes her grandmother had packed had been sitting around the house for days. She looked around her bedroom. She was not going to start packing her things until her grandmother told her she'd found a place and given her a moving date. Then, all that she had to pack, her clothes and music, she could complete in one day. But the move was not the only thing overwhelming her.

She had received a letter from her mother—really, it was more of a note—apologizing for not writing more but she had no money to buy paper from the commissary. What she wanted to know was if Tia would come and see her again.

Tia found herself wishing her mother would just leave her alone, but the irony of her wish was that Ida *had* left her alone—for twelve years. And now, here she was, wishing for the very thing that had caused her so much pain in the first place.

She sat in the middle of her bed with her legs crossed staring at the letter. Why did everything have to be so difficult? Why was it that every time she turned around, she was faced with having to make a decision? Should she visit her mother or not? Should she forgive her? What about her grandmother? Should she try to get closer to her? And then there was still the issue of sex. To do it or not to do it. It was all getting to be too much.

She looked at the yellow sheet of paper again. Each letter had been neatly written, and she noticed how the ending of every sentence ended with a circle instead of a dot. She looked up at the ceiling. It had been a few weeks since she'd gone to see her. Maybe this second visit would be better. Her eyes returned to the letter, and she followed the words down to the end of the page. Ida had ended the note with the single word, *Mommy*.

Tia stared at the word, and then she heard it—a small voice.

"Mommy."

Barely audible, the voice spoke again.

"Mommy."

Its whisper increased in volume until she realized she, herself, was the one calling out the name. She squeezed her arms tightly and began rocking back and forth as the word passed from her mouth, repeating itself over and over. She had found the answer to one of her questions. She wanted and needed still her mommy.

Chapter Twenty-nine

"Let's go. I ain't got all day," Mavis said heading for the front door of her living room.

Tia looked at her grandmother. She didn't have anything *but* all day.

"It's Monday, Grandma. Visiting hours at the prison don't end until eight-thirty."

"Did I ask you what time the visiting hours end? Or did I say, 'Let's go'?"

Tia took a deep breath, and then answered, "You said, 'let's go.'"

"That's right. And besides, it ain't when visiting hours are over with. It's what time that charter bus pulls out of that parking lot, and it pulls out in forty minutes."

"Yes, ma'am."

"And, on top of that, it's gonna take us thirty minutes just to get to the parking lot. So let's go."

"How come Henry couldn't drop us off?"

"Because I didn't ask him to," Mavis said sharply. "I didn't need him to drop me off the last time I went to see Ida, and I don't need him to do it this time either." She hesitated. "Besides, this don't have nothing to do with Henry. This right here is between me, you, and Ida."

Tia picked up her purse. Her grandmother could have still asked him. Just because they were separating didn't mean she couldn't ask for a ride, did it? And why was her grandmother so grumpy?

She should have known the nice way she had been acting for the past few days would not last for too long. If she had known she was going to be like this, she wouldn't have even bothered asking her to come with her to see Ida again.

"I'm ready," Tia said quietly.

"And speaking of Henry," Mavis said as they headed for the door, "when I get back I got some business to take care of with him."

"What business?"

Mavis looked at Tia. "I said *I* got some business."

Tia rolled her eyes and sped up her pace. "Well, why'd you even say anything about it in the first place then?" she mumbled.

"Excuse me?" Mavis said.

"Nothing," Tia replied as she waited while Mavis locked the door, then turned the knob and pushed it to make sure it was locked.

It was the middle of the day, and the sun shone brightly. Tia put on her sunglasses as they walked to the bus stop.

"You know," she said looking straight-ahead as she walked, "you never did tell me what you and my mother talked about, Grandma."

"It don't matter," Mavis said. "What we talked about was between me and her. And when we get there today, we're just going to have a nice conversation. The three of us."

Tia looked down. *The three of us are strangers.* "Okay," she said.

They reached the bus stop. There was no bus in sight, so Mavis took a seat on the wooden bench that was partially enclosed by Plexiglas. Tia sat down next to her in an effort to calm the jittery feeling in her stomach.

They waited in silence for the city bus that would take them across town to the minimart where they would then board the charter bus for the hour-and-twenty-minute ride to the prison.

After some time, the city bus appeared, coming to a slow halt in front of the stop. As Tia took her seat, she couldn't help but wonder how many more of these trips she would be making.

They made it to the parking lot in front of the minimart on time. As they stood in line waiting to board the bus, it seemed to Tia that she had spent most of her life waiting. She remembered as a little girl waiting alone at night for her mother to come home. Then, after she was taken away and placed in a foster home, she remembered waiting to be reunited with her. Later, after going to live with her grandmother, she continued to wait, only she was getting older, and the image she had been waiting for had begun to change.

She had begun waiting for her hero, the one who would rescue her from the life she had. The one who would love her unconditionally and never leave her. And as time passed, and he too did not show up, she went searching for him only to not find him. Something was wrong. Was it with her? She didn't know. But something was wrong, and she did not know how to fix it. She stuffed her hands into her pockets and shifted her weight from one leg to the other. Why did they have to be so slow? If her grandmother hadn't been standing next to her, she knew she would have probably said out loud what she was thinking, *Can y'all hurry up?* She was fed up with waiting. Fed up with it all!

"Good afternoon," the driver said as her grandmother handed him their tickets.

"It's about time," Tia mumbled.

"What?" Mavis said.

"Nothing."

"I can't be doing this every week," Mavis said as she searched for a seat. "These tickets are kind of expensive."

For once, this was something they both agreed on. A round-trip ticket cost twenty-seven dollars and twenty cents. If they went to visit Ida once a week, it would be over one hundred dollars a month for each of them, and that was too much.

"You think she'll be getting out soon?" Tia asked.

"She should be," Mavis said. "This is her twelfth year. Maybe I'll ask her about it when we get there."

Tia let out a sigh of relief, realizing that if her mother would soon be released, she would not have to make this visit a weekly thing.

The bus driver announced that there would be another five minutes before they took off. Tia stood up and began heading toward the exit.

"Where you going?" Mavis asked.

"I'm going outside to smoke a cigarette."

"Well, don't be long. You heard what the bus driver said. Five minutes."

"I know."

She stepped off the bus and fumbled around inside the pocket of her slightly worn leather jacket. She felt the almost empty plastic package and took it out. She pulled one long cigarette from out of the container and slowly raised it to her mouth. What would happen if she didn't get back on the bus, if she just started walking away? She reached into her other pocket and found the lighter. What would she be walking away from anyway? Her past? Or would it be her future? Was this her chance to finally have what she had been waiting for all this time?

She inhaled deeply from the cigarette and noticed a woman who appeared to be not much older than her own mother coming toward her. Her clothes were wrinkled and stained, and a tattered scarf was wrapped around her head. She spoke softly as she looked at her.

"Excuse me, ma'am, I lost my bus pass, and I need some money to get home with. Do you have any change you can spare?"

Tia hesitated. Why was this woman who was clearly old enough to be her mother calling *her* ma'am? And why should she help the older woman? No one had ever helped her. Except for the time she had briefly stayed with a foster mother as a child, she could not recall anyone ever really trying to help her, and even that time period was a vague memory. She couldn't say with complete honesty that her grandmother was looking out for her well-being either, because up until recently, she had made it clear that Tia was going to have to move out when she turned eighteen.

"Nah," she said without looking at the woman, "I don't have any change."

"All I need is fifty cents or whatever you can spare."

Tia looked at her. The woman's eyes were clear and focused . . . and sad. Tia let the cigarette, still burning, dangle from between her lips as she sighed and dug deep into her pocket. She pulled out two silver coins and handed them to the older woman.

"God bless you," the woman said and turned to walk away. She turned back around just as Tia blew smoke from her cigarette out into the air. "Oh, would you be interested in buying some perfume? I got a couple of bottles right here." She unsnapped her tattered jacket and reached into one of the inside pockets. Two small glass bottles filled with a clear liquid emerged in her hand.

Tia dropped the cigarette on the ground and stepped on it. "I thought you said you needed some money for bus fare?"

"I do, but I gotta eat too, don't I? I bet you eat, don't you?"

"Yeah, I do," Tia said, rolling her eyes. "And I work, too!"

"All the more reason why you should help me out," the woman said holding her stare. Tia stared back at the woman, ready to tell her off and send her on her way, but there was an unmistakable sadness in her eyes that reminded her too much of her own mother.

"How much?" she asked.

"Fifteen dollars apiece," the woman answered. Then, before Tia could reply, she rethought her answer and said, "Ten dollars. You can have them both for ten dollars. Now *that's* a deal."

"All right," Tia said, defeated by the look in the woman's eyes. She dug down into her pocket for the second time and pulled out a ten-dollar bill.

The woman blessed her again and left.

She opened one of the small bottles and inhaled the strong, sweet fragrance. Then she stuck both of them into her purse and headed back toward the bus.

She rode in silence, taking in the scenery that spread itself out rapidly on either side of her. Miles of open fields alternated with outlet malls, weigh stations, and small restaurants. Occasionally, she would catch a glimpse of homes still under construction that were nestled within a subdivision far off from the highway.

Billboards adorned this stretch of road nearly every mile or so, advertising everything from the apple farm just a quarter of a mile up the road to the largest indoor/outdoor rummage sale in the state.

After awhile, her eyes grew weary of trying to keep up with everything passing before her. She shifted in her seat and let her eyelids close. Soon, she heard her grandmother sniff, allowing a few seconds to pass before she sniffed again.

"Are you wearing perfume?" she asked.

"Uh-uh," she answered without opening her eyes.

"You sure?"

"Not me." A few minutes passed before she remembered the two bottles of perfume she had put in her purse earlier. "Oh, yeah," she said. "I forgot I put two bottles of perfume in my purse. You probably smell that."

"What are you doing with two bottles of perfume in your purse?"

"I bought them from a lady who was outside when I got off the bus."

"You did what?"

She opened her eyes and looked at her grandmother. "I bought them from a lady who was outside when I got off the bus."

Mavis stared at her.

"What?" Tia asked.

"Girl, what's wrong with you? Don't you know better than to be buying stuff like that from strangers on the street?"

"It was a good deal. I got two for ten dollars."

"How do you know you didn't just pay ten dollars for some sweet-smelling toilet water?"

She frowned, "I don't. But do you think she might like it?"

Her grandmother raised her eyebrows in amazement. She was about to ask who *she* was when she realized Tia was talking about Ida. She didn't want to hurt her feelings, but it was the cheapest smelling perfume she had ever smelled and was probably not even worth the ten dollars she had paid for it. Still, the last thing she wanted to do was interfere with what she hoped was the beginning of a reconciliation between her daughter and granddaughter.

"Yes," she answered, "I think she will."

Tia smiled slightly as she returned her gaze to the world swiftly passing her by on the other side of the glass window.

Chapter Thirty

Tia and her grandmother arrived at the prison on time and went through the check-in process that they were both now familiar with. They were led to the same visiting room that they had each been in on separate occasions with Ida and were instructed once again by the guard to take a seat on two of the three chairs surrounding the table with its peeling vinyl edges.

There were multiple groups of chairs throughout the large room that were paired off with tables that differed from each other only to the degree of how much vinyl had been peeled away from their round edges. There were several rectangular-shaped windows in the room that Tia had not noticed during her first visit with Ida. And they sat right at ceiling level with metal bars covering all of them.

Bright lights flooded the room, and just like last time, there was a guard standing near the entrance where he was occasionally visited by a second guard.

Some of the inmates were already engrossed in conversations with their loved ones who had come to see them. Others engaged in playful activity with small children, and Tia wondered if each one of them was the mother of the child they were playing with.

Even while the women played and talked, she noticed they all held one thing in common—sadness. The kind of sadness that becomes a permanent by-product of some traumatic event or events. It was the kind of sadness that was not erased. Even after healing had taken place and amends made, it still lingered on, and the person didn't even realize that they were still sad. It was the type of sadness that she was sure she had seen in her mother's eyes as well.

As she and her grandmother sat at the table she noticed a guard escorting a small-framed woman toward them.

"Hey, Momma," Ida said exposing her crooked teeth. She gave Mavis a quick hug, and then she turned her attention to Tia. She stared at her in silence. Tia stared back until finally, Ida spoke. "How you doing?"

"I'm okay," Tia answered flatly. "How about you?"

Still smiling, Ida raised her arms slightly, and then pushed them back. "I'm here."

Tia looked around the room and wondered what she had to be smiling about. Ida waited for Tia to sit down before she took her seat. Mavis, caught off guard from the unexpected hug Ida had given her, remained standing.

"You know you can sit down, Mama," Ida said jokingly.

Mavis felt a wave of heat stretch across her face. She looked down at the empty chair. A nervous giggle passed her lips as she sat down. She cleared her throat. "So how are things going in here, Ida?"

"They're going okay. I'll be getting released in six months. Other than that, it's the same old, same old. You know."

Tia frowned. *How would Grandmother know that? She's never been in prison.*

"You're getting released in six months?" Mavis's eyes sparkled.

Ida nodded her head. "Yep," she said as she stretched both of her arms out and smiled. "In six months I'll be a free bird."

"That's wonderful, Ida." Mavis looked down at her own hands resting in her lap. "And if you need a place to stay . . ."

"We can talk about that later," Ida said quickly. "There's still time."

Mavis turned sideways to look at her granddaughter. "Tia brought you a present," she said, "but they wouldn't let her bring it in with her."

"Oh yeah? What is it?"

Tia could feel them looking at her as she studied the cracked pattern on the gray and white tile floor beneath her shoes. The palms of her hands were getting moist.

"Tell her what it is, Tia," her grandmother was saying.

She shifted in her seat. "Just some perfume."

"Just some perfume?" Ida said. "I would ask what kind, but it's been so long since I had any perfume. Even if you tell me, I probably won't know who you talking about." She was smiling again. Had she ever stopped since they'd gotten there?

"Well, you know, it ain't nothing special," Tia said, letting her voice trail off.

"It's special to me," Ida affirmed. "And if they let me, I'ma wear it until it's all gone. Thank you."

"You're welcome." She wanted to reach over and hug her mother right where she sat, right then and there. But something held her tightly in her seat, kept her glued to it.

Mavis watched the two of them as the spark of reconciliation tried to become ignited. Her eyes grew misty, but she did not want to cry. She had her own news to tell.

"I'll be moving pretty soon," Mavis said.

"Oh yeah? Where y'all moving to, Mama?"

"*I'm* planning on moving into the house across the street. You know, the one you used to live in."

"Oh really? Why you trying to do that? And why'd you say, *I'm*? Henry ain't moving with you?"

"Because it's empty, and been empty for a while. And since I need a place to stay, I may as well stay there. And no, Henry is not moving with me."

Tia pressed her lips together and began chewing on the inside flesh. So that was her grandmother's plan.

"How come Henry ain't moving with you?" Ida asked. "Y'all getting a divorce or something?"

"I ain't said nothing about no divorce, but I am moving out. I just pray I can get him to let me stay there."

"What you mean *let* you?" Ida straightened her posture. "You his wife, so that property is as much yours as it is his."

"That's true," Mavis said thoughtfully.

"So why y'all gettin' a divorce?" Ida repeated.

"I didn't say we were getting a divorce. I said I was moving out."

"Why?" Ida pushed the question. She shifted in her seat. Did it have anything to do with that stupid letter she'd sent her mother years ago telling her to tell Henry she was sorry about the baby? How could she have been so hateful? Vengeful! That's what she had been feeling at the time, but the truth was that she really didn't know who the baby's father had been. She'd simply implied that Henry was the father just to spite Mavis. Now, here Mavis sat telling Ida she was leaving him, and Ida prayed it was not because of the letter she'd sent.

"It's just time," Mavis said. "It's been time . . . for a long time."

Ida sighed. "What did he say about it?"

"Nothing. He couldn't care less. We ain't had no real marriage in a long, long time."

Tia just listened. So she would be moving back into the house where everything had begun. The house where her mother had left her. The house where her baby brother had died. That house, with all its awful memories of hunger, pain, roaches . . . Her heartbeat quickened.

She wanted to tell her grandmother that living there would not work. She wanted to tell her to find another house. What was her grandmother thinking? But Mavis had just finished explaining what she was thinking, hadn't she? So Tia just sat there, sweaty palms and all, trying not to show the fear that had crept into her heart. She was oblivious to her name being called.

"Tia!" Mavis was saying. "What's wrong with you, girl?"

"Huh?"

"Didn't you hear your mother?"

She wiped her hands on her pants. "Oh, nah. I must'a been daydreaming."

"Daydreaming!" Mavis rolled her eyes at her.

"Leave her alone, Mama," Ida said. "She probably was daydreaming about some boy."

"Boy?" Tia said rolling her eyes. She was about to tell her that she didn't deal with boys her own age because they were too silly and immature. She was going to tell her that when she did deal with guys, they were always much older than her, and then she realized that her mother wouldn't know that because she didn't know *her*. And besides all of that, her grandmother was sitting right there and would not like what she heard.

"You don't have a boyfriend, Tia?" Ida was asking.

"Nope."

Ida looked at Mavis whose only expression was two raised eyebrows.

"Well, keep it that way. Ain't no rush. Men, boys, whatever." She waved her hands in the air. "They gon' always be here. They ain't going nowhere. And most of them don't even know it. You'll see."

She smiled slightly. She *had* seen, and she would have told her so if it had only been the two of them. But it was her grandmother that she had to go home with, and so she kept that information to herself.

She was her mother's child. Tia was slowly accepting this fact. Why? Because she wanted to, needed to. She was eighteen years old, and she could not say that she had ever experienced a true mother-daughter relationship. The time for that had passed, and they had both missed out on it. What she and her mother were establishing now was more like a friendship, and it was all that she had. She was going to take it. She had to.

She didn't know how Mavis felt about her relationship with Ida, but she must have felt something because ever since that first visit, she had changed, become softer somehow . . . well, some of the time. But there was definitely a noticeable change.

They sat in the visiting room a little while longer talking about how Ida spent her days within the confinement of the prison walls. They talked about minor news events while Ida systematically shot glances at Tia throughout the entire conversation. It seemed as though she followed every move Tia made. If she raised her hand to scratch the side of her face, Ida's eyes traveled with the hand right up to the very spot where it scratched. If she turned her head to look at the toddler sitting next to them, crying to be held by his mother, Ida's head turned in that direction as well.

The lights flickered for a few seconds, signaling the end of the visitation period. The small glint of something that had been in Ida's eyes faded as the flickering lights went back to being one steady stream of brightness. Everyone began standing. Ida hugged her mother first, this time with more intensity than at the beginning of their meeting. And this time, Mavis hugged her back, not wanting to let her go. But Mavis knew there was someone else in the room who needed hugging as well, and so she released Ida, who walked around the table toward Tia.

Tia stood with her arms hanging at her sides. Her legs had developed a will of their own and would not allow her to take a step forward in order to meet Ida halfway. Her arms, paralyzed where they hung, would not raise and place themselves around Ida's waist. So, she just stood there, unable to move, feeling the unmistakable transfer of emotions from her mother's hug flowing into her.

She could not deny that it felt good. Awkward but good. And so, she struggled with the battle between herself and her arms, and at the last minute, as Ida began releasing her hold, taking back her emotional energy, Tia overcame her battle and placed her arms around the bony prominence of her mother's hips. It was all she could do. But it was enough.

All other movement seemed to stop as the two held onto each other. She became deaf to the sounds around her, blind to the lights. She was in a different place, a place where the rapid beating of her heart and the spinning sensation in her head were *good* feelings. She whispered words of love that only her mind heard. Then it was over.

"Come back and see me, okay?" Ida whispered.

"I will," she said, then added softly, so softly that she almost did not hear it herself, "Mama."

They left the prison in silence and rode the bus home the same way. Tia relived every second of the visit, adding or deleting certain segments that, in turn, altered the remainder of her memory.

But one part stayed the same, and she closed her eyes each time she got to it—the part where she and Ida embraced. It felt just like it should feel . . . or at least how she imagined it would feel for a mother and daughter to hug each other.

Mavis was satisfied with their visit, convinced she had done the right thing. She thought about how and when she would present her plea—well, it wasn't really a plea because she wasn't about to beg Henry for anything—regarding her desire to move into the house, *their* house, across the street.

And when she had moved in, and Ida was released, Mavis would invite her to stay with her until Ida could get back on her feet again. That house, with its old memories, would have no effect on them, now or then. They would be starting fresh, and there would be no desire to relive any of the past events. God would see to that.

She looked at her grandchild sitting next to her. Her eyes were closed as though she was asleep, and Mavis smiled. At that moment, she felt something that she couldn't say she had honestly felt in a long time. For once, Mavis felt happy.

Love had gotten to Ida. Plain and simple. It had bypassed its way around the cold, gray steel of the prison bars, drilled a hole through the wall of protection she had built around her heart, and had gotten to her. It was an emotion that she was not used to and had not easily embraced for a long time.

For twelve years she had not allowed herself to feel anything for her daughter. In her mind, the pain would have been too great. Feeling nothing at all was better than feeling something for someone she did not have, could not see, and who maybe didn't even want to see her.

Now, by the grace of God, it had happened. On this day in the visiting room with her daughter, in that moment of embrace, a lifetime of repressed feelings had taken hold of her. And she did not want it to let her go. She was scheduled to be released in six months, and for the first time, she was looking forward to it.

Belinda looked up as she entered the small cell. "Had a good visit, huh?"

"Yep. It was nice." Ida smiled her crooked smile.

"Yeah, I can tell."

She snickered. "How can you tell?"

"Because you got that silly grin on your face. But it's cool."

"I'm glad you like it," Ida said as she stretched out on her bunk. "My daughter came back again with my mother."

"How she doing?"

"She doing good, I guess. At least she looks like she doing good. Kind of quiet. But I guess I'd be kind of quiet too if I was visiting my mother in prison after not seeing her for years." The crease in her forehead deepened. "Come to think of it, that *is* what I'm doing. Only I'm on the other side of the wall."

"Is she gonna come back?"

"She said she was."

"I guess that means you'll stop biting your nails now, huh?"

"Don't start," she said as she closed her eyes, still smiling.

Chapter Thirty-one

Henry woke up from his nap and came downstairs. He stood in the middle of the dining-room floor surveying the boxes strewn about. Where was his wife planning on moving to? She didn't have a job and no money that he knew of.

A small smile crept across his face; it was a smile of victory, of having conquered something. But what had he conquered? The smile faded. Where was the victory in having his wife tell him that she didn't want to be his wife anymore? He shrugged. She still didn't have a job and no way to support herself. And he was sure not going to take care of her. If she left, she would be on her own. And then his smile returned because he knew she wasn't going to go anywhere. How could she? She had nowhere to go.

It was then that he realized he didn't have anything to worry about—not that he had ever been worried in the first place, but if he had, he could put all of that to rest. He didn't care if she did have boxes stacked up all over the place. The bottom line was that she had no place to go.

He kicked one of the boxes aside as he made his way to the window. Where was she anyway? His stomach rumbled as he turned to make his way to the kitchen. There was nothing cooked and waiting for him on the stove this time. He grabbed an unopened package of saltine crackers, a few slices of bologna from the refrigerator, and sat down to eat his meal.

He hadn't been sleeping well lately and had resorted to taking over-the-counter sleep aids on a regular basis. But they had little effect. When he did fall asleep, he could still feel himself tossing and turning, and he was always aware of the empty space beside him where Mavis used to lay. It was not a restful sleep. Daytime fatigue had begun to interfere with his responsibilities as a pastor. And today was a perfect example of that. He'd found it impossible to concentrate on writing his next sermon or focus on any other matters at the church because he had just been too sleepy. He had to come home and take a nap. There was just no getting around it. It had done him some good, but he still did not feel completely rejuvenated.

He put the last piece of bologna on top of the cracker and stuffed the whole thing into his mouth. After that, he stood up and immediately felt light-headed. He sat back down, and after a few minutes had passed, he rose again. If this light-headedness and lack of sleep continued, he would have to pay a visit to the doctor.

Slowly he made his way through the house, past the boxes, and back upstairs to his bedroom. He was just about to drift off to sleep when he heard the front door close, and then the sound of footsteps on the stairs. He heard Tia's bedroom door close, and then moments later, heard someone moving around in the kitchen. He got out of bed and went downstairs.

Mavis stood vigorously wiping the crumbs from the crackers he'd eaten off the kitchen table. She shook the crumbs from the dishcloth into the kitchen sink, and then threw the empty package of bologna that he'd left on the counter into the wastebasket. He waited for her to turn around, but she continued to busy herself, keeping her back to him.

"Hey, where've you been?"

The sound of his voice startled her. She hadn't heard him come in. How long had he been standing behind her?

"We went to visit Ida."

"Oh yeah?"

"Yeah."

"And?"

"And what?" He had begun to irritate her already.

Henry sighed. This is how it had always been with Mavis. She volunteering little, him pulling and tugging for whatever he could get. "How is she?"

"She's doing all right, all things considered. She'll be getting released in October."

He stood silent, waiting.

Mavis was waiting too. She was waiting for the rapid beating of her heart to slow down. Why was she so nervous anyway? That house across the street was as much hers as it was his. She stalled for time.

"When did you come in anyway? I didn't hear you."

"I've been here. I was upstairs taking a nap."

She took a deep breath. "Listen, Henry, I've been thinking. That house, *our* house across the street has been empty for a while now. It's just sitting there and . . ."

"And you want to move into it, right?"

She stopped wiping the already dry countertop and turned to look at him. He stood emotionless next to her, and she felt sorry for him though she did not know why. "Yes," she answered. "I want to move into it and take Tia with me."

"Well, what's the point of moving right across the street? You may as well stay right here if that's the case."

"Henry, don't start . . ."

"Look, Mavis, we've been together for twenty-four years. What's the point of leaving now?"

"Because I'm not happy, Henry. And I haven't been for a long time. I told you that."

"Yeah. You told me that *after* you'd already made up your mind to leave. How come you didn't tell me that sooner?" His eyes were bulging. "How come you didn't tell me that when you first started feeling that way?" His emotions began to escalate. "That's your problem, Mavis. You hold everything in. And I mean *everything!*"

"Look, Henry . . ." The last thing she wanted was a shouting match between the two of them. She felt her emotions rising inside of her as well and slowly paced her words. "I'm not gonna go over all of this with you again!"

And just like that, he had been diffused, dismissed, defeated. Her calm, emotionless demeanor had shut him down again. A few minutes passed before he spoke, this time in a lower tone. "So you think moving across the street will make you happy?"

She gave the countertop one last wipe, then folded the dishcloth in half and draped it over the faucet. "It's a start," she said.

"A start to what?"

"A start to a better life. For me, and maybe even for you."

"Instead of trying to tell me what kind of life I need, maybe you should have been trying to be a better wife!"

She felt a slight piercing in her heart. "Henry," she said quietly, "you and I both know that there were some problems in our marriage. So, I'm not going to take all the blame for this."

"So you don't love me anymore, right?"

"No, I don't." It was easier to agree with him than to admit that there was still some confusion in her heart.

He turned and headed for the front door.

"The house is as much mine as it is yours," she said to his back.

He didn't answer as he closed the door behind him. She watched him walk out. He had to have seen this day coming, *should* have seen it coming, and he could have done something to prevent it just as much as he said she could have. But he hadn't.

He'd chosen to do what he'd done, and she'd made her choices. And she'd heard her husband quote the words of Jesus Christ in the book of Matthew 12:25 many times: "Jesus knew their thoughts and said unto them, 'Every kingdom divided against itself will be ruined, and every city or household divided against itself will not stand.'"

She sighed as she thought about the ending of that verse: *a household divided . . . will not stand.*

Henry didn't know why he went outside. He knew he was tired, more so now than he had been earlier. His whole body felt heavy, as if there was some load resting heavily on his shoulders. He stood on the front porch trying to decide if he should return to the house or head for his car.

He fumbled around in his pants pockets and realized he didn't have the keys to the car. He stood looking at the house across the street until he had convinced himself that it probably would be a good idea for Mavis to live there. She hadn't lived alone in twenty-four years, and this way, he could still keep an eye on her and make sure that she was safe.

He crossed the street to do a close-up inspection of the house. The orange glow from the setting sun made it look warm and inviting. And even though it had gone through another cold, harsh winter, everything was still intact, and there was no peeling paint or loose roof shingles that he could see.

He would have to check the gutters and make sure they were not clogged with any fallen twigs or wind-blown leaves though. He knew the damage clogged gutters could do if they were not repaired, and he did not want to have to deal with any rotting wood issues, cracks in the foundation, or worse, a leaky roof.

The newly appearing grass surrounding the front and back of the house seemed to Henry much more vibrant than that covering the lawns of his neighbors, and he marveled at the fact that not even the coldest, harshest temperatures could permanently subdue the life that had been created by God. He decided that it would not subdue him either.

He knew he couldn't hold on to Mavis. The fact of the matter was that he had never really tried to. She had been his wife, mainly in name only, and on those rare nights when no one else had been available, he would come to her and, after much prodding, she would allow him to relieve his tension as she lay stone-cold in the bed.

The more she became disengaged sexually, the less he desired her until it got to the point where he stopped coming to her at all. And when Ida was not available, he would just find someone else to satisfy himself with.

It wasn't that he hadn't loved her. He had. And he knew he should not have done the things he'd done. He'd studied and preached the Word of God every Sunday and knew better than anyone just how wrong he had been. Still, he was only human. And had she paid attention to that little fact, she would not have neglected him the way she had. A woman just can't do a man like that!

He rationalized that she should have known better. She should have known that to neglect the physical needs of her husband was just as good as forcing him to commit adultery. So, in his mind, she was just as guilty as he was.

He headed back across the street, remembering how tired he felt. All he wanted to do was go to sleep. If she wanted to move into the house, so be it. He was through with it . . . and her.

Mavis heard the front door open and shut. She looked out from the kitchen and saw Henry making his way toward the stairs.

"It's yours," he said without looking at her.

She smiled as she watched him climb the stairs. God is good. He had made a new beginning possible for Mavis that not only included Henry agreeing to her request, but had also allowed her, Ida, and Tia to take the first steps that would lead them, she hoped, to an emotional freedom.

Although no one had actually said the words "I forgive you," Mavis felt like she had been forgiven. They had been able to embrace one another after so many years of nothing, and that was a start.

She knew in her heart that God had heard her prayer that night in the easy chair, and He had forgiven her. And she knew something else as well. She knew that in order to be forgiven, she too must forgive. And her forgiveness would have to extend to Henry.

She watched him climb the stairs. His steps were slow and heavy, but with each step he took, she felt her own burden growing lighter and lighter until it was almost nonexistent.

Tia sat on the side of her bed still replaying the visit she'd had earlier with Ida. She could not deny how warm, and free, and good she'd felt in the arms of her mother. She needed more of that feeling, and that was why she had made the promise to return. Everybody deserved a second chance. She would give her one.

She'd heard her grandmother and Henry arguing downstairs. His voice loud, her grandmother's restrained. Now, she heard Henry's heavy footsteps coming up the stairs. Her door was halfway open, and she saw his medium-sized frame slowly pass by. Then she heard his bedroom door slam shut.

The restrained tone she'd heard her grandmother using with him downstairs was just like something she'd do. Even in an argument, Mavis maintained all control. Maybe if she would have just yelled once, just showed some kind of emotion, things would have been different all the way around. Maybe.

She thought about her grandmother's plan to move into the house across the street. There had been no relationship between the two of them back then, and now, just like then, her grandmother had no idea of what had gone on in that house when she and her baby brother had lived there with Ida. Her heartbeat quickened as she recalled the hits, slaps, and items that had been thrown at her . . . not to mention the countless days of hunger.

"Help me, Lord," she heard herself whisper.

She closed her eyes and thought about her mother. Ida's twelve-year absence from her life outweighed the few years of abuse she'd endured when she'd lived with her. Tia believed her to be a changed person now. But she would never know that for sure if she didn't give her another chance.

What had that pamphlet said about God? That He gave second chances? That He would forgive us if we came to Him and asked Him to? The beating of her heart returned to its normal rate, its rhythm strong and steady. She would see her mother again. Soon. And with God's help, she would try her best to forgive her.

Chapter Thirty-two

Tia awoke to the sounds of a new day. She got out of bed and walked over to the window, listening as the birds chirped out their calling to acknowledge the beauty of another spring morning. Peering through the curtains, she could see the golden hue of the sun just above the horizon, its light radiating across the sky.

She opened the window completely and inhaled the fresh scent of spring as an early morning breeze sifted through the screen. Although it was moving day, her soul felt as light as the breeze that had just carried itself into her room. She was thankful.

Everything that needed to be packed had been and was now lined up neatly by the front door downstairs. Henry had hired two men to move all of the heavy pieces of furniture—a bedroom set, sofa-sleeper, a recliner, a thirty-two-inch television set, and the kitchen table and chairs—across the street.

Since Henry seldom cooked, he had no real need for the kitchen set, but he had become accustomed to preparing his sermons at the dining-room table. So, it had been decided that he could keep that particular piece of furniture and do both—prepare his sermons and eat—at that table. Besides, the house they were moving into was much smaller, and the kitchen was not big enough to fit a table of that size.

Tia took a quick shower and brushed her teeth. She put on a tee shirt and a pair of sweatpants she'd left unpacked the day before and headed downstairs thinking of the new beginning this would be.

She had rekindled a relationship with her mother, felt just a little bit closer to her grandmother, and maybe someday somewhere she would fall, trip, stumble . . . or whatever, into that other kind of love that she was still waiting for. Maybe it would stumble into her. But she didn't want to think about that now. Today was moving day.

"Soup's on!" Mavis sang out to her as she entered the kitchen.

"Soup?" Tia asked.

"Well, that's just a figure of speech. I managed to find a pot so I cooked some oatmeal."

"Oh," Tia said looking at her sideways. Was she mistaken, or was this the most cheerful she had ever known her grandmother to be?

"This'll be the last time I cook anything in this house," she said still smiling.

"Sure will." Tia looked around and noticed some of the boxes missing from the front door. "Where's Henry?"

"He went over already. I guess he wanted to get an early start."

"Eager, huh?"

Mavis shrugged her shoulders as she placed a bowl of oatmeal before Tia. The steam rose slowly upward like a tornado in reverse.

"Eat," she said. "You're gonna need all your strength today. We got a lot of work to do. And while you're eating, I'm gonna take a few of those boxes over."

"Okay," she said before gently blowing on a spoonful of oatmeal, and then placing it into her mouth. Just then, her phone rang.

"Hello?"

"Hey, girl, what's up?" The voice on the other end bid its familiar greeting. It was Monica.

"Nothing. Just eating some oatmeal."

"Oatmeal?"

"Yes . . ." she hesitated. "You do know what oatmeal is, right?"

"Ha-ha," Monica mimicked. "As a matter of fact, I do. That's that slimy stuff that sticks to your tongue even after you swallow it, right?"

Tia sighed. *Why does she always have to relate everything to sex?* "Get your mind out of the gutter," she said.

"What? I'm serious. It *is* slimy, and it *does* stick to your tongue. I don't know what you're talking about, but I'm talking about oatmeal."

"Yeah, okay."

"Maybe you need to get *your* mind out of the gutter. But I guess if you ain't had none in a while you can't help but go there from time to time, huh?"

"You know what, Monica? I gotta go. It's moving day, remember?"

"Oh yeah. Where's your grandma?"

"She took a couple of boxes over already. I'm gonna start as soon as I finish eating. And my slimy oatmeal, as you put it, is getting cold, so I'll talk to you later."

"Yeah. Nothing worse than cold oatmeal. Then it *really* gets sticky."

"Bye, Monica."

"Bye."

Tia hung up the phone, slightly annoyed by the conversation. The oatmeal still held some of its warmth, but the tornado-like steam had disappeared. As she finished eating it she wondered if maybe it *was* her mind that had been in the gutter, and maybe Monica's comments had really been about nothing more than oatmeal.

She quickly dismissed the thought. There was no point in thinking about something that she did not have the answer to. But it continued to linger in her mind until she heard her grandmother calling her.

"Tia! Are you done eating? I need some help!"

"I'm coming!" she yelled back.

The fact that they were only moving across the street made the move a little easier. They had to make countless trips back and forth, but still, it hadn't been so bad. It had not gone unnoticed by Tia how Henry had seldom made eye contact with either one of them throughout the move. She had lived under the same roof with him for twelve years, and although they had never grown close to each other, she almost felt sorry for him on this day.

It had also not gone unnoticed how this move had seemed to transform her grandmother into someone whose smiles now appeared more frequently, and every word out of her mouth was no longer laced with sarcasm or disapproval. When had she first noticed this change in her personality?

After a few minutes, she realized the change had begun after her first visit with Ida and had continued right on up to this day. There was a lightness to her grandmother that had not been there before. Almost as if she had been set free from something that had been holding her down. Tia was glad for the change because that would make it much easier to live with her in the small space that they both would soon be occupying. She picked up another box to take over to the new house. *Thank God for freedom.* Or whoever was responsible for this change in her grandmother.

***

Mavis thought about scriptures as she busied herself with the move, placing each box in whichever room the letters indicated it should go. She thought about one scripture in particular and what God had said: *"I will repay you for the years the locust have eaten—the great locust and the young locust, the other locusts and the locust swarm—my great army that I sent among you"* Joel 2:25.

She remembered once hearing a preacher say that if something of value was not protected in the first generation, it would be neglected in the second generation, and completely rejected in the third generation. That was the case in her life. The damage had been done, and she was not the only one with wasted years. She was not the only one in need of a reversal. Each generation after her would inadvertently inherit the same loveless trait. The trait of detachment.

But now, all those wasted years of her being unable to love or truly care about anyone else were slowly being reversed. Praise God! Through her, He was proving His Word to be true.

It was late afternoon when Tia brought in the last box. It was marked with a "K," and she set it down in the kitchen. She stood for a moment at the window, vaguely remembering the bassinet that had sat in that same spot years ago. She tried to remember her brother's face, but she could not. She stood at the entrance that led from the kitchen into the living room.

The image of her mother throwing the bottle of soda toward her, the sound of it smashing against the wall and the feel of the sticky liquid running down her face came rushing back into her memory. She walked into the room. There was no evidence of soda stains on any of the walls. Everything had been given a fresh coat of white paint, and the room had a bright and clean look about it.

As she made her way to the bathroom, she remembered the dingy walls with the peeling paint and the toilet seat that always moved whenever she sat on it. Then she remembered the mouse and hesitated while she did a quick inspection of all the corners and baseboards of the small room.

She tiptoed in and was surprised once again to see how bright and clean everything was. There was no peeling paint, and the toilet seat maintained its position as she firmly gave it a nudge. The cabinet and sink had been replaced, and a matching vanity had been added. This was not the same flat that she had spent the first six years of her life in. Nothing was the same. And again, she thanked God for the changes.

Chapter Thirty-three

Henry thought about what he would do that evening. The moving had all been completed, and now he was in his house alone. He had another sermon to preach tomorrow, but his mind was in no condition to concentrate.

Every Sunday it was the same thing: one sermon after the other. And was anyone really listening? Was anyone really trying to follow the doctrine that he preached? Was he? He stopped short because he already knew the answer to his question. He didn't want to dwell on his wrongdoing. His marriage was ending, *had* ended, and that was that. He was not going to allow himself to dwell on it.

He walked into the kitchen, then walked back out and stood in the center of the dining room. From the window he could see that the lights were on in the house across the street. He wondered what Mavis was doing at that very moment. He rubbed the top of his receding hairline and thought about going to bed until his stomach began to growl, reminding him that he hadn't eaten anything all day.

He went back into the kitchen and opened the refrigerator door. There was nothing quick and easy that he could cook. He opened the freezer and found an assortment of uncooked packaged meats and vegetables, but nothing he could throw in the microwave for a quick meal. He sighed as he closed the door. He returned to the dining room and sat down at the table.

The silence was loud. He thought he saw something move from the corner of his eye, but when he turned his head, nothing was there. His stomach growled again, and he made a third trip to the kitchen, this time pulling out a package of sausage links from the freezer and placing them in the refrigerator. Hopefully they would be thawed out by the morning. Finally, he made his way up the stairs to his bedroom.

He stopped as he got to the bathroom and went in. He saw the container as soon as he opened the medicine cabinet; it held ten small pills that promised sleep to those who took them. Usually, he only took one, but tonight, he decided that two would be better. He swallowed them without water and placed the cap back on the bottle.

Now he would be able to enjoy the luxury of sleep like everybody else. And when he woke up in the morning he would make himself something to eat, and then work on his next sermon. Life goes on. As he lay his head down on his pillow, a scripture entered into his thoughts: *"Whoever pursues righteousness and love finds life, prosperity and honor"* (Proverbs 21:21).

But what do you find if you don't follow after righteousness? He knew what God said about that too.

"The acts of the flesh are obvious: sexual immorality, impurity and debauchery; idolatry and witchcraft; hatred, discord, jealousy, fits of rage, selfish ambition, dissensions, factions and envy; drunkenness, orgies, and the like. I warn you, as I did before, that those who live like this will not inherit the kingdom of God" (Galatians 5:19–21).

And he decided that his next sermon would be titled, "You reap what you sow."

***

Mavis went to the living-room window and looked out. Her gaze traveled to, and stayed on, the house across the street. She had seen the bathroom light go on, and a few seconds later, it went off. Almost immediately following, a light in the bedroom—the one she and Henry had once shared—came on. Minutes later, it too went off. She knew he was probably hungry, and she wondered if he had eaten or had just gone to bed hungry. In all the years they'd been together, she'd never known him to cook. Yes, he might have fried up some bacon or sausage and maybe some eggs, but that had been it; nothing too complicated. She sighed and closed the curtains. Maybe she would go over and cook a nice meal for him tomorrow. That was the least she could do.

She turned to survey the small living room. Her chair had been placed in one of the corners so that she could have a full view of the television set when she sat down. She looked at the bare walls and thought about what she could hang just above the sofa-sleeper to make the room look more lived in. The smallness of the flat was a far cry from where she had spent the last twenty-four years, but it allowed her enough space to come to terms with all that was going on in her life.

"I'm hungry," Tia's voice from behind caused Mavis to turn quickly.

"Girl, don't scare me like that!"

"Sorry. But I'm hungry. What are we gonna eat?"

"I know you don't think I'm gonna cook after all of this moving?"

"No." She hesitated. "But what are we gonna eat?"

Mavis was silent for a few seconds. "Do you want to go get some chicken?"

"That'll work."

"Here," Mavis pointed toward the sofa-sleeper, "hand me my purse."

"I'll pay for it, Grandma."

"Well," Mavis stared at her, "big spender, huh?"

Tia snorted as she headed for the door. "Not hardly."

The door closed behind Tia and immediately silence took over. For once, it was not a forced or unnatural silence. It was not the kind of silence produced from having too many unresolved issues, too many resentments left unaddressed until they began to pile one on top of the other until all Mavis could do was be quiet. No, this silence was just the opposite, and she welcomed it.

"Thank you, Lord," she whispered.

Chapter Thirty-four

Tia stepped off the front porch and remembered how she had stepped off that porch twelve years ago when the policemen had come, and the social worker had held her hand as she'd led her out of the house into a waiting car. She remembered how afraid and unsure she'd felt, afraid of the darkness that had engulfed her as the car had slowly driven off, taking her to an unknown destination.

Now, making her way down the steps, there was no fear of the dark, and she was not thinking of the future. At that moment, she was only thinking of her hunger and of satisfying it. She smiled slightly. It was funny how things went sometimes.

The restaurant was only two blocks away, and although she was tired, it felt good to be out walking in the fresh evening air. She almost felt like whistling, and that reminded her of Henry. She turned to look back at the house and wondered if he was whistling now. The harsh sound of a car horn forced her to turn quickly.

"Hey, girl." It was Monica. "Where you walking to?"

"Why'd you have to blow your horn so loud? You scared me!"

"I know," she said laughing. "I thought you were gonna jump off the sidewalk. I would've turned it down, but then I remembered this horn don't have a volume level!"

"Humph."

"Where you going?"

"Just around the corner to get some chicken."

"Oh, I'm just in time then, huh?" She pulled up to the curb and reached over to unlock the passenger door. "Get in."

Tia hesitated. She had been looking forward to the short walk.

"Get in," Monica said again. "What? You think I'm gon' eat up all the chicken?"

Tia smiled as she slid into the passenger seat. "Nah, I ain't worried about that. I was just looking forward to the walk. It feels good out here."

"Well, you can walk tomorrow. And roll your window down if you want some air."

The breeze created from the moving car felt good brushing against Tia's face. "I see you got your mama's car again, huh?"

"Yep."

Tia closed her eyes and inhaled the fresh air.

"So what's up?" Monica asked.

"Nothing. We just finished moving in, and it's time to eat. You know what I mean?"

"Uh-huh. How did everything go? The move, I mean."

"It went fine. He even helped us."

"Oh really!"

"Yep."

"You think your grandmother is gonna be happier now?"

"She acts like it, but I guess we'll just have to wait and see."

As Monica pulled into the restaurant's parking lot, the red and white sign shone brightly, advertising the latest deals on various parts of chicken. She steered the car into a parking space and turned it off. "You know the music festival is coming in June, right?"

"Oh yeah, that's right."

Tia had been looking forward to this event since the beginning of the year. It was an annual festival that came to the city to kick off the beginning of summer. There were going to be a variety of musical groups performing on different stages, at different times. Some of the groups were well known. Others were local bands trying to establish a name for themselves. The first festival had been so successful that this would now be the third year it was returning.

"One more month."

"That's right," Monica confirmed.

"So, we're going, right?"

"Duh! Why do you think I'm telling you?"

Tia got out of the car. "I'm just making sure," she said closing the car door. She looked at her friend and realized it had been months since she had been on a date—since she had *told* her about a date—with anyone.

Monica was pretty by most men's standards. She had a small almond-shaped face with big baby eyes that made her look like a doll. She kept her hair short, and the shorter it was the more naturally curly it became. The cut suited her face, and her weight was proportionate to her short height.

"Why are you looking at me like that?"

"I was just wondering," Tia began, "why you haven't mentioned a guy to me in a while. I mean, I know I told you *I* didn't wanna hear about no more men, but what about you? When's the last time you been on a date?"

"Date?" Monica frowned. "What's that?"

Tia smiled. "I hear you. But what happened to finding Mr. Perfect? Mr. He-gotta-be-all-that?"

"He ain't all that, and I stopped looking," she hesitated, "for now."

"Okay."

"I'm serious. I'm trying to get my education so I can move on up and out of here." She tossed the car keys up into the air. "Ain't no men in this city."

"I don't know about that."

"I know. Trust me."

"Okay."

As they stepped into the restaurant, the aroma of frying chicken greeted them. There were several customers in line ahead of them, and that gave them time to survey the menu.

"How many pieces are you gonna eat?" Tia asked Monica.

"Just get a ten-piece." Monica answered.

"Is that gonna be enough for all three of us? Remember, my grandma is eating too." Monica said.

"That should be enough. I'll go half on it."

"Humph," Tia giggled, "since you going half, can I get some fries with that?"

"Nope, but you can get a biscuit."

"You're cheap."

"Not anymore." She cut her eyes at Tia and watched as it took her a few seconds to catch her real meaning. Then, in unison, they laughed again.

As Tia waited for the clerk to take their order, her mind went back to the festival. She needed to hear some good music and just have fun. She rubbed her shoulder. *Who knows what else can happen?* She might even meet a nice man there.

As if she was reading her mind, Monica turned and said, "I hope they have some nice men, I mean acts, at the festival."

"Me too," Tia said smiling.

Chapter Thirty-five

Tia didn't like flipping burgers, taking orders, and cleaning anymore. It was time for a change. Working in a restaurant just wasn't going to cut it any longer. She had been communicating regularly with Ida through letters and visits, and it was Ida who had suggested that Tia think about what it was she really wanted to do, and then go about doing it. But that was the hard part.

She didn't exactly know what it was that she wanted to do. She knew what she *didn't* want to do, and that was flipping burgers. She liked nature and being close to Lake Michigan. She liked being surrounded by grass, trees, and flowers. How could she take all of that and turn it into a career? She asked her mother this question as they sat across from each other during visiting day at the prison.

"You like flowers and nature, huh?"

"Uh-huh."

"Well, they're pretty," Ida said, tapping her slender fingers against the table.

"Yeah, but what can I do with that?"

Ida was silent for a few minutes. "Well, let's see. Flowers got to be grown; then they get cut, and some of them end up in a flower shop for sale."

"Oh, you mean like a florist."

"Yeah. So maybe you could be the one to sell them."

"Or grow them."

"That too."

"I think I need to go to school if I want to grow them. I don't know the first thing about growing flowers."

"Did you talk to your grandma? She might know."

"No, I didn't. But you're right. She might know."

"It's a start."

Tia smiled. She was feeling better already. She ran her hand across her face. She could almost believe that there really was something better out there for her, waiting just for her.

She looked at her mother's face. It was beginning to show signs of aging. The half-moon circles under her eyes seemed to be just a little bit darker each time she came to visit. Her eyes still held a certain sadness in them, yet somehow, they were able to hold a small spark as well. She had grown to love the tiny light in her mother's eyes, and she looked for it every time they visited. Somehow, it gave her hope.

She reached across the table for her mother's hands and glanced down at the table as she whispered, "Thanks, Ma."

"For what?" Ida wondered. *For all the pain I caused you over the years by first neglecting you, and then getting myself locked up and you taken away from me?*

Tia stumbled over her words. "You know, for . . . just talking to me and, you know . . . giving me advice."

Something I should have been doing all along. "Believe me, if I wasn't in here, I'd be doing a whole lot more for you," Ida said wistfully, and her eyes became moist, too moist for her liking.

Tia squeezed her hands. "I know you would."

"I'm sorry."

"I forgive you," Tia said. "Now, you can forgive yourself."

Ida quickly wiped each eye with the back of her index finger. "That's the hardest part," she said smiling sadly. "But I'm learning."

Her eyes lit up again. "There's this group of Christians that come in once a month. I can't remember the name of the church that they from, but I'll find out next time. Anyway, they come in and talk to us, and we have Bible Study. And the Bible says that if we admit that we're sinners, repent, and accept Jesus Christ into our life, we can ask God to forgive us, and He will."

"What's repent?"

"Okay, let me think for a minute." Ida looked up at the ceiling. "To repent means that you are sorry for the sins you've committed, and that you want to stop sinning. So, you talk to God and admit you're a sinner, and you *been* sinning, and you ask Him to forgive you, and you ask Him to come into your life and take over and change you. And if you mean it in your heart, He hears you. And the next thing you know, you start feeling different, you start *thinking* different because Jesus Christ is working on you and *in* you."

Tia looked at Ida sitting across from her. Was it just the lighting in the room that was causing her face to glow?

"Is that what's happening to you?"

"I think so."

"What makes you think you're a sinner?"

"It's not just me," Ida said smiling as she pointed at her. "It's you too. It's every single one of us. Do you have a Bible at home?"

"I don't, but Grandma does."

"When you go home, read it. Go to . . .," she looked up at the ceiling again. "I think it's Galatians, chapter five. Yeah, I'm pretty sure that's where it is, but I can't remember the verse. But just start reading chapter five and you'll come to it. Somewhere in there it starts talking about all the things God don't like. And if you doing something that goes against God, then it's a sin."

"Hmmm."

"You know, I'm still learning. But you should go to church and get with a Bible Study group too."

Tia thought back to the pamphlet the lady had given her at the drive-through window months ago. "You know, I was at work one day, and this lady drove around to pay for her order, and she gave me a pamphlet about Jesus Christ. I still remember the name of it. It was called, 'Is Something Missing?'"

"Did you read it?"

"At first I wasn't even thinking about it. I was gonna throw it in the garbage as soon as she pulled away from the window. But then I just stuck it in my back pocket, and I ended up reading it."

"What was it about?"

"I can't remember all of it. But I know it did talk about the things we do, I guess when something is missing in our life."

"And I bet it said that the something missing is Jesus Christ, huh?"

"I can't remember. But I still have it. Maybe I'll read it again."

"Yeah, you should. That's God trying to get your attention."

The lights flickered, and they both knew what that meant. Visiting time was over. They stood up slowly.

"Well, give me a hug," Ida said. She was thankful for this amount of physical contact. She was thankful that Jesus Christ had caused a change in her which had led to her *wanting* to hug and be hugged, a change in her that was blotting out her negative behavior and replacing it with a positive way of thinking.

Now, every night she thanked God for the changes that had occurred and were still occurring in her. And every Sunday she looked forward to the visit from the Christian group and the Bible Study they would have. They had told her that God is good. And she could see it for herself. She was living proof because only God could have broken through the block of cement that even *she* knew had been surrounding her heart. Nobody but God.

Chapter Thirty-six

The saxophonist for the opening act began playing a slow, mellow tune. Tia sat alone listening to the music, disappointed that Monica had bailed out on her at the last minute. They were supposed to have come to the music festival together. They had talked about it a month ago, and Monica had been as excited about going as Tia had been. Then, at the last minute, she'd called to cancel, saying she didn't feel good and was tired. Her last-minute cancellation irritated Tia. She did not want to go to the festival alone. Still, the thought of missing it altogether just because she didn't have anyone to go with bothered her even more, and so she made the decision to go. Now, she was glad she had.

She turned to look out at the growing crowd behind her, and her eyes made contact with the eyes of a young man sitting directly behind her. After several eye exchanges, they had graduated to smiling at one another and finally, he spoke.

"Enjoying yourself?" he asked.

"Yes, I am." She smiled. His eyes looked gentle and kind.

"My name's Lorenzo."

"I'm Tia."

"Tia?"

"Uh-huh."

He smiled. "That's a pretty name."

The dimples produced from his smile sank deep into his cheeks, and she thought she would melt. "Thank you."

He nodded.

"You have a pretty smile," she said. He smiled again, and it was confirmed . . . she was melting.

"Is this your first time here?" he asked.

"No, I came last year."

"This is my first time. I really just drove down to see War."

"Oh. Where do you live?"

"Chicago."

She felt a twinge of disappointment. Chicago was a long way away. *But why does that matter? I don't even know him.* As they talked, she found out that he was twenty-six years old—seven years older than she, and had just graduated from college with a degree in electrical engineering. He would be starting a new job the following week.

He pointed to the empty plastic cup she was holding and offered to replace whatever had been in it.

"Just strawberry lemonade," she answered in the most nonchalant way she could, but her heart was racing. What was it about him? Was it his smile? The dimples? His gentle behavior? Or the way he shyly glanced at her? She didn't know. All she knew was that they had just met, but it seemed as if she had known him for a very long time. She forced her gaze away from his tall, medium-sized physique as he left to get her another drink, and surveyed the crowd around her.

There were hundreds of men and women who had come out to hear the main musical act, War. Pillows of cigarette smoke drifted up from the crowd and were carried away by the warm breeze of an early-summer evening. Sounds of laugher and nonstop chatter were intermixed with applause and moans of delight when the musician hit a particularly soulful note. Then the drummer began performing a solo act, and the rhythm caused her head to move in unison with each beat.

She looked past the long stretch of people sitting in her row and saw his tall frame coming toward her. She could not find a word to describe how she was feeling. The applause grew louder from the crowd, and she returned her attention to the stage. It was an unfamiliar emotion. Her heartbeat quickened when she felt him tap her on the shoulder.

"Here you go," he said, handing her a plastic cup filled with the sweet, yet slightly tart red liquid.

"Thank you."

"You're welcome," he said smiling.

She tried to ignore the attraction that she was feeling toward him, but his smile made it almost impossible. The more he talked, the more she found her gaze drifting to his full lips, the strong jawline, the flawless cinnamon-colored face, and, of course, those perfectly situated dimples in his cheeks. Looking at his face gave her pleasure. It was a strange, quiet type of pleasure that she thought she could enjoy forever. She didn't want to admit it, but his was the kind of face that made her want to reach out and stroke it gently. Even his eyes spoke to her after his voice had long become silent, and she found herself being mesmerized by the sincerity that she saw in them.

"So, would you like to go and get something to eat after this?" he asked.

"Well, I don't know. I mean, I just met you. How do I know you ain't some kind of pervert?"

He laughed softly, sweetly, and she found herself smiling as well. How could she not smile? His laughter was contagious and the sweetest sound she'd ever heard.

"I'm not," he said. "I promise."

"Well, of course, you'd say that. I mean, you're not just gonna admit it."

Again he laughed, and her heart did a somersault.

"Okay." He pulled out his wallet. "What do you want me to do? Show you some ID?"

"Sure, you could do that, but that's not gonna do me any good if I'm lying somewhere in a ditch dead, is it?"

"You got me there. Guess you're just gonna have to trust me, huh?"

"Humph," she swallowed the last of the drink. "I'll trust you, but we're just gonna get something to eat, and then you can take me home."

"That's cool," he said, then with a serious look added, "but there is something I wanted to ask you."

She stiffened. "What?"

"Have you ever been to Chicago?"

"Yes," she answered slowly.

"Did you like it there?"

"Actually, I did."

"When do you think you'll be coming back?"

She was confused. "Back? You mean to visit?"

"Yeah."

"I don't know. Why?"

He was silent for a few seconds. "I thought it might be nice to see you again. You know, after tonight."

She smiled. "Yeah, that would be nice." And then suddenly—she would never be able to explain why—she reached over and stroked his arm. Just a quick stroke, but not so quick that she didn't feel how firm and tight it was.

He looked at her. She looked away. He leaned in closer, and she tried to concentrate on the form in front of her on the stage. She could sense him still staring at her, and she continued staring at the stage, the lights, the equipment, and the back of the woman's neck in the row in front of her until finally the main act was announced and his attention was diverted.

After forty-five minutes of enjoying nonstop music, and the band's frequent encouragement to the crowd to sing along, the concert ended. The music had stopped, but she felt like dancing as he took her hand and covered it with his own. They stood to make their way through the crowd, and the ground beneath her feet felt like air.

He led the way as she followed, holding his hand tightly. He continued to talk, but she could barely make sense of what he was saying because every time he turned to look at her, her mind would go blank, numbed by that smile of his.

For all she knew, he could have been saying, "So, yeah, I'm really not going to take you home. I'm going to kidnap you, cut you into little pieces, and *you're* going to be the dinner," and she would have happily gone to her demise, blinded by that lovely smile.

Yet it was more than just his smile. She sensed something beautiful in him that stretched far beneath his skin, its true source lying deep in the pit of his soul. She had a feeling it was vibrant, and kicking, and colorful. She imagined a beautiful blend of passion, soul, fire, and wisdom, of rhythm and emotion, protectiveness and pain.

She felt safe with him, even though she did not know him. Something had touched her soul and was tugging on her heart. She could not ignore it, and she definitely couldn't explain it, but standing next to him, holding his hand, she knew she could not deny its existence. She thanked God for this feeling and realized how often she had been thanking Him lately.

They stopped to grab a bite to eat, and as he had promised, he took her home. They sat in his car talking and smiling well into the night, and Tia had been seduced by his aura, his wonderful blend of beauty. They exchanged phone numbers, and he kissed her on her forehead. She stiffened. No man had ever kissed her there before. She didn't know what to do.

"Good night, Tia," he said. "Or should I say, good morning?"

She laughed, "Good morning, Lorenzo."

As she closed his car door, she somehow had the feeling that no matter how this relationship turned out, she would, for the first time in her life, know what it felt like to be loved.

Chapter Thirty-seven

It had been a little over a year since Tia and Lorenzo had first met, and even though Lorenzo lived in Chicago, they had been able to maintain their relationship by visiting each other on the weekends since it was only an hour-and-a-half drive either way. This was Tia's weekend to visit him, and they embraced each other as they walked along Navy Pier, located on Chicago's shoreline just off Lake Michigan.

The weather was unseasonably warm for the month of May, and a variety of outdoor vendors had set up booths that displayed everything from jewelry to Chicago's infamous all-beef hot dogs. Tomorrow she would have to go back home. She didn't want to.

She loved being with Lorenzo. She loved that he was still smiling. She loved the fact that they could talk about anything . . . and they had. She had told him all about her mother and why she had been in prison, her time spent in the foster home, and what it had been like growing up with a detached grandmother. She had even told him about the abortion, and he had not condemned her but had simply listened and offered an apology for it all as though it had been his fault.

Today, they had somehow gotten on the topic of her mother and why she had gone to prison.

"People do the bad things they do because of sin," he said. "God created us and loves us, so He knows what's best for us, but God has an enemy, and that enemy is the devil, Satan. And Satan is the one responsible for all the sin in this world and in us."

"Yeah," Tia said, "my mother said something like that. But what I want to know is why does God let it go on?"

Lorenzo looked at her hard as he thought about his answer. "So many people ask that question," he said. "I used to be one of them. But you know, I read a tract one of my coworkers gave me a couple of months ago, and then he invited me to church. And ever since then, I started going to the Bible Study, and I've been learning. And I'm learning that when some people can't get the answer they're looking for, they have a hard time believing and trusting in Jesus Christ. It's a mind thing." He pointed his index finger upward. "Or maybe it's a pride thing."

"Well, I can't really blame them."

"Yeah, but you can. See, because God said that the mysteries of God belong to God, and that His ways are not our ways, and His thoughts are higher than our thoughts. And if you think about it, that makes sense. How can we really be able to fully understand somebody who created us?"

She was silent.

"So," he continued, "that's where the faith comes in. You just *have* to trust Him."

"If you say so."

"Well, it's not me saying it. It's God. But check this out. There *is* a way out. God sent His son, Jesus Christ, to die for us and take all our punishment so we wouldn't have to. Because if we had to take the punishment," he continued, "we'd all be going to hell.

"Now, if we would just *believe* Jesus Christ is the Son of God, and accept the fact that we *all* are sinners, we could repent, come to God, and ask Him to forgive us.

And He will. And then we can spend our eternity with Him in heaven after we die instead of spending it with you-know-who."

She stared at him. "What's repent?"

"Repent means you're sorry for your sins, and you want to stop doing them."

"Oh yeah, that's right," she suddenly remembered. "My mother told me about that. But it doesn't make sense to me."

"What? Repent?"

"Yeah," she scratched her head. "The whole thing."

"Look at it this way," he said. "God created us, right?"

She nodded her head.

"So we're His creation, right?"

"Right."

"So," he pointed at her, "if something you created breaks, you know how to fix it, correct?"

"That would be correct."

"Well, sweetheart, we're all broken because of sin. Every one of us. And we need fixing. We need somebody to fix us, to save us from our sins. Something's missing inside of all of us. It's like a void. And only one person can fix us and fill that void at the same time, and that's Jesus Christ."

He was silent now. His face seemed to take on a glow as he looked straight-ahead. Maybe it was the light being created by the sun as it slowly began to set, but to her, he seemed more beautiful than she had ever recalled him to be.

She remembered the tract the lady at the drive-through window had given her last year. Funny that he should say something's missing when that had been the name of the tract she'd been given. She still had it at home in one of her drawers.

"Do you think you'll get to heaven one day?" Tia asked.

"According to God's promise, if I keep obeying His Word, I'm sure banking on it. And see, we're never gonna be sinless. That would make us perfect, and then we wouldn't need a Savior. But the idea is to try, and in your heart, want to be as Christ-like as you can. Because God can't tolerate no sin in heaven."

He sighed. "But it ain't easy, baby." He took her hand, "I want you to get to heaven too." Then he smiled, "but not for a long time. Maybe when you're a hundred, I'll be ready to let your old, wrinkled butt go by then."

They both laughed as she slapped him on the shoulder.

"How long *would* you like to live?" he asked.

"I don't know." But that was a lie. As she looked into his eyes, she knew she didn't want to die until the day he did.

She thought this might be what love felt like. She hadn't told him though. She was waiting to see if the feeling would die down, waiting to see if he would stop being so nice, waiting to see if he would leave her. And all while she waited, he stayed put, creating a pathway to her heart. And there wasn't anything she could do to stop it. *How am I supposed to stop something like that anyway?* she thought.

He led her to an unoccupied bench facing the lake. "Let's check out the sunset," he said.

There was nothing but water and sky for miles around. The sounds of music hovered in the distance as clusters of seagulls soared midway in the sky amid a background of faded blue and golden streaks that decorated the sky. She loved being close to the lake. Loved it even more now that she had someone special to share it with. She lowered herself slowly to the bench, his hand guiding her backbone. A slight breeze caressed the side of her face.

"You all right?" he asked.

She looked up at him and smiled, nodding her head.

"Whatcha' smiling about?"

"Huh?"

Placing careful emphasis on each word, he repeated himself. "What are you smiling about?"

"Nothing. I was just looking at you."

"What? I look funny or something? I got something sticking out of my nose?" He laughed. "You could've told me."

"You don't have nothing in your nose," she smiled. "I was just looking at you, and you started smiling and that made me smile."

"Hmmm," he said, "if you say so."

He kept watching her until finally she turned to him. "Stop it!" She nudged him gently with her shoulder.

"Stop what?"

"You know what."

He put her hand in his and turned to watch the sunset. Silence overtook them as the sun made its slow descent, leaving behind a golden myriad of hues that stretched across the horizon. Soon, the moon replaced the fiery hues with its own reflection of light that bounced off the water.

"So what are we gonna call my little man?" he asked, smiling.

She let her hand sweep down the side of his face. She really didn't care what they would call the new life that had begun growing in her four months ago. All she knew was that if Lorenzo ever stopped smiling, that would be the death of her.

"How do you know it's a boy?"

"Well . . ." he said, rubbing her stomach that had begun to swell.

"Well, what?" she interrupted. "It could be a girl, you know."

"I know." He squeezed her hand. "But as soon as you told me you were pregnant, I just automatically thought about a boy. So, let me have my fantasy." He smiled. "Please?"

She looked out toward the lake. "We can name him *or her* any name that you want."

He thought for a minute. "How about Tiombe?"

"What?" she laughed.

"Tiombe."

"How do you even spell that?"

He thought for a few minutes. "T-i-o-m-b-e or maybe T-i-o-m-b-y. I don't know. We'll figure it out."

"Yeah, right. And our kid'll be a senior in high school before *he* figures it out!"

"Our kid," he smiled. "That sounds nice."

He was silent for several minutes before he spoke again. "You know we got to make this right."

"Make what right?"

"You and me."

She stared at him. "That's what my grandmother is always saying."

"And she's right," he said.

"You know she wasn't too happy when she found out I was pregnant." Tia closed her eyes and shook her head. "The old Mavis would have probably put me out . . . on the spot!"

"Yeah, but your mom is okay with it, right?"

"I guess." Tia opened her eyes and shrugged. "I mean, what can my mother say? She wasn't around for twelve years of my life, and now that she's out of prison, I think she just wants to support me in whatever way she can."

"That's cool," Lorenzo said, and then added, "I don't want you to leave, Tia."

"I don't want to leave either."

"So, like I said, we have to make this right . . . in God's eyes."

"Are you talking about getting married?"

"Yeah, Tia, I am. We can't keep having sex without being married." He wasn't smiling now.

Her heart started beating wildly. The weather had cooled slightly, and she felt a gentle breeze caress her clammy skin.

"What about school?" she asked.

"Well, you haven't started the next semester yet, right?"

"Right."

After one of the conversations she'd had while visiting with her mother last year, Tia had decided to enroll at the Floral Design Institute located in the midtown section of Milwaukee. She planned to learn all she could about floral designing and had included a business course along with the rest of her studies. Her hope was that she would be able to open up her own small flower shop one day. Enrollments for new classes began every six weeks, and her next set of classes was not due to begin until July.

"So could you continue your classes down here?" Lorenzo was asking. "Maybe transfer your credits?"

"I don't know." Her excitement was mounting. "If there isn't an institute here in Chicago, I'd probably have to finish taking the courses online, if that's possible," she said.

"And as far as visiting your mother goes . . . actually, the distance would be about the same, give or take an hour."

"That's true. I see somebody's been thinking about this."

"Yeah, well, somebody had to. Trying to wait on you, a brother be waiting forever."

She looked surprised. "Trying to wait on *me?*"

"Yeah, you. I mean, we need to be together in the same city. You, me, and baby. Forever, I'm thinking."

"So are you saying that you were waiting on me to say something?"

He looked at her in feigned astonishment. "Aha! You hit the nail on the head!"

She rested her head on his shoulder. *Forever.* She couldn't fathom forever. Had no idea what it felt like. Still, she would let her guard down. She would bare it all and pray to God that He would not let her live to regret it.

"Will you marry me?" he asked.

It's now or never. "I love you," she whispered. "If you want me here, then this is where I'll be."

"I love you too. And I do want you here." He held her tightly. So tight that the fear she was feeling seemed to be squeezed right out of her.

Chapter Thirty-eight

On the bus ride back to Milwaukee, Tia rehearsed in her mind how she would tell her mother and grandmother about Lorenzo's proposal. Since Ida's release, the three of them had grown closer over the past year, and it was not fear that caused her to play out the scene in her mind, but rather the thought of disappointing Mavis and Ida when she told them she would be leaving.

At least Tia could take some comfort in knowing that Mavis would not be living in the house alone. After Ida had been released, she'd moved in with Mavis and Tia. It had been a little cramped, but Mavis had purchased a queen-sized sofa sleeper for the living room, and this is what Tia and Ida had been sharing. Mavis had also placed her membership with a new congregation, and Ida followed along, regularly attending Bible Study classes on Wednesday nights.

Although Henry's health had begun to decline, he still managed to maintain the house that the women occupied. He kept the grass cut in the summer, and the sidewalks clear of snow and ice in the winter. If there were any indoor maintenance issues that the house required, he would hire someone to take care of it. In return, Mavis made regular trips over to him to take him plates of food whenever she cooked.

They had never proceeded with the divorce, and now that they occupied two different houses, Mavis and

Henry seemed to be much friendlier toward each other than they had ever been when they'd lived under the same roof as man and wife.

Tia's feelings toward Henry were much as they had always been; she didn't like or dislike him. The two of them had never been close. He was just there. But she was glad that he had continued to support Mavis in the small ways that she needed him to.

Mavis had also found part-time work in a clothing store which she said she enjoyed because it gave her a chance to get out of the house more. She had even lost a few pounds—although Tia didn't know how she'd managed to do that because she was sill cooking those fat-laden, down-home, soul food dinners that she'd been cooking when she'd been living with Henry.

Tia entered the small flat and walked over to the wall unit, where the Mother's Day card Ida had given Mavis was still on display, even though it was now the middle of July.

"Tia, is that you?"

"Yes." She stood looking at the card. "Guess who wants me to move to Chicago," she said as Mavis walked into the room.

"Oh yeah?"

"Yeah."

"Is he talking about marriage?"

"Yes."

"Who's talking about marriage?" Ida asked walking out of the bedroom.

"Lorenzo," Tia said, turning toward Ida.

"When?" Ida asked.

"We didn't talk about that."

"So, what are you gonna do?" Mavis asked, shifting her weight. "Live together?"

"I don't know." Tia stumbled. "I guess . . . maybe . . . at first."

"You know you shouldn't be living with no man unless you're his wife," Mavis reminded her.

Tia turned to face her grandmother, rubbing her swollen stomach. "Well, I guess the damage is done now, Grandma."

"That don't mean you can't make it right," Mavis said sternly.

Tia sighed. "Yeah, that's what he said."

"Do you think you're ready to get married?" Ida asked.

"I don't know. I guess I'm as ready as I'm gonna get."

"What did you tell him?" both Mavis and Ida asked in unison.

"He said he wanted me in Chicago and that we should get married to make it right in God's eyes."

Mavis nodded her head. "And what did you say?"

Tia loosened the collar around her neck. "I said okay."

"Do you love him?" Ida was standing beside her now with her arm around Tia's waist.

There was that love question again. "I think I do."

"Uh-uh," Mavis said shaking her head. "You gonna have to do better than that. Either you love him and you know it, or you don't."

"I do," Tia said quietly.

Mavis was not convinced. "You know, having a man's baby is no reason to get married."

Tia looked at her grandmother in disbelief. "But you're the one that just said we need to be making this right, Grandma!"

"I know what I said. And I know you're still young, and marriage is hard work."

"I know."

"No, that part you don't know." She wanted to tell her that all she had to do was look at her own marriage and how that had turned out. But she realized that her past did not have to be her granddaughter's future. And so she bit down on the inside of her lip and said nothing.

"So, you don't think I should do it?" she asked both of the women.

"I *know* you shouldn't be living with him," Mavis said. "And I definitely don't think you should move to Chicago, period . . . unless you're already married."

"Put a ring on it," Ida said with a quiet laughter.

Tia sighed.

"Don't do that sighing with me," Mavis said. "I'm just telling you the truth."

"She really is, Tia," Ida said softly.

"Well," Tia said, "Chicago's not that far away."

"No, it's not. But sometimes common sense is."

"What's that supposed to mean, Grandma?"

Mavis gently pressed her index finger into the center of Tia's forehead. "It means don't you be no fool. Learn from yesterday. Accept Jesus into your life today, and I promise you He'll be there for you tomorrow."

"Amen," Ida said.

Tia frowned. "I'll try," she mumbled.

"You better do more than try," Mavis said. "Now, take off that jacket and sit down. You look like you about to pass out."

One week later, Lorenzo was at Tia's door exactly at six o'clock just as he had promised he would be. Mavis and Ida stood in the middle of the living-room floor making small talk with him while their eyes sized him up for the last time. He shifted his weight from side to side, and then began rubbing the back of his neck. Tia took that to be a sign that he was getting impatient and carried her two large suitcases over to the front door.

"I'm ready," she said standing next to him.

"Don't mess over my granddaughter," Mavis said.

"I wouldn't do that," he said with a half smile. "I really like Tia. She's a good girl."

Tia looked at him. *Did he say girl?*

Ida raised her eyebrows. "Like? What you mean, *like?*"

Mavis chimed in. "She's getting ready to move all the way to Chicago. Shouldn't the word be *love?*"

"Yeah. Yeah," Lorenzo stuttered. "That's what I meant. I meant love. I love Tia."

"I hope so," Mavis said, "because you know she's still got a lot of growing up to do."

"Don't we all?" he tried to laugh.

"Yeah," Mavis squinted her eyes, "but some of us more than others."

"Come on now, Grandma," Tia said. She was starting to feel a little uncomfortable herself.

"Okay. But I mean what I say. You be good to her, you hear?"

"I will."

"Don't make us have to come down there," Ida said jokingly.

"I won't."

Tia walked toward Mavis. "Give me a hug, Grandma."

"God bless you," Mavis whispered as she held her tight. "And remember what I told you."

"I will," Tia said. Then she turned to Ida. "I love you, Ma," she said as she hugged her.

"I love you too, Tia. We'll come down there and visit as soon as you get settled, okay?"

"Okay."

Ida released her grip, and Tia picked up the two suitcases. The fact that she was even able to ask her grandmother for a hug, and receive it, was, for her, a blessing already done. And there had been others too. Like her renewed relationship with her mother and being loved by Lorenzo.

"Aren't you going to carry those for her?" Mavis was asking him.

He gave a slight chuckle, then reached over and took the bags out of Tia's hands.

"Thank you," Mavis said.

"Bye," Tia sang. "I'll call y'all."

"Okay," they both answered.

When they had reached the end of the sidewalk, far enough away so that Mavis would not hear him, Lorenzo said, "Man, your grandmother is tough."

Tia smiled. "She just cares about me, that's all."

"And you think I don't?"

"Of course not." She looked at him. "If I thought that I wouldn't be leaving with you, would I?"

"I guess you wouldn't," he smiled.

She settled into the passenger seat of the car and rubbed her stomach. This was it. In an hour and a half, she would be in another place with a man that she had come to love and who said that he loved her. Well, in the house he'd used the word *like,* but she'd known what he'd meant. Mavis had just been trying to give him a hard time, and even though Tia had witnessed a great change in her grandmother, she knew that some parts of her would always stay the same. But it was okay now because the parts that had changed had softened her grandmother and allowed that brick wall she'd built around her heart to come crumbling down, and now Tia was the recipient—she and Ida—of more than a decade of love not given: blessing number one.

She watched Lorenzo from the rearview mirror as he loaded the suitcases into the trunk. He looked tense, and she wondered if Mavis had gotten to him. He got into the front seat next to her and put the key into the ignition.

She patted his thigh. "Don't worry, baby. You know that's just how she is."

"Oh, I'm not worried," he said turning the key. "She'll be a long way away from us."

The car sat idling as he let down his window, and then the window on Tia's side. As she sat waving good-bye to her grandmother and mother, an unwanted image began to form in her mind. It was the image of her when she was a little girl, and someone was ushering her out of the house that she now sat in front of. She was tired and had been crying. The panic she'd felt about having to leave without her mother that dark night years ago began to resurface, and she struggled to control her breathing.

She remembered the questions she'd asked, the cool night air, the darkness, the faint cry of someone familiar calling out her name as the car pulled off. She closed her eyes to try to erase the memories. All of that was old news; the past. Yet, here she was about to leave her mother and this same house again. Why was she thinking about it now? And what had her grandmother told her about the past?

He interrupted her thoughts. "You all right?"

"Yeah. Just a little tired."

"Ready?"

"As ready as I'm going to be."

He steered the car away from the curb slowly. He did not wave good-bye. And then, just like that dark night years ago, the vehicle picked up speed and headed for a new destination. Only this time she hoped it would be filled with happiness and joy.

Chapter Thirty-nine

An hour and thirty minutes later, Tia entered Lorenzo's apartment; their apartment. She walked past the narrow kitchenette right off the living room and headed straight for the bedroom.

It was fully furnished with a king-sized bed, dresser, and chest, and was large enough to accommodate the two of them without a problem . . . at least after they were married. Lorenzo had made it clear that there would be no more intimate contact between them until they were legally man and wife, and they were going to exchange vows before a judge in Cook County the following week.

She sat down on the edge of the mattress and rubbed her lower back. If she and her grandmother had had a bedroom this large, they too could have shared it, and she wouldn't have had to sleep on the sofa. She went from room to room, seeing what she had seen a hundred times before. Only now, she was seeing things through the eyes of an occupant instead of just a visitor.

To get to the bathroom she only had to walk out of the bedroom and turn left. It was fairly large with a rectangular-shaped mirror above the sink that stretched the length of the countertop, and there was about a finger's-width of space on both sides of the toilet, separating it from the sink on one side and the bathtub on the other. The lower portion of the wall that surrounded the tub was covered with yellow and green tile, and the floor had been covered with yellow linoleum. All of the walls were painted a neutral off-white color and were clean and intact.

She left the bathroom and took a short walk down the hall into the living room. It was slightly larger than the bedroom and was shaped like a square with one side missing. A tan, leather sofa and glass end table occupied one side of the wall. A wall unit with a television and stereo occupied the opposite side. A matching chair sat on the outskirts between the two. This room, like the bedroom, had a dark brown carpet covering the floor.

She sat down on the leather sofa. She had always felt so comfortable in this room whenever she had come down for the weekend. Now that this was to be her new home, it seemed as though her comfort level was fading. She looked down at her hands and made a conscious effort to stretch out each finger. *Why do I feel so nervous and uncomfortable?* She thought about the week prior to her move.

She had finished her first set of exams at the Floral Design Institute, and had passed all of her courses with a B average. Prior to moving, she had confirmed with the institute's advisor that the courses she needed to take in July would be offered online.

She had to admit that she hadn't been too thrilled about taking online courses; she liked having the ability to physically see and talk to someone if she needed to. But with the baby due in October, she began to think that maybe the online courses would not be such a bad idea after all.

Since she was only in her fourth month of pregnancy, she decided to look for a part-time or seasonal job. She picked up the newspaper that had been left on the floor and pulled out the employment section.

Lorenzo sat down next to her. "What are you looking for?"

"A job."

"A what?"

"A job." She smiled. "You know, something that you do on a regular basis and get paid for doing it."

"I know what a job is," he said with a serious look on his face. "I have one, remember?"

"I know."

"Well, then," he said slowly, "why do you want a job? You haven't even gotten yourself situated here yet, and you're talking about leaving already."

"Who said anything about leaving? I'm just talking about bringing in some extra money." She hesitated, waiting for his response. When there was none she continued. "Besides, it'll give me something to do."

"Oh, you'll have plenty to do. Trust me."

"Like what?"

"Well," again he spoke slowly as if he were measuring every word, "like taking care of me, for one."

"You don't need no taking care of," she said laughing. "You're a grown man."

"Yes, I am. I'm a grown man who wants his woman at home when he comes home from work."

She studied his face for a few seconds before asking, "Are you serious?"

"I'm serious. And I'm also hungry, so what's for dinner?"

"It's kind of late, Lorenzo. Why don't we just go out and get something to eat?"

"It's not that late. And why shell out money for food when we have a refrigerator full of it right here?"

Her smile was fading. "Because I'm tired maybe?"

"Ah, come on, girl. You ain't that tired, are you? Go on and whip us up something to eat. I would say I'll make it worth your while," he winked at her. "But we have to wait until after we're married."

She snorted.

"You'll see. Besides, I want to see how well my woman can cook."

She slowly made her way to the kitchen. "What do you want?"

"Surprise me."

With even slower movements, she opened the door to the refrigerator. Inside, she found an opened package of ground beef, a half head of lettuce, a package of cheese, and several small potatoes.

"This is what you call a refrigerator full of food?" she shouted into the living room.

He shouted back. "Look in the freezer."

She opened the freezer door to a better selection. There were packages of pork chops, chicken, more ground beef, and fish. As she sorted through the items, she found bags of frozen vegetables, pizza, and an assortment of TV dinners.

"Well, that's better, but guess what?"

"What?"

"This stuff is all frozen."

"Take something out."

She was getting impatient. Before, when she was just a visitor, they would always eat out because he didn't want to waste precious time having his woman in the kitchen cooking.

"Lorenzo, do you know how long it'll take for something to thaw out? It'll be midnight before we even *start* eating." She stood staring at the frozen items. "I could just throw one of these pizzas into the oven."

"That's not home cooking."

"Well, I'm sorry, baby, but you're going to have to do without a home cooked meal tonight. The only thing thawed out is this ground beef. I can make you a burger if you want."

He said nothing.

"Lorenzo?"

Still, he said nothing.

She looked around the corner. "Lorenzo," she repeated, "do you want a burger or not?"

"I guess," he answered without looking at her.

"Does this mean that you won't make it worth my while now?" She tried to lighten the mood.

He only shrugged and mumbled something that she didn't understand.

She walked over to the sink and washed her hands. *What does he expect me to do? Perform a miracle?*

She opened the package of raw meat and scooped out a handful. Then she began sharply patting and shaping it into round patties. *He knew he was going to be hungry when we got back.* She reached for the stainless steel skillet hanging above the stove and slammed it down onto the gas burner. *If he hadn't planned to go out to eat, then he should have taken something out of the freezer before he left.* She tossed the meat patties into the skillet, and then began peeling the potatoes that would be transformed into slender strips of french fries. They ate their meal in silence, and then she announced that she was going to bed.

"What about the dishes?" he asked.

"What about them?"

"Aren't you going to wash them?"

"They'll get done in the morning," she called out over her shoulder.

"They really need to get done when I ask you to do them."

She pretended not to hear him as she shut the bedroom door. Why couldn't *he* wash the dishes? It should have been enough that she'd cooked the meal! She snatched the comforter back on the bed. And what was that comment about them *"needing to get done when I ask you to"* all about?

Chapter Forty

It was October, and five months had passed since Tia had moved to Chicago and married Lorenzo. It had just been the four of them at the courthouse—she and Lorenzo, and his parents. Her grandmother had not been able to make it; Henry had been sick, and although they still lived in separate houses, she had not wanted to leave him completely alone. Ida had just gotten a temporary job in a factory, and she could not get the day off.

After the ceremony, everyone had gone back to doing whatever they had been doing prior to the occasion, as if the whole thing had been just a minor interruption, a detour from their daily activities. It had been no more significant than that, and so for Mavis to be absent had not really been that big of a deal.

Tia, herself, had felt oddly detached from the entire thing, and there had been nothing special planned afterward, no celebratory dinner, no champagne toast, no walk in the park, nothing. Lorenzo's parents seemed friendly enough when she'd met them at the courthouse on the day of the wedding, but she felt as though she hadn't made a real connection with them and didn't feel comfortable calling them just to say hello or see how they were doing.

Time passed slowly. She had completed all of her online Floral Design courses with a final grade of A. And since Lorenzo did not want her to work, had actually *forbidden* her to work, she had nothing left to occupy her time.

She talked frequently by phone with her mother, grandmother and Monica, but she missed seeing them. She had not been to visit any of them since she'd gotten married, even though Lorenzo had implied that she would still be able to.

She seldom left the apartment unless it was to go grocery shopping or attend Sunday morning services at the neighborhood church two blocks down the street. At first, both she and Lorenzo attended the services together, but little by little, he began to make excuses for not going on Sunday morning.

"I'm tired today, baby," he'd say. "It's my only day to relax. You go."

Although his attendance was decreasing, he continued to encourage, almost insist, that she go. And she did. She found that she liked going to church. She liked the spiritual hymns she heard, and often when she would be feeling down she would walk through the church doors, take a seat, and the pastor would get to preaching a sermon that seemed as though it was meant specifically for her. She'd also felt a sense of welcoming from the first time she'd walked through the doors.

Some of the women from the church had given her a surprise baby shower, and the items she'd received for the baby were much needed. There were packages of disposable diapers, onesies in neutral colors, pajama sleepers, and bottles. One of the church members, Georgean, had even bought her a baby carrier. It was the kind that would allow her to carry the baby strapped either to her front or back.

That had been one of the few occasions that Lorenzo did not mind her leaving to attend a social event, and

Tia was thankful for all the gifts. For whatever reason, Lorenzo did not seem to be too concerned about securing all the necessary items they would need once the baby was born. He had bought the crib, but that had been all, even though he knew she was in her ninth month. *What's he waiting for?* More and more, she found herself wondering what was wrong with him. And she was getting tired of hearing herself ask that question.

She had also begun to see another side to Lorenzo that he had obviously succeeded in keeping hidden from her. He was often gone, but when he was home he was moody, easily agitated, and mean-spirited. She had secretly begun to keep tabs on how often they made love, and the last time he'd touched her or even attempted to had been two months ago. And he had been unsuccessful.

"What's wrong, Lorenzo?" she had asked him when he'd abruptly stopped.

"I, I don't know."

"Why'd you stop?"

"I can't . . . I think it's your stomach. It's in the way."

She'd suggested other positions that would have eliminated the need for him to lie on top of her fully rounded stomach, but he was not receptive to her ideas. It seemed to her that he was not interested in touching her or pleasing her in any way, and this belief caused that familiar emotion that had plagued her all her life to awaken. She felt it stir with the twinge of not being wanted by someone . . . again. *After all, hadn't my own father abandoned me?*

She rubbed her lower back. It had been aching off and on throughout the night, and was continuing to ache. She thought about her father's faceless image as she sat by the window smoking a cigarette. She knew smoking wasn't good for either her or the baby, but she was only smoking one a day, and she reasoned that was better than smoking seven or eight of them a day. She exhaled forcefully with her face almost pressing against the gray metal screen and watched the stream of smoke gently flow through the tiny openings out to the other side.

Her imagination took her to a scenario where her smiling father was holding her on his lap. Then he was tucking her into bed, his tall figure looming over her in a nonthreatening manner as he kissed her gently on the cheek and said good night. Next, she was in her teens, and she saw herself asking for his permission to go to the prom, or out on a date, or over to a friend's house. *What would he have said? How would he have said it? What words of advice would he give me now about my present situation?* She rubbed her forehead. Had she grown up with a father to begin with, she would probably not be where she was now, stuck in a new city, alone and pregnant.

A wave of cramps passed through and around her stomach. She looked up at the sky, trying to focus on the irregular shapes of the gray clouds. Lorenzo was not the man he had pretended to be. He had stopped attending church, but insisted she attend saying he wanted a godly wife. *But what about a godly husband?*

At first she'd attended services reluctantly, silently resenting his choice to stay home. But hearing the Word of God preached every Sunday was doing something to her. She couldn't put her finger on it, but something was changing. She began to feel like she was in the right place every time she walked through the church doors. She wanted to hear and learn more about the Word of God, and she began to look forward to the Bible Study held there every Sunday morning.

They were studying the thirteenth chapter in First Corinthians. It was about love, and she was learning that love is patient and kind. She was learning that it is not selfish or mean. And the more she learned about love, the more she realized her husband's love was not matching up with how God said love is supposed to be.

She would sit in that apartment, waiting for Lorenzo to come home; hoping that when he walked through the door, he would be the Lorenzo she'd fallen in love with. The Lorenzo she'd married. The one who used to treat her so nicely. She wanted to have conversations with him like they used to have. Yet, strangely enough, when he would finally come home, she could find nothing to say other than to ask him where he'd been and what he'd been doing. That line of questioning, of course, irritated him. And then the arguing would begin.

"I don't appreciate you trying to put me on a leash, Tia."

"And I don't appreciate you leaving me home by myself all the time," she'd counter.

The gentle feelings they once shared were slowly being replaced with arguments, and the closeness, with distance. *What's happened? Did he really love me?* She began to question all that he had said—that she had believed—to her. She remembered him telling her that he had to make things right between them now that she was pregnant. The dull ache in her back was increasing. *Did he marry me just because I'm carrying his child?*

She looked down at the cigarette between her fingers. The once round filter was almost flat from the tight grip she had on it. She tried to justify the daily cigarette by convincing herself that it was the only sliver of freedom she had left since marrying Lorenzo. It was her only vice, and one she was not willing to give up completely. She took one last puff and quickly made her way to the bathroom where she flushed the remaining evidence down the toilet.

In the living room she searched for any remaining evidence, anything forgotten that would incriminate her. She saw the five empty candy wrappers crumpled on the end table that had once held bite-sized, chewy pieces of chocolate. Next to that sat the empty porcelain cup that she had sipped hot tea out of. Forbidden. All those things forbidden for her to have by Lorenzo. According to him, candy would make her fat, and the caffeine in tea was not good for the baby.

In one motion, she scooped up the wrappers, then grabbed the teacup and took everything to the kitchen. She pushed the wrappers deeply into the trash bag, and rinsed the teacup out.

She went back into the bedroom. Back to the window. *And he has the nerve to say that I'm trying to put him on a leash.* Why did she have to hide things like chocolate and tea just because he didn't want her eating or drinking them? She wasn't a child. She was *having* a child, but she was not a child, and she should be able to eat and drink whatever she wanted to.

She felt another spasm in her stomach. She closed her eyes and rubbed her temples. She was certainly able to enjoy chocolate, tea, and more before she'd met him and all while she'd been dating him. Shuddering, she closed the bedroom window. Why had he changed?

She thought about the cigarettes. He didn't know about that, and she planned to keep it that way. She remembered the time when she'd almost gotten caught. He had come home early, but that hadn't been the

problem because she always covered her tracks for unexpected times like that. The problem began when he
called her to the bathroom, and she found him standing over the toilet bowl pointing.

"What's this?" he asked harshly.

She remembered standing next to him, looking into
the bowl, watching the half-smoked cigarette floating
calmly, peacefully, in the water. She remembered the
tiny beads of sweat forming on her forehead as she
conjured up a quick lie to tell.

"Oh, that," she said as nonchalant as possible. "The
lady next door came over to use the phone, and she
didn't have anything to put her cigarette out in so she
must have put it in the toilet." She remembered reaching over and flushing the toilet, watching the cigarette
dance in a circular motion before finally getting sucked
down into the strong, tornado-like current, all the
while feeling his eyes staring at her intensely, praying
that him staring at her would be as far as it went. And
she'd been prepared to stick to the lie. What else could
she have done?

To admit that she'd been smoking would have also
been admitting to disobeying his rule, and there would
have been a heavy price to pay for that. She'd found
that out just one month earlier when she had gone to
the grocery store and deliberately defied him by buying
a small box of tea bags. When she'd returned, he'd gone
through the groceries, and upon seeing them wanted to
know why she'd bought them. When she didn't answer,
he'd slapped her in the face with the back of his hand.
Stunned and confused, she stood there watching as he
threw the tea bags into the wastebasket one at a time.

"Didn't I tell you not to drink anything with caffeine
in it?"

All she could do was nod. She was speechless.

She touched her face, remembering the pain as if it had just happened, remembered standing in the front of the bathroom mirror the next morning trying unsuccessfully to suck in her swollen bottom lip so that she could go to church without anyone noticing the deformity.

She remembered the heavy sadness she'd felt when she had finally been able to look at him as he apologized over and over and convinced her to stay home from church. With him. He would stay home too. Not that he went to church anyway, but he wouldn't go anywhere else that day either. He didn't know what had gotten into him. He said it was just that he had so much love for her and the baby that he didn't want to see anything hurt either of them. And she remembered thinking, *But you just hurt me.*

So when he'd stood before her questioning a cigarette butt floating in the toilet, she'd lied. God forgive her, she lied, and she had done it well.

She looked at the sky again. The clouds were getting darker. She got up and went into the bathroom. The frequency of her stomach cramps was increasing. She stood staring at the white porcelain sink. This was too much. She could not go back to being abused like she had been as a child. Why did he treat her like one? She was a grown woman, now. What had her grandmother said about yesterday? To learn from it. And Jesus? She said to keep Him with you today, and He would be there for you tomorrow.

"Oh, Lord," she whispered, "forgive me for my sins." The tears began to trickle down her face. "Help me, Lord. I don't know what to do." She was on her knees now, rocking back and forth.

"I know I'm not perfect, and neither is Lorenzo. And I'm asking you to touch us, Lord. And fix us. Save us. And save this marriage. Help us to make Jesus the head of our home. Please, Lord. Touch Lorenzo's heart and bring him back home to me. And to you. In Jesus' name I pray. Thank you, Lord. Amen."

The phone rang as she finished her plea. She wiped the tears from her eyes.

"Hello," she sniffled.

It was Lorenzo on the other end. "Hey, what are you doing?"

"Nothing," she tried to sound normal. "But my stomach's been cramping all day, and my back was hurting all night."

"You need to take it easy," he said casually.

"Humph," she tried to sound light. "If I take it any easier I'll be dead." She hesitated. "When will you be home?"

"I don't know," he answered dryly. "I have to meet with some of the other engineers to go over some testing procedures we're working on. It might be awhile."

She sighed. "You know, Lorenzo—"

"Don't start," he interrupted.

"But I think I'm having lab—"

"I have to go. I'll talk to you later. Bye."

The tears began rolling down her cheeks again. Had they ever really stopped? She hung up the phone and sat listening to the wind outside. It was no longer a gentle breeze, but had increased its force considerably. *What meeting? Where?* She could see the leaves on the trees being pushed relentlessly from side to side. Back and forth. *How long?* The leaves held on, and she stopped crying. Her stomach began cramping again. *When will he be home?*

She turned on the lamp in the living room, and then turned the television on to the evening news. The weatherman was predicting rain with strong winds. As she sat down on the sofa, the cramps spread to her sides. She inhaled deeply, then slowly released the air. *Not yet. Please, not yet! He's not here. Why can't the pain just go away?* The ache in her back intensified. *Why can't he just come home?* Another wave of pain thrust her forward. The rain had begun to fall outside. The force that propelled the liquid down from the sky caused it to beat a furious tune against the windowpane. The wind was howling, and she was sweating. The weatherman was talking, and it hurt so bad . . . Where was her husband?

She picked up the phone and called her obstetrician. The after-hours operator answered and said she would relay the message to the doctor. Minutes later, her doctor called back. She told him her pains were occurring every two minutes or so. He told her to go to the hospital. She was in labor. She called Lorenzo on his cell phone. There was no answer. She ended the call, and then dialed 9-1-1.

Chapter Forty-one

The paramedics came and drove her to the hospital with the sirens flashing. She was wheeled into the emergency room where she was admitted. She gave the nurse all of the necessary information and answered all of her questions, but when she asked the last question Tia had no answer for her.

"Do we need to contact your husband?" Tia simply shook her head. "He's in a meeting," she said.

The contractions were now coming less than a minute apart. "Oh God!" she moaned. "I can't do this. I can't!"

She began twisting her body from side to side. With each contraction, she felt her entire torso immobilized by the burning, searing, viselike grip of pain that showed its mercy only in the amount of seconds it allowed her to catch her breath before the next wave of cramps engulfed her.

"I can't breathe!" she cried out between pants. "I can't breathe!"

The nurse took her hand. "Just take deep breaths, now," she said calmly. "Breathe in, breathe out."

Another wave of pain shot through her without warning, and she was convinced that this was the one that would finally kill her. She heard someone say this was going to be a quick delivery, and that was unusual since this was her first pregnancy.

"A-h-h-h! O-h-h-h!" She violently shook her head from side to side. "I need my husband," she screamed. "I need my husband!" She took her hand back from the nurse's. It should have been Lorenzo's hand she held. It should have been *his* voice telling her to breathe in and out. She closed her eyes. It should have been . . .

She tried to endure the pain of a life that was trying to make its way out, a life that the two of them had created together. *But where is he?*

"Oh, Lord," she moaned, "please let this be over with."

After what seemed like an eternity, they said it was time for her to push. But she would not. A glimpse of a life now flashed before her. *How could he do this?*

"Push!"

She moaned, but she did not push. *Where is he?*

"Push!"

She panted, but she did not push. Her mind wheeled forward to a future unknown. She knew that she would always be here for this new life that was about to be born, but would Lorenzo?

Through her pain, she thought she was looking into his eyes, eyes that were glossy with tears. Or were they her own eyes?

"I'm here," he said.

"Lorenzo!" she cried out, and she realized it was not a fantasy. He was standing there, and she didn't know how long he'd been holding her hand or rubbing her forehead, but she was relieved she wouldn't have to go through the delivery alone.

"I'm sorry," he whispered.

And she pushed. Pushed until she thought she would pass out. Pushed until every muscle in her body felt as though it had been tried and tested far beyond its limit. Pushed until she had nothing left to give. And the head of the infant emerged, ready or not, to greet the world.

It was a girl, soft and warm and full of emotion. A girl who, in those first few moments, had already experienced the first of many experiences to come, but none would ever trump this first one: the beginning of life.

The nurse briefly placed the small infant, full of sound, into Tia's arms. Tia smiled and leaned over to place a gentle kiss on a tiny area of skin on her baby's forehead that had been cleansed from the aftermath of the birth. Lorenzo was smiling too as he stroked the side of his newborn daughter's cheek. Then the nurse took her back to fully clean and clothe her.

Tia looked up at Lorenzo. "How'd you know I was here?"

"I thought about what you said on the phone. About the backache and the cramps. I left the meeting because I was gonna come home, but when I called you back and you didn't answer, something told me to just turn around and go to the hospital. I'm glad I did."

"I was trying to tell you that I thought I was in labor."

"Yeah, I know that now."

She looked away. "You know that now," she repeated. "But now was almost too late."

"Again, I'm sorry."

The medical team had given Tia a bed bath, changed her linen, and tidied the room before they left. She turned to her side facing away from him.

"I'm tired," she said.

"I'm glad I made it."

She sighed. "Yeah. Me too."

Just before she dozed off, she recalled the image once more of two people smiling and loving their baby whose cries had been temporarily silenced by a kiss on the forehead and a stroke on the cheek.

***

Hours later she was awake, staring at the scenery spread out before her on the other side of the window. The sprawling treetops held a mixture of blood-orange, nectarine, and amber-colored leaves. And the sun had begun to announce its presence, creating a blazing light that would soon claim the entire sky.

A flock of birds spread their wings and departed from the branches they had been coveting. They flew aimlessly at first, and then suddenly came together in unison to form a bottomless triangle. Their departure caused a sprinkling of leaves to fall to the ground, and Tia thought about fairy godmothers and the magical dust they sprinkled that would cause the person it fell on to find beauty and love everlasting.

If only it could have been that easy. Her life had certainly not been a fairy tale. But it had not been the worst either. She looked at her daughter lying in the bassinet next to her. She would have to call Mavis and Ida in a little while and share the good news with them.

She watched the rhythmic rise and fall of the tiny newborn's stomach as she slept. She looked so calm and peaceful, and she and Lorenzo had decided to name her Serenity. Yes, something good had happened to Tia. She was looking at her right now. And she did not want to pass on the legacy of her own messed up past to her daughter.

She returned her attention to the sky. She yearned to feel the freedom of gliding across the treetops just like those birds, parallel with the horizon, at peace with God. She knew that with God's help it didn't just have to be a yearning. It could be a reality. She could have the freedom and peace of Jesus Christ living in her.

Her grandmother had told her to stay close to Jesus and He would stay close to her. The preacher at church said the same thing practically every Sunday. The pamphlet the customer had given her when she'd worked at the restaurant said that Jesus was the answer, too.

Even her own mother, who, upon her release—no, even before that—had undergone a transformation. Tia had witnessed the changes in her from the first visit they'd had to the last one, when Ida had sat at the prison table glowing as she'd talked about Jesus Christ. And to this day, Ida was continuing to be renewed.

All of them could not be lying! If they could be changed by the Word of God, she could be changed too. She was going to put her trust and faith in Jesus Christ for the peace she had never been able to find. With His help, she *would* be free from her past.

She heard a stir behind her and turned to find Lorenzo repositioning himself in the chair next to the bed.

"Beautiful, isn't it?" he said.

She turned back toward the window. "Yes, it is."

"I mean the baby."

"Well, you said, 'it.'"

"I know," he smiled. "I gotta get used to saying 'her.'"

She turned to look back at him. "That's not the only thing you need to get used to."

He stared at her.

"Some things are gonna have to change if we're gonna stay together."

"I know."

"I hope you do." She rubbed her forehead as she thought about the challenges before them.

"I know one thing that needs to change right now," he said.

She stared at him, waiting.

He put his hand on her shoulder. "I need you to forgive me. I love you. I do."

"How come it doesn't feel like you do?"

He dropped his head as if he'd been defeated.

"Lorenzo, when we got married we were supposed to be united, as one."

He nodded his head.

"We're not united. We're not one. There's you. And then there's me." She had finally found her voice, and now her words were unstoppable. "I feel like you don't care about me. You don't listen to me. You just do what you want to do, and everything has to be your way. I can't go anywhere. I can't talk to anybody. You don't even go to church any more, but you're always talking about how you want a godly wife." She paused. "I've been thinking—"

"Wait a minute, wait a minute." He held up his hand. "Don't say it. Please don't say it."

But she had made up her mind. She was going to take the baby and move back to Milwaukee.

He got out of the chair and lowered himself to his knees in front of the bed.

"Please forgive me, Tia. It's just that you've been through so much in your life. I just wanted to protect you. And . . . I don't know. I guess I felt like I had this huge responsibility to be all things to you. And you gotta remember, this is my first time being married too."

"I forgive you, Lorenzo. I have to. But you went too far. I'm not a child. You can't treat me like one."

"I know." His head shook from side to side. "I know I went too far."

"Yeah, you did. And I can't stay with things the way they are."

"But it's not too late, Tia. I know what I need to do to change, baby." He gently took her hand and bowed his head. "Pray with me," he said.

"Heavenly Father, please forgive me for my sins. I haven't been a good husband, and an even worse servant for you. Help me to put you first, Lord, and seek you in everything I do. You said if we would confess our sins, you would forgive us. You said we can do all things through Christ who strengthens us, Father, so I'm asking you to give me strength.

"Make me a better man than I was yesterday, Father, but not as good as I'll be tomorrow. Starting today, Lord. Starting right now. Please help me to be a better servant for you, a better husband," he squeezed Tia's hands tightly, "and a good father. I'm asking you to help me, Lord, because I know I can't do it on my own. I thank you, Father. I thank you for Serenity, and for my wife. In Jesus' name I pray. Amen."

"Amen," Tia whispered.

She had prayed for this moment many times. She had asked God to touch Lorenzo's heart and prepare him to return to Jesus Christ. She had prayed for so long until it seemed that God was not going to answer her prayer, and that's why she had decided to take the baby and leave. But God *had* heard her prayers. And today, He answered them.

Lorenzo leaned over and kissed the tears rolling down Tia's cheek. "Starting today," he said, "there will be no more looking back at yesterday. Not for me and not for you. Okay?"

She nodded her head as they held onto each other, and she knew that it would not be easy, but she also knew that the love of Jesus Christ changes people. She had living proof of that in her own life, and in the lives of her grandmother and mother.

With the power of Jesus Christ on their side, she and Lorenzo would be able to overcome many things. And flying above the treetops just might be one of them.

Discussion Questions

1. Do you think the real reason Ida slept with Henry was for money?

2. Do you think Henry would have slept with Tia if given the chance?

3. Do you think Mavis made the right decision to separate from Henry? Should she have divorced him?

4. Do you think Henry's health began to decline because of all the wrong he'd done?

5. Why do you think Tia never attempted to contact Ida while she was in prison?

6. Do you think Ida should have gotten more time in prison for the death of her baby? And should she have attempted to reconcile with Mavis much sooner than she did?

7. Mavis decided not to ask Ida if Henry was the father of her deceased baby. Do you agree with her decision?

8. Do you think it was okay for Tia to forgive Ida and accept her back into her life after such a long absence?

Discussion Questions

9. Do you think Ida was really a changed person when she was released from prison?

10. What do you think about Lorenzo's change of attitude after he marries Tia?

11. Lorenzo physically abused Tia and became distant and controlling. Do you think Tia should have left him?

12. Do you think Lorenzo will change?

13. Can you relate to Mavis and her inability to express her emotions?

14. Do you believe that love really does conquer all? If yes, why? If no, why not?

15. Do you believe that God can heal and change people? If so, under what conditions, if any?

16. Are *you* still holding on to a painful memory/ event from your past? If so, do you think it's time to let it go?

About the Author

Catherine Flowers currently resides in Wisconsin with her family. She was a registered nurse for sixteen years before deciding to change careers and pursue her lifelong goal of writing. She is the creator of www.freefrombondage.wordpress.com, an online Christian blog. When she's not writing, she enjoys spending time with her family and learning to play the violin. For more information about the author, you can log on to www.authorcatherineflowers.com or contact her at catherineflowers@aol.com. *Yesterday's Eyes* is her first novel.

UC HIS GLORY BOOK CLUB!

www.uchisglorybookclub.net

UC His Glory Book Club is the spirit-inspired brain-child of Joylynn Jossel, author and acquisitions Editor of Urban Christian, and Kendra Norman-Bellamy, author for Urban Christian. This is an online book club that hosts authors of Urban Christian. We welcome as members all men and women who have a passion for reading Christian-based fiction.

UC His Glory Book Club pledges our commitment to provide support, positive feedback, encouragement, and a forum whereby members can openly discuss and review the literary works of Urban Christian authors.

There is no membership fee associated with UC His Glory Book Club; however, we do ask that you support the authors through purchasing, encouraging, providing book reviews, and of course, your prayers. We also ask that you respect our beliefs and follow the guidelines of the book club. We hope to receive your valuable input, opinions, and reviews that build up, rather than tear down our authors.

WHAT WE BELIEVE:
—We believe that Jesus is the Christ, Son of the Living God

Urban Christian His Glory Book Club

—We believe the Bible is the true, living Word of God
—We believe all Urban Christian authors should use their God-given writing abilities to honor God and share the message of the written word God has given to each of them uniquely
—We believe in supporting Urban Christian authors in their literary endeavors by reading, purchasing and sharing their titles with our online community
—We believe that in everything we do in our literary arena should be done in a manner that will lead to God being glorified and honored

We look forward to the online fellowship with you. Please visit us often at *www.uchisglorybookclub.net*.

Many Blessing to You!
Shelia E. Lipsey,
President, UC His Glory Book Club